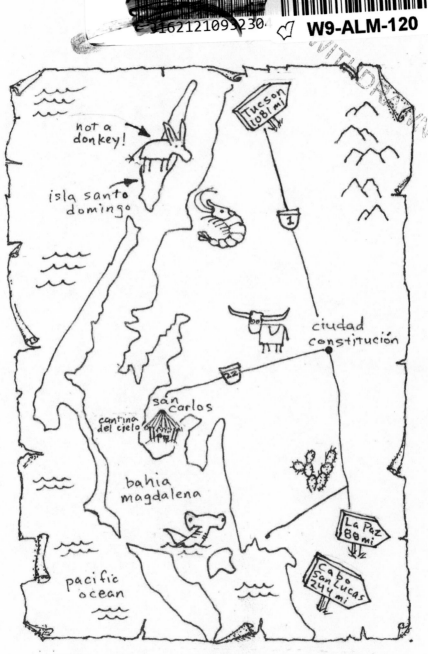

Fish's map of the habitable universe

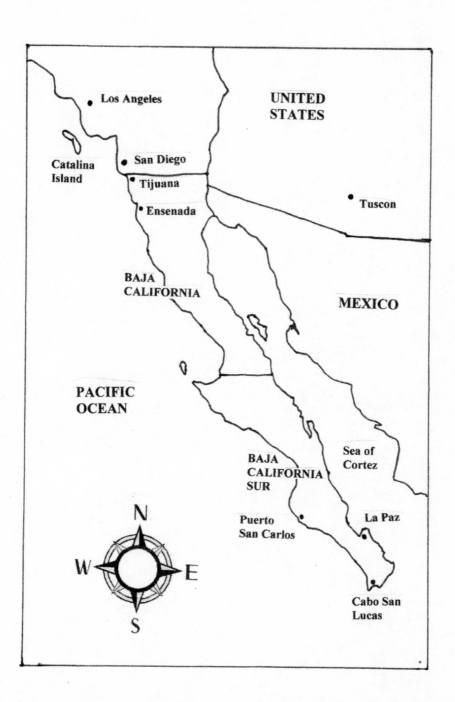

WAHOO RHAPSODY

WAHOO RHAPSODY

SHAUN MOREY

PUBLISHED BY

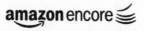

The characters and events portrayed in this book are fictitious. Any similarity to real persons, living or dead, is coincidental and not intended by the author.

Printed in the United States of America.

Published by AmazonEncore
P.O. Box 400818
Las Vegas, NV 89140

ISBN-13: 9781935597872
ISBN-10: 1935597876

"The very air here is miraculous, and outlines of reality change with the moment. The sky sucks up the land and disgorges it. A dream hangs over the whole region, a brooding kind of hallucination."

—John Steinbeck, *Log from the Sea of Cortez*

To Amanda, my muse, my love, and the smartest, most interesting woman I know.

PART I

PART I

CHAPTER 1

SEA OF CORTEZ, MEXICO

Weevil Ott had not slept in days. Dark hammocks of skin hung beneath his eyes, eyes etched in red, eyes juiced with stimulants. His temples pulsed. Bits of frozen fish gills clung to the chest of his waterproof overalls.

"Lime heals all wounds," Weevil chortled into the empty bunkroom. He held an oval green fruit in his gloved hand. His other hand held a nest of razor-sharp hooks.

Weevil hunched his gaunt frame and stared at the unmade bed, confident its occupant remained on midnight watch.

"Two weeks at sea," he continued, "and the rookie still doesn't get it."

Weevil blinked into the shadowy murk. The fishing boat banked heavily into a spray of windblown waves. Seawater whipped against the lone porthole window.

Weevil paused.

He reached out and wiggled two of his fingers, dropping a single three-pronged fishhook to the mattress. He glanced down and felt suddenly sentimental. He was familiar with these surroundings: small, dank, and bare. The bunkroom had been his twenty years ago, back when he was a teenage deckhand scrubbing

1

salt and slopping stalls. It was a room designated for the lowliest crewmember—a newbie on unsteady legs.

This season it was populated by a greenhorn. A land lug who lacked any sea sense. An aspiring marine biologist and summer intern named Willie Pike.

In Weevil's view, Pike was an annoying, know-it-all college boy. Lazy, arrogant, and rude. Weevil had warned the captain not to hire the graduate student. Fishermen fished, Weevil had told him. Scientists scienced. But the captain thought otherwise. He told Weevil that fish were part of a fragile ecosystem, that university types understood this, and that with early intervention future biologists like Willie Pike could become an angler's best friend.

Set the hook properly, the captain advised, and friends like Pike could keep them clear of the government's bureaucratic nets.

Weevil wiggled free another tiny grapnel of steel and watched it bounce across the bed. "Just setting the hook, Captain."

Outside, the sea sparred with a rising northbound breeze. Cresting waves threw watery uppercuts. Windy jabs sent whitecaps airborne. The dark sea wavered, caught its breath, and like an aging heavyweight, lumbered in for another round. On most deep sea nights this melee went unnoticed, but on this occasion Mother Nature had a group of unwitting participants—fifteen recreational fishermen who had chartered the eighty-two-foot fishing boat, *Wahoo Rhapsody*, and who now slept fitfully in their staterooms. All had flights to catch in a few hours. From Cabo San Lucas to San Diego, where two days later they would reconnect with the *Rhapsody* and its cargo of yellowfin tuna.

As the heavy boat heaved starboard, Weevil hovered like a mantis in the low-slung room. The boat righted itself, and Weevil dispersed the remaining fishhooks across Pike's empty bunk. He raised the lime to his mouth, resembling a native peeling a coconut. He tore the rind with his teeth. The tart juice stung his cracked lips. Weevil blinked, barely aware of the pain. He held out the broken lime and squeezed it across the hooks.

"Chum," he giggled.

Weevil stepped back. He arched his brow and whisked dribbles of sweat from the ridge of a woolen cap. An awkward swell caught him off balance, and as he made a stumbling recovery, fish scales broke free from his overalls and fluttered like confetti in the starlight.

"Sweet dreams, Willie Boy," he said, tilting back his head and squeezing the remaining lime juice into his mouth.

He pitched the emptied fruit into the corner and hurried back to his refrigerated workstation set deep in the belly of the charter boat.

Weevil had work to do.

Solitary work.

Smuggler's work.

⌞ ⌞⌞ ⌞

Willie Pike, the *Wahoo Rhapsody*'s novice deckhand, stood watch at the stern of the ship, guzzling the remnants of a can of diet soda. His mood matched the end of the blustery night. Hours of monotonous deck wandering proved more loathsome than his daily Los Angeles commute. "A semester at sea" was the original plan, but after two weeks with a boatload of crazed fishermen, Pike was having second thoughts. Twice in the last hour he'd almost veered inside to his warm bunk. But both times he'd encountered Weevil, the ship's flaky first mate, foraging in the galley for munchies and beer.

Pike felt doomed.

He hadn't expected this temporary assignment to be so aggravating—so nauseating. Not back when he boarded the boat in San Diego. But after working day and night for the crazed boatman, Pike's hope of a worthwhile stint at sea had been jettisoned like stormbound jetsam. Pike had never been so miserable.

Now, as the *Wahoo Rhapsody* neared Cabo San Lucas, Pike was abandoning ship. The passengers would soon disembark for their return flights home, and Pike planned to join them. He'd gathered enough data, had learned all he needed to learn. Another week shadowing Weevil would be calamitous. Pike planned to inform the buggy-eyed tatterdemalion of his decision to depart early. Barge into the fish hold and quit. Pike was finished with the seafaring life.

As he considered his Weevil-less future, Pike's wristwatch obediently pinged the end of the night watch. He glanced up and spotted Big Joe, the relief watchman, stepping from the helm. Pike waved. He took a step toward the galley and paused. The boat pitched, and Pike rolled his knees in a balanced rhythm, surprised by his newfound sea legs. He rushed halfway across the deck and stopped beside the bait tank. The next swell struck amidships, and as he reached out he squished the remnant of a dead anchovy. The smell catapulted him back to the fish markets in Korea Town near his apartment in downtown Los Angeles. Waves of nostalgia washed over him. He hadn't expected to miss home so much, not with its plethora of smog, its fat tails of traffic, its constant buzz of neon and noise. But two weeks with Weevil made downtown Los Angeles a veritable Shangri-la.

Pike's reminiscence didn't last long. He plunged his fishy hand into the bait tank, wiped it across his jeans, and hurried into the galley. He padded across the emptiness humming his favorite Jimmy Buffett tune, descended into the narrow passageway, opened his bunkroom door, and stepped inside. At only five foot six he barely had to stoop in the low-slung room. He leaned into the corner to remove his shoes and socks and then stripped from his jeans and pulled off his sweatshirt. He could almost feel the softness of the sheets, the pillowy mattress, the deep glorious sleep. Crooning about his upcoming change in latitude, Pike misjudged the motion of the boat and tumbled sideways into his booby-trapped bunk.

"Ahhhh!"

Though zombied with fatigue, the zip of lime-basted, triple-pronged hooks jarred his central nervous system. Dozens of acidic stainless steel spines cut into his right arm, his rib cage, and down his lower back. One migrated into the back of his boxer shorts. It caught in the gap of his glutei maximi, pinning the lobes of skin together like a pair of fleshy bookends.

Pike shrieked.

He slapped at the back of his boxer shorts, unaware that a third prong jutted from his haunches like a cobra in a crack. Pike's hand slipped over the hovering hook. The sharpened end snagged the webbing between his thumb and forefinger and sank past the barb.

"Aghhh!"

Pike bounded from the bed. Red rivulets coursed from his wounds. Lime juice blazed into his torn flesh.

"Scorpions!" he yelled, confused by the searing pain.

Pike charged from his room. He clambered swiftly but unsteadily up the stairs, through the galley, and sprang barefoot onto the dew-covered deck. As he did, a rolling swell lifted the stern and dropped the bow. Pike attempted to steady himself, but as the swell passed beneath the hull, the stern dropped and the bow breached. Pike flopped to his belly and skidded headfirst down the deck, his left hand firmly attached to his backside as if in mid-scratch.

The lone witness to Pike's near-naked toboggan run was morning watchman and chief engineer Big Joe, who swore the sound of Pike's head hitting the stern wall was reminiscent of a fish bat thumping a 150-pound tuna squarely between the eyes.

CHAPTER 2

MAGDALENA BAY, BAJA CALIFORNIA, MEXICO

Atticus Fish sat on the back of his saddleless mule and watched another dead stingray wash in with the Pacific tide. He was a few miles south of Puerto San Carlos in Magdalena Bay along a remote stretch of Baja California coastline. He wore a guayabera shirt opened to the waist and a pair of tan-colored dungarees. His face was shaded by a fishskin cap, and his six-foot frame towered above the rare Appaloosa half-breed. Shoulder-length hair spilled across his collar, and a fisherman's crimp held the end of a braided goatee. One glance and most passersby would assume the barefoot man on the mule was just another gringo running from *norteamericano* obligations. They would be wrong.

Fish was certainly running from his past, but not because of alimony or unpaid taxes. Fish had once been the most vilified lawyer in the world. He was also the wealthiest. Born Francis Lee Finch, the handsome ex-lawyer turned expatriate fled south of the border after settling the largest class-action lawsuit in history. His fee of nearly a billion dollars did little to appease the masses. Having sued God and won, millions of fanatics wanted him dead.

And so Francis Finch—avid fan of his fictional namesake and arguably the world's most beloved, albeit fictional lawyer, Atticus Finch—became Atticus Fish, and the six-foot former Golden Gloves middleweight boxer settled into a life of exile on Isla Santo Domingo, a ten-mile-long sand dune island located on the Pacific coast six hundred miles south of San Diego. Its rolling dunes guarded Baja's famed Magdalena Bay, and a miasma of mangroves protected its quartz-white sand from even the hardiest tourists.

For two weeks he slept in the back of his seaplane and surveyed the surrounding dunes. Satisfied by its desolation and its raw beauty, he slogged through miles of mangroves at low tide and hitched a *panga* ride to the small fishing village of Puerto San Carlos to load up on supplies. To avoid trudging back through the mud flats, he bought his own twenty-two-foot *panga* with a 150-horsepower Evinrude and waited for the tide to rise. The mule, however, was an impulse buy. White with gray splotches, the rare Appaloosa was a bargain for a hundred bucks.

That had been years ago, back before the latest tidal wave of development transformed the tip of Baja into a Mexican Fort Lauderdale. Droves of drunken Americans descended weekly into the bowels of Cabo San Lucas to consume and copulate. A few louts were bound to drift off course to Puerto San Carlos hoping to harass a whale or hoard the rare seashells scattered across miles of unmolested beach. Which is why the sight of the mass killing washing up around him was not entirely surprising. Dozens of dead stingrays glistened in the sun like cobblestones on the beach. All of them speared point-blank, the telltale sign of a three-pronged Hawaiian sling tattooed on their backs.

Fish tilted back his mullet-skin cap and squinted down the shoreline. A lone black pickup truck rested on half-buried tires just above the waterline. Fish rolled up the sleeves of his shirt, rubbed out a rope of sweat coiling down his neck, and sighed. He'd planned to fly south to Cabo San Lucas that morning and surprise the captain who found him floating in the ocean all those years ago. Board the *Wahoo Rhapsody* before its departure north and give Captain Winston, his one and only business partner, a cash birthday bonus. Now it looked like the trip would have to wait.

Fish gently heeled a bare foot into the mule's flank and picked up the trot. The truck was parked beside a badly constructed tent near an avalanche of empty beer cans. A depression of sand with remnants of charred wood marked the previous night's campfire where a cooler held an iPod and a foot. The iPod blared profanity masquerading as music. The foot waggled masquerading as rhythm.

Fish rode into the camp and stopped. A college-aged kid sat in an expensive beach chair, his eyes closed, the big toe of his gyrating foot red and slightly swollen.

"*Hola!*" Fish hollered over the music.

The kid snapped open his eyes. "What the fuck, man!" He pushed himself upright in the chair. "You think that's funny? You scared the shit out of me."

Fish ran a calloused hand along the edge of his sun-bleached goatee and let his fingers fall to the metal crimp beneath his chin. He motioned toward the iPod. "You mind?"

The young camper scowled and turned down the music.

"You should soak that toe in hot water. Takes away the pain. Also pulls out any leftover barb."

"Doc recommends beer." He reached into the sand for his can of Tecate. "What can I do for you, cowboy?"

"Those your friends out there?" Fish nodded toward the two snorkelers splashing along the shoreline.

"My cleanup crew? Wouldn't go anywhere without them."

"They sure enjoy the spearfishing."

"Spear*killing*'s more like it." He chugged half his beer. "Doc's the one making all the noise. He's pre-med. Deadly with a Hawaiian sling. Knows all about snakes and venom and shit." He finished the beer and fished another from the cooler. "Fucking rays are a menace, man."

Fish dismounted in a single, swift motion, landing softly on the sand just inches from the camper. "Only when you step on them."

Beer sprayed from the young man's mouth. "What the—!" He took a quick breath and glanced around. "Weren't you just on that horse?"

"Mule."

"Whatever, dude."

"I counted thirty dead rays so far."

"The locals can thank us later…" His voice trailed off as Fish stepped to the back of the pickup truck and reached into the bed. "Hey, you can't do that!"

Fish hefted a thick tangle of rope and dropped to one knee. From the corner of his eye he saw the camper stumble from the chair and grab a half-burnt log from the ashes.

"I'm serious, man. That's my truck. My rope. Don't make me hurt you."

Fish twisted the rope a few times, stood, and casually flung a lasso, cinching the loop tightly around the camper's chest and arms. The camper dropped the log and screamed.

Fish stepped casually to the mule, looped the tag end around the animal's neck, and pulled himself astride. Then he turned up the beach toward a small inlet of water left by last month's spring tide. The estuary was less than a quarter mile away, brimming with baby stingrays, safe from predators until the next new moon and the following spring tide that would flush them out to sea.

"Whoa, dude!" the lassoed man yelled as the rope tugged him forward. "You can't do this. I'm American! I got rights!"

Fish didn't answer. He eyed another flat, round corpse drifting onto the wet sand.

"Hey, asshole! I'm injured back here!"

"You'll live."

"My buddies'll be coming out of the water any minute!"

"Hope so."

"Let me go, goddammit!"

"Count on it," Fish said, and he slapped the mule hard on the flank.

CHAPTER 3

SEA OF CORTEZ, MEXICO

"Bedtime for Willie," Weevil quipped as he checked his waterproof watch. "Wish I was up top to enjoy it."

It was the beginning of the tuna season, and the near-freezing room capable of storing twenty tons of game fish was less than half full. Weevil had spent hours organizing a workstation among the stacks of icy, hundred-pound tunas. He'd adjusted the temperature to just above freezing and piled the fish like cordwood, their crescent tails stiff as smiles in a morgue. At the far corner of the room was a rickety workbench with a battery-operated lantern giving out a soft glow. A miniature castle of bricked marijuana rose from the center of the workbench. Beside the marijuana were a jar of frozen cockroaches and a stack of cloth baby diapers.

"Think our friend Willie's been snagged by anything yet?" Weevil asked the roomful of dead fish.

He waltzed toward a waist-high stack of tuna carcasses. "Hook-up!"

Weevil spun in a circle high-fiving the frozen tuna heads. He removed his woolen cap and scratched his thinning pate of stringy brown hair, laughing at the thought of Pike crawling into a bunk of hooks. Weevil had tried to reason with the man. Do what the captain wanted. Show the collegiate bigmouth how things were aboard the *Rhapsody*. How well he and Big Joe handled the fish. How they released the small ones. How they didn't dump sewage or trash into the sea. Scientific goodwill, the captain had emphasized, was priceless.

But it was soon apparent to Weevil that the new guy was inept at everything fish related. Worse, the lackey hadn't stopped bragging about his brilliant future since boarding the *Rhapsody* a week earlier. The boat had barely begun its slow troll of the fishing grounds when Pike informed each of the passengers that he was studying marine biology at USC.

University of SoCal was how Pike had said it. No abbreviations. Extra emphasis on the word *So*. Like anybody cared. *University of Spoiled Children* was what Weevil was thinking. The fishermen didn't seem to care until Pike followed up his pedigree with the pronouncement that he intended to get some "bona fide exposure to the big blue."

Bona fide? Big blue? Weevil bowed his head in disgust. The muscle-headed fratboy was a blowhard. Weevil became even more incensed when the bite turned hot and Pike began to accost the anglers with a smorgasbord of scientific gibberish.

"Female *Thunnus albacares* of the yellowfin variety," he would say, leaning close to the proud angler. "Fat one, too. Egg sacs loaded. Probably should have let that one go, bub."

Sometimes he would kneel to the end of Big Joe's long-handled gaff and pat the yellowfin tuna on its head, peer up at the fisherman, and say, "Nothing better than hunting and gathering out here on the big blue."

Weevil had warned Pike to keep quiet. Told the intern that the guests on board spent their money to catch fish, not listen to some academic mumbo jumbo. He'd even taken Pike aside and patiently explained that a deckhand's job was to assist the fishermen, without comment, and to congratulate them on their catch. Pike just nodded and continued his annoying ways.

Weevil gave up. The guy was worse than a flock of screeching gulls.

The final few incidents came on their last day of fishing. Pike had abandoned his post on the aft deck and was found snooping around the engine room claiming to be lost. Later that same day, Weevil caught him near the helm asking the captain questions about navigational systems and radar capabilities. Both times Weevil had shooed Pike back to the deck. But later that evening, when Pike followed him to the hatch leading to the fish hold asking about fish-packing and flash-freezing, Weevil had had enough.

"Back inside!" Weevil demanded.

"But the captain—"

Weevil narrowed his eyes. "I report to the captain. Not you. And trust me, so far the reports about you have been abyssal."

"Is that even a word?"

"It is if I say it is."

"Just one little peek inside the fish hold?"

"Scram!"

"But I need to know about fish processing for my final paper."

"I'm warning you."

"But—"

Weevil unsheathed his filet knife. "You've got to the count of three, book maggot."

That was the last Weevil had seen of the intern.

Now, as Weevil skipped across the stainless steel floor, he felt vindicated. The world's worst seaman was about to learn the fine art of hook removal.

Weevil smiled at the thought. He paused at another stack of tunas and lifted a clear plastic baggie of crystalline powder from the top of a frozen fish tail. Weevil brushed the icy skin with a gloved hand, unsealed the baggie, and spilled the powdery contents across the fin. Weevil removed his gloves. He raked the pile into a crude line and surveyed the room.

"Don't worry about your marine biology buddy," he told the scaly corpses. "I'm an expert at removing hooks." Weevil choked back a laugh, his weedy chin hairs fluttering like corroded wires. "Of course, the authorities could always arrest me for baiting and assault." Laughter sprayed from his lips. "Get it? *Baiting* and assault!"

Weevil's body convulsed. Red-lined lids boomeranged over his bloodshot eyes. Small icicles of snot broke free of his nostrils. He doubled over to calm himself and then raised halfway and touched his nose to the frozen fish tail. He pressed a thumb against a nostril and followed the line of powder like a tracker through snow.

As narcotics swirled into his bloodstream, Weevil felt invigorated. He licked at the residue clinging to the tail.

"Sashimi," he said, and jitterbugged across the room.

CHAPTER 4

TIJUANA, BAJA CALIFORNIA, MEXICO

"The skinny *gabacho* told you both beacons *failed?*" La Cucaracha demanded.

"*Sí,*" Guillermo "Memo" Villa told his boss, flat teeth grinding as he spoke into the cell phone from a hotel balcony above Avenida Revolución in downtown Tijuana. "I pretended to believe him, but complete failure is impossible. I had backup batteries, backup beacons, even added a half inch of insulation to cushion the initial drop into the water. And all of that *after* I double-waxed each radio pack with heavy-duty paraffin."

"Find what is missing," La Cucaracha snapped back. "The *Wahoo Rhapsody* will be leaving Cabo San Lucas for San Diego by tomorrow morning. Our cannery man is prepared for the special delivery, no?"

"Always."

"Then we must not let him down."

Memo clacked his teeth. "I will fly to Cabo San Lucas and talk with the lying goats who would dare steal from La Cucaracha."

The voice at the end of the line lowered. "Remember, Memo, the gringos will be needed in San Diego. Keep them alive."

"Of course."

"A thousand cans' worth of our highest quality product have been promised to Topwater Tuna. Because of this sudden development, you must inform the cannery man of our shortage."

"I will contact Mr. Sparks immediately."

"I trust you understand my concerns regarding the lost shipment?"

"I understand," Memo hissed.

"You will involve Socorro, yes?"

"Of course."

The phone went dead. Memo glared out at the dusty Tijuana street below. There were two daily flights to Cabo San Lucas. If he caught the afternoon flight, he could be dockside by sunset.

Just in time for a private happy hour aboard the *Wahoo Rhapsody*.

CHAPTER 5

MAGDALENA BAY, BAJA CALIFORNIA, MEXICO

Atticus Fish urged his mule from the estuary back to the lone black pickup truck. His first captive was a few hundred yards away hogtied at the shore of the estuary soaking his stingray-stung toe in the saltwater. The two friends were still snorkeling with their deadly Hawaiian slings.

As Fish approached the campsite, he thought of the mountains of cash he had hidden around the world. How he'd squirreled away his fee after winning the world's largest class-action lawsuit. How he'd fled the zealots who wanted him dead, after the tabloids started calling him "Lawyer Lucifer" and "Billionaire Beelzebub." Fish couldn't blame them, really. After all, he'd sued the Almighty and won.

So Fish started buying things. Paid for in cash. Offshore properties and unlikely repositories. There was the seaplane with its fat belly of precious gemstones—a hundred pounds of emeralds, rubies, and sapphires. The pristine sand dune island and its three-story hideaway built into the rolling sand and insulated, literally, with panels of cash.

But then he was just getting started.

There was the Catalina Island storage unit stuffed with green-backs, the miles of Canadian coastline owned free and clear, the Caribbean marina, the Paraguayan mountaintop, and the ecolodge in Guatemala. He owned a fly-in fish camp in Honduras and a Learjet near Mexico City—in case the extremists honed in on his hermitage. And he'd purchased the eighty-two-foot charter fishing boat whose captain had saved his life. Paid three million for the boat and agreed to be the captain's silent partner—for an annual salary of one dollar. Then, when the captain and crew were on shore leave, Fish secretly stored ten million in cash inside the *Rhapsody's* double steel hull. Shrink-wrapped in twenty-pound bundles each worth a million and sealed in waterproof skins.

And then the infamous lawyer started to relax. He grew his hair, burned his courtroom clothes, and changed his name to Atticus Fish. He settled onto his sand dune island, rode his mule, flew his seaplane, and fished. What else could the world's wealthiest expatriate need?

A bar, it seemed.

The fact that he hadn't had a drink since his midnight fall from the railing of the *Rhapsody* ten years earlier did nothing to dissuade him. The port of San Carlos needed a place that served local booze and good seafood. A watering hole where the locals felt comfortable and the vagabonds were welcome. A place where the proprietor wouldn't quaff the profits.

And so, a year after settling his lawsuit against God, Atticus Fish opened Cantina del Cielo.

Heaven's Bar.

Thirty miles south of Fish's sand dune home and 125 miles northwest of La Paz, Cantina del Cielo was built on a marled lot on the outskirts of San Carlos steps from the largest expanse of

Magdalena Bay. Built to resemble an open-air courtyard with a sand-packed floor and a palapa roof, the one-story structure had a rounded front one hundred feet long with top-hinged windows and a steady bay breeze. Below the windows was a waist-high wall paneled in cactus ribs and topped with a counter fashioned from the hull of a shipwrecked schooner. Dozens of stools carved from palm tree trunks lined the open windows, each with a view of the bay.

A small kitchen in the back housed a flatiron stove where Mamacita Espinoza cooked her famous sanddab tostadas and twice-baked tortillas. Her daughter Isabela managed the bull's-eye-shaped bar constructed from pier planks that encircled the palapa's center support beam. The bar was stocked with hand-crafted mescal and solar-chilled Mexican beer. Above the bar high in the palapa's rafters lived a macaw named Chuy and a pair of domesticated iguanas named Pancho and Lefty. The parrot was fond of perching on unsuspecting shoulders until a peanut was offered. The lizards cruised the perimeter, lapping up spilled beer and passing out on the sandy floor.

Within months of opening, praise spread like sails in a storm, and soon the big bay was strewn with boats anchored inside for a respite from the Pacific and a taste of Mamacita's famed tortillas. Even the parking lot began to overflow with landbound *norteamericanos* willing to brave the thirty-five miles of washboard dirt from Highway 1 for a shot of mango-infused mescal and fresh fish tostadas. Bad roads made for good people, and most of the newcomers were harmless adventurers eager to spend a few pesos. Campers looking for barren beaches. Surfers in search of unmolested waves. Drunks and drifters, dropouts and wanderers. All with a story. Most with a smile.

But these campers were different.

Deadly different.

Fish stopped his mule in the shallow water and watched the two snorkelers exit the surf. They wore flippers and masks, and each held a six-foot-long Hawaiian sling. One boy jabbed the pronged end of his sling into the sand, leaning over it like a savior on a staff. The other boy proudly hefted his into the air where a juvenile stingray flapped awkwardly at the end, its wings contorted by the piercing prongs.

"Death to the devilfish!" the kid called out, and he hurled the wounded ray through the air. It Frisbeed to the sand and lay still.

Fish, who had rummaged two more ropes from the back of the campers' truck, nudged the mule up the shoreline. He watched the spearfishermen high-five each other and then tug the masks from their faces. They blinked away the saltwater. One glanced up and elbowed his friend. They both turned.

"Howdy, boys," Fish called out. The mule moved in close and stopped. "Good fishing?"

"Hell yeah!" the taller one with the bloodied sling declared. "But watch out for your horse, man. Stingrays are everywhere."

"*Were* everywhere," the other boy corrected, and the two high-fived again.

Fish leaned forward. "She's a mule, not a horse."

"Cool," the boys said in tandem as they took a flippered step forward. "Hey, where's Luke?"

"Tied up at the moment."

"Tied up doing what?" the tall one asked.

"Making amends. You boys planning on eating those rays?"

"No fucking way!" they said in concert.

Fish raised a rope in each hand and began to twirl the lassoes.

"Hey, those are our ropes!"

Fish pitched the left-handed lasso and caught the tall boy first. The second boy tried to move quickly, but his flippered feet caught the sand. He fell to his knees, and Fish sent the second lasso over his shoulders and pulled tightly. Obscenities drowned out the sound of the small waves lapping higher with the incoming tide.

Fish worked quickly. He looped the ropes over the mule's head and turned the animal toward the inlet a few hundred yards away. The mule yanked the two spearfishermen forward. Both belly-flopped to the sand. They stopped yelling.

"Ready?" Fish asked.

The first lassoee kicked off his flippers and scrambled to his feet. "Ready for what?"

"Desert sleigh ride."

"Huh?"

"Closing your eyes is highly recommended."

Fish slapped the mule's flank, and a few minutes later he pulled up at the estuary where the first camper sat with his toe in the shallow water, his hands trussed behind his back. His shirt was torn, and raw, sandy sores tattooed his arms and shoulders.

Fish freed the ropes from the mule's neck and hopped to the ground. He strolled barefoot to the two sandy lumps and leaned down. "Best to soak those sand burns in the saltwater as soon as possible." He untied the prisoners and motioned at the placid estuary. "Watch out for the rays, though."

"He's crazy, man!" hollered Luke, jerking his swollen toe from the water as a pair of oval shadows glided past. "Totally fucking whacked."

The two new arrivals spit sand from their mouths. Their swim trunks were twisted low on their hips, and the skin around their waists and upper backs was covered in sticky red swaths. Each stared about wild-eyed.

The shorter one said, "Whatever it is, man, take it. You want the truck, it's yours."

Luke spun on his knees. "It's not your truck, Jesse! It's mine, so shut the fuck up!"

"He's gonna kill us, bro," Jesse pleaded. "Don't be stupid. It's just a truck. Your old man will buy you another one."

"Nobody's getting killed," Fish said. "And I don't want your truck." He yanked the boys to their feet. "Start walking."

"Where?"

"Into the water and all the way across. It's time to learn how to shuffle."

"That's it?"

"That's it."

Luke released a throaty laugh. "Water's full of stingrays, you idiots. I've been watching while Indiana Jones over there rode off on his donkey. Thousands of little fuckers in here swimming around like mini pancakes, only with fangs and shit. One just tried to bite my foot."

"Lesson number one," Fish said, prodding the two boys toward the water. "Rays don't attack people. They're shy creatures. Hate being stepped on. The trick is to shuffle your feet. That way they feel you coming and swim away. No better place than a stingray nursery to learn the lesson." He motioned toward Luke, who still sat hunched at the edge of the estuary. "You too, Skywalker."

"Fuck you," Luke said, hugging his knees defiantly.

Fish took two lunging steps, grasped Luke by the waist, and flung him easily into the shallow water. Luke belly-flopped. He splashed to his feet in cartoon speed, howling in pain. His arms, still knotted behind his back, ratcheted up and down. Stinger welts rose on his thighs and chest. He stared into the clear water and froze. The estuary floor was carpeted with miniature rays.

Fish brushed his hands across his dungarees and turned to the other two. "Next?"

Both boys quickly shuffled into the water, their feet dragging across the bottom like leaden shoes.

"All the way to the other side," Fish ordered, absently twisting the tip of his crimped goatee. He whistled for the mule standing in the shade of mesquite trees. The mule trotted over, and Fish pulled himself astride. "These rays are only pups," he explained. "Stings won't last long." He nudged the mule with a bare heel and said, "Lesson number two: Being American doesn't mean squat down here. In Baja you want rights, you earn them."

The one named Jesse released a sudden wail.

"Try to focus on the first lesson," Fish called out.

Jesse shuffled quickly, the water rising to his thighs, then his waist. He let out a second scream as the saltwater lapped against a rose petal of skin.

"What, are you retarded?" Luke asked, catching up to his friend.

"Fuck off," Jesse said, and he shoved Luke in the chest. Both boys stumbled off balance and screamed. They turned and started shuffling toward shore.

"Wrong direction," Fish warned, nosing his mule to the water's edge.

Jesse and Luke shuffled back toward the middle of the estuary. The third boy, who had resorted to swimming a modified breast-stroke, suddenly cried out. He splashed to his feet, surprised to be in ankle-deep water. He raised his arms and glanced at the tiny trickle of blood slaloming down his rib cage.

"Sandbars," Fish called out.

The boy nodded theatrically.

"The mule and I'll be back after lunch. Your campsite better be cleaned up by then. I find so much as a tread mark and you'll wish you were back in the estuary."

"Yes sir," all three said with conviction.

"Kill another stingray and you'll wish you never heard of Baja."

"Okay."

Fish patted the mule on the neck and cantered through the mesquite trees toward the beach. He glanced up at the sun. An hour before noon. Still time to catch the *Wahoo Rhapsody*.

CHAPTER 6

SEA OF CORTEZ, BAJA CALIFORNIA, MEXICO

Minutes after Weevil's drug-induced jitterbug across the frozen room, the hatch cover flung open. The wan light of dawn added little to the glow of the lantern. Big Joe descended into the shadows, his face hardened, his ridgeback shoulders hunched as he squeezed beneath the deck.

"Damn it, Weevil," he said, unable to straighten to his full six and a half feet. "Pike's full of hooks. His head's cracked open. And right now the captain's not amused. It's his birthday, for Christ's sake." Big Joe dragged a hand through his mop of curly red hair. "I called ahead for a doctor to meet us at the dock." He glanced at his watch. "That's in an hour."

Weevil, who had ducked behind a stack of fish, poked out his head. "Pike's head cracked open?"

"Like a Dungeness. Ran on deck screaming something about scorpions just before he slipped. I thought he was dead."

"Ouch."

Big Joe stared menacingly at Weevil, who seemed preoccupied.

"What?"

"Ouch is all you have to say?"

Weevil fast-tapped his middle finger on a glassy fish eye, the rat-a-tat-tat loud in the insulated room. "Sorry."

"This was a one-time deal, Weevil. Your deal! Your goddamn gambling debt! I'm just backup. Remember? The captain takes a nap, I alter course, and *you* pick up the fucking pot! That's it." Big Joe's face was snapper-red. He took a series of deep breaths. "Now it's getting complicated. Pike's hurt bad. That means the *federales* might want to come aboard and sniff around."

"Come on, Joe. The *federales* don't give a damn about injured gringos."

Big Joe pointed his finger at the oblong bricks of marijuana stacked on the plywood table, the black cellophane packages tinged with frost. "They might give a damn about that. You're supposed to be done by now."

"Before we get to port. I promise." Weevil shuffled to the cluttered workbench and cleared away the assorted detritus: rusty fishing gear, empty soda cans, candy wrappers, a dog-eared *Mad* magazine. What remained was a single propane burner under a copper kettle and an oversized plastic jug of petroleum jelly, its rectangular top festooned with ointment. There was also a stack of cloth baby diapers and a pail of icy water. Weevil lit the burner.

"If the feds do come aboard, just offer them some free tuna?" Weevil offered hoping to cut the tension. When Big Joe didn't respond, he added, "You know what they say? A fish a day keeps the cops away." He slapped a tuna on the head and gave a short laugh.

Big Joe scowled and glanced across the room. He spied the clear baggie of white powder. "What the hell is that?"

"Just a little pick-me-up. It's frigging cold down here."

"Jesus Christ! You've been cranked up for days. No wonder Pike's so banged up." He threw his hands up in the air. "A scoop of dead bait would have been a good prank. The hooks were almost lethal."

"I think he might know about the drugs, Joe. As soon as I got the bales onboard, he started asking weird questions. Followed me everywhere. It was worse than a goddamned Coast Guard inspection."

"Pike was in his cabin when you pulled the bales. I was on watch. I checked before I relieved the captain."

"The guy was still acting weird."

"It's the baggie of white powder, Weevil. The drugs are making you paranoid."

Weevil shrugged. "Schoolboy was really screaming about scorpions? What a pussy."

Big Joe glared at his friend. "Forget about Pike. You need to finish what you started. Then you need to explain to La Cucaracha how you missed his fourth bale of pot."

"I didn't exactly miss it."

"You did. I confirmed it this morning."

"You talked to La Cucaracha?"

"You left your phone in the galley. I picked it up after Pike hit the wall."

"You answered my phone way out here? The roaming charges are going to kill me."

"Focus, Weevil! Some guy named Memo was calling. Said to tell you he knows."

"Knows what?"

"Knows you missed a bale. Said the signal on the fourth bale went dead."

"Shit," Weevil complained. "I'm toast."

"Pike might kill you, but not La Cucaracha. Memo said there's a backup signal. He wants you to go back out and retrieve it."

"Oops."

"I know. You don't have a lot of time. As soon as we get to Cabo, you can rent a super-*panga*. At full speed you can be back out there in a few hours. I'll tell the captain you had to go into town for supplies and a little R&R. That will give you most of the day to search."

The kettle of water began to hiss, and Weevil hurried to grab it. "No, I mean oops as in I smashed the signal box before I dropped the bale back into the water."

"You what!"

"How much do you think that pot's worth, Joe? A half million at least."

Weevil hoisted the funnel and poured boiling water down a tuna throat. "Don't worry, I re-marked it. Attached a tracking signal to coordinate with my handheld GPS. We can go back and get it in a few weeks."

Big Joe stared blankly as Weevil retrieved a stack of shrink-wrapped marijuana from the workbench. He spread a handful of ointment across the plastic sheathing, placed the bricks one by one inside the fish's mouth, and shoved them belly-deep with the butt of a fishing rod. Then he wet a cloth diaper and jammed it into the throat where it would freeze and close off any slippage of the drugs.

"Tell me you didn't steal from a drug lord, Weevil."

"Joe, you need to relax. It was just a little bait-and-switch beacon. I'll tell Memo that the backup signal wasn't working. Nobody will know. Next trip down we'll retrieve the pot. Hey, I'll even split it with you—after I pay off the loan shark. Then we'll be done with Memo and the bugman."

"Fuck!" Big Joe groaned.

"That's what I'm talking about," Weevil said, turning in a circle and shadow-boxing a dead tuna. "Make a little love, do a little dance, get down with it."

As Weevil spun back around, he heard the hatch door slam shut. When he looked up, Big Joe was gone.

CHAPTER 7

SAN DIEGO, CALIFORNIA

Edwin Sparks, manager of Topwater Tuna, puffed at the moist end of a Swisher Sweets cigar. It was midmorning, and already his extra-large bowling shirt had come untucked from his polyester pants. He rubbed a plump hand over his balding head and opened the window of his second-story office. A cheekful of sugary smoke flowed from his mouth as he stared past the 5 Freeway across Mission Bay toward Fisherman's Landing, the southland's largest fishing wharf and home to the majority of California's long-range recreational fishing fleet. In all there were dozens of Southern California charter boats bringing in tons of tuna fish a year, and Topwater Tuna canned nearly all of it.

Recent competition, however, had forced Edwin to think creatively—something he loathed more than the smell of simmering tuna. Edwin extinguished his cigar and returned to the small black-and-white television at his desk. The familiar infomercial was playing again, its aging actress imploring viewers to send money to help her foundation feed the world's starving children. Edwin closed his eyes and retraced the moment last month when he'd marched down to the factory floor where his workers were shoveling hundreds of pounds of fish sludge into wheelbarrows.

The waste was destined for the storm drain leading directly to Mission Bay, a free daily disposal in direct violation of city regulations. Edwin, who was normally happy to allow the breach of law, halted the wheelbarrows. Not because he was worried about fines or punishment; Mission Bay already stunk of persistent discharge from neighboring SeaWorld, heavy boat traffic, settling freeway exhaust, and the not-so-covert nightly bridge dumpings. Edwin was confident no one would notice the deluge of rotting fish skeletons bubbling up with the muck.

He stopped the illegal dumping because instead of fish waste Edwin now saw cheap nutrition—and job security. Edwin instructed his workers to reboil the waste, load it with salt, and can it as Salisbury Tuna. Then he returned to his office and phoned the number on the television screen. He offered the new product to the charity at a hefty discount and soon had the aging actress on the line. She was so grateful she even promised to promote the idea to other food charities. Soon Topwater Tuna became the exclusive exporter of ground-up, overcooked, finny byproduct. And the third world couldn't get enough.

In countries whose citizens' lack of protein was matched by their leaders' surplus of greed, the needy could now get omega-3s at a fraction of the cost of a standard can of tuna. Never mind that the world's poor may have been choking down the occasional bone shrapnel and bits of fish bile. As far as Edwin was concerned, cooking tuna innards into a barely edible paste was a win-win. Topwater Tuna had a market for its fish waste, and people without food got fed—albeit in a barely palatable form of tuna Spam.

Within months of Edwin's brainstorm, profits at Topwater Tuna surged. Edwin's employer, an elderly art collector named Doris Dockweiler, was ecstatic. She may have abhorred all things fish-related, but she adored money. Having inherited the cannery from her husband after he'd croaked from a mercury-rich diet of free canned tuna, she immediately appointed Edwin as top fish at the cannery.

"Make me money, Edwin," she'd said, "or suffer the consequences of unemployment."

Thus, when she'd called to congratulate Edwin, she told him he could not only keep his job as manager, but as a bonus, instead of paying wholesale for his canned tuna, he could have all the free tuna he wanted—so long as he took it for personal use only.

"Just think of the savings, Edwin," she remarked happily. "You can put those extra food dollars into your retirement account and let interest do its daily work."

That had been a month ago, but the words remained as unpleasant to Edwin as the stench of boiling fish. He forced away thoughts of his penurious boss, relit his Swisher Sweets cigar, and returned to the window. He stared out at the incessant traffic clogging the freeway, each new car a rolling ton of plaque along San Diego's asphalt artery, and marveled at his newfound endeavor.

The *Wahoo Rhapsody* was on its way back from the fishing grounds, and Edwin was anxious. He knew his cousin, longtime pot smoker and part-time drug dealer, would be waiting at the docks, heavy-duty dolly in hand, to unload the potbellied fish. He knew the two of them would spend the night in the cannery loading the leafy contents into lead-lined cans, each custom-made to match the weight of a real can of dolphin-safe tuna. And he knew the delivery instructions would arrive days later in a nondescript manila envelope, the only indication of its sender a wax stamp with the initials L.C. affixed to the clasp. He just wished he knew more about the drug boss. He had a theory that it had nothing to do with the brutish middleman named Memo who had contacted Edwin's cousin about the idea of canning cannabis.

Edwin, who knew a little Spanish, theorized that La Cucaracha was a businessman like himself. He felt the connection the moment he had first opened the wax-stamped envelope. The moment he saw the dead bugs. He supposed that La Cucaracha was some tortilla magnate headquartered south of the border. And like Edwin, the man probably had an office at his factory. But instead of flies buzzing around dead fish, the drug lord had to contend with cockroaches scurrying through his maize.

In fact, the only real difference Edwin saw between himself and the tortilla magnate—other than the fact that the man was a notorious drug lord named after a popular Mexican song—was that La Cucaracha lived in a country without health codes.

What else could explain the dead cockroaches?

CHAPTER 8

MAGDALENA BAY, BAJA CALIFORNIA, MEXICO

After leaving the three campers to hone their stingray shuffle, Atticus Fish rode his mule back up the bay a mile and a half to his bar, Cantina del Cielo. He stopped briefly at the black pickup truck, dumped out the contents of a suitcase that had been jammed between cases of beer and bundles of store-bought firewood, and cleaned the shoreline of dead stingrays.

By the time he arrived at the bar's shell-packed parking lot, the lunch crowd was in full Baja mode. Two Avis rental Jeeps and three dust-covered Volkswagen Vanagons accompanied the usual junkers. The deepwater bay was also beginning to fill with the recent arrival of four sailboats and a private yacht. Through the open air of the cantina he could hear Janis on the jukebox lamenting her loss of Bobby McGee.

Fish tied the mule to a serpentine branch of mesquite where a bin of oats and a bucket of water rested in the shade. A sign tacked to the tree read "Mephistopheles." Beyond the tree was the small dinghy dock and the seaplane moored in the bay. Fish pulled the suitcase from the mule's back and started for the entrance. He made it halfway when the honk from a 1980 Buick station wagon slowed his stride. As the car pulled into the lot, a familiar face leaned through the driver's side window and grinned.

"Maybe not so healthy moving into a bar," the driver said, parking beside the dust-coated Volkswagens. "Then again, you own the place, so what do I know?"

Fish set down the suitcase and pushed back his mullet-skin fisherman's cap. "Good morning, Skegs."

The man called Skegs stepped from the Buick and squinted into the sharp sunlight. He stood tall for a Seri Indian, at least a foot taller than most, with blue jean eyes and hair that resembled clumps of dried seaweed. Odd hair for an Indian, but Fish had become accustomed to the oddness of Baja. Skegs was no exception.

From his height and hair color, to his penchant for recreational fishing, nothing about the man seemed indigenous Indian. Fish suspected Skegs was more Native American than Seri Indian, probably a casino dropout from San Diego who migrated south for personal reasons. But Skegs never wavered about his full-blooded heritage. He was quick to tout his tribal connections originating across the Sea of Cortez, where he claimed family members still foraged for the ironwood that made the Seris famous. Skegs wore moccasins in the winter and huarache sandals in the summer. He was an expert in all things cactus-related, and he smoked tobacco from a peace pipe rumored to be made from the bone of a chupacabra, the mythical goat-sucking demon of the Sonoran desert. He was also a compulsive fisherman.

Fish was happy to play along. The ruse was harmless. Plus the man had the heart of a monk. He also sold the best homemade mescal north of Oaxaca. And lately, when he wasn't busy hawking his bootleg tequila and faux ironwood carvings, he was showing Fish where a quirk in the undersea geography brought exotics within a mile of Fish's sand dune island. Dorado, marlin, wahoo, and even the occasional tuna. Deepwater game fish lured into the shallows by a confluence of current and upwelling and an abundance of year-round bait.

"Dodos are schooling heavy," Skegs said excitedly, glancing over at Fish's seaplane moored in the bay. "You and that big silver bird could get us there in ten minutes, tops. Splashdown outside the action and get them with the dinghy. I'll row."

"Not selling any cactus juice today?"

"There you go again. Thinking my people sit around with a bottle of hooch all day. Ask me about the buffalo hunt, too. Man, I thought you were a friend."

"I'll take a case of mescal and all the ironwood marlins you got. They're a hit with the rental car crowd." Fish raised the suitcase and stepped toward the shade of the bar's towering palapa.

Skegs frowned. "I see you're still riding that smelly old mule. Man, that's an embarrassment. Let me find you a horse. Strong one. Indian-bred."

Fish stepped to the raised entrance and dropped the suitcase, sloshing bloody water from its zipper.

Skegs stepped back. "Never mind the horse, man. I knew you were acting weird. Who you got in that thing? Ex-wife? Business partner? Pushy salesman?"

"Stingrays," Fish said.

Skegs quickly crossed himself. "*Muy mala suerte.* You mess with the rays, the rays mess with you. You gonna get whacked by a momma ray you keep this up. When you do, you remember it was Skegs who told you so."

"Never knew you were Catholic."

"What?"

"You crossed yourself."

"Naw, man. I was performing a sacred cleansing ritual. The elders taught us when we were kids. Secret Indian stuff."

"Elder white guys wearing black robes and talking about Jesus? We call them missionaries where I come from."

Skegs scowled. "Go ahead, make fun. But you better hope the stingray *jefa* forgives you, man. That's all I can say."

Fish wiped a switchback of sweat from a sun-bleached sideburn and reset his fishskin cap. "I didn't kill them."

"No need to justify it, hombre. It's your bad mojo."

"I'm walking away now."

"Only one case of mescal?"

"It's what I always order."

"A few more might fix that bad mojo."

"Yeah?"

"And I'll put in a good word with the stingray fish goddess."

"Better give me all you got then." Fish swung the heavy suitcase through the bar's open front door. Up in the rafters Chuy squawked.

"I got a filet knife in the glove compartment," Skegs called out.

Fish turned back and eyed the salesman curiously.

"The stingrays," Skegs said, pointing at the suitcase. "Help you filet them."

"I thought they were bad luck."

"*Yours* not mine."

Fish glanced back at the shiny red fishing rod poking from the back window of the Buick. "Schooling dodos you said?"

"Big ones."

"I need help painting the new community center next week."

"Next week? Sorry, rayman, I got a conference in Mazatlan."

"Then I could use a copilot today. I'm flying to Cabo in an hour. To deliver a fortieth birthday surprise to an old friend before he heads back north. Been avoiding the place for years, but this is a special occasion."

Skegs's eyes parted like clamshells. "Cabo? In the afternoon? That's crazy whiteman talk. You know what it's like down there these days? Nonstop happy hour. *Animal House* on the water. The whole bay filled with crowds of drunken Jet Skiers and whacked-out parasailers. No way, man. Take a seaplane in there, you gonna kill someone."

"That bad?"

"Worse. Add the endless train of cruise ships and hundreds of fishing boats and you'd be lucky to find an anchorage within a mile of the marina."

Fish gave a disappointed nod. He knew Skegs spent more time in Cabo than anyone. With a new bar opening every week, it was a mescal-maker's utopia.

"Maybe I'll radio him instead," Fish said. "Offer to fly out tomorrow as they pass by. Splashdown if the water's not too rough."

"Now you're thinking like an Indian."

Fish stole another look at the new fishing rod. "Frees up my afternoon to head into town to wrangle up a volunteer painter."

Skegs scowled. "I love painting. Used to spruce up all the tee-pees back in the day."

"You lived in a teepee?"

Skegs threw his hands in the air. "There you go again. Thinking only Apaches and Pocahontas were good enough to live in teepees."

Fish gave a dismissive wag of the head. "What about that conference down in Mazatlan?"

"I can cancel. Mazatlan's as crazy as Cabo these days."

Fish hefted the suitcase over his shoulder. "The sooner I get these stingrays skinned the sooner we get that new fishing rod of yours wet."

"Roger that."

As the barefoot man in the mullet-skin cap threaded the crowd of patrons, Skegs hurried to the trunk of his Buick and unloaded a box of cement marlins painted ironwood-brown, half a dozen cases of home-brewed mescal, and the sharpest filet knife in southern Baja.

CHAPTER 9

CABO SAN LUCAS, BAJA CALIFORNIA, MEXICO

The midday heat hurried Weevil along Cabo San Lucas's main cobblestone street toward the Giggling Marlin Bar and Restarante, one of the town's most popular tourist cantinas. Weevil had finished his fishbelly work aboard the *Wahoo Rhapsody*, and by noon no *federales* had arrived to investigate the injuries to Willie Pike, who Captain Winston had taken to the hospital for sterilized hook removal.

Weevil left a hasty telephone message with Memo explaining that the backup signal on the missing bale was dead, and that they would deliver the partial load to San Diego as scheduled. Then he cancelled Big Joe's plans to hire a super-*panga* to go back out for the pot and headed into town, promising he would return well before sunset. He'd also promised not to take along any drugs. Big Joe had checked his pockets anyway.

Now, as Weevil weaved a course along the broken sidewalk, his tongue felt chalky. His eyes burned beneath his baseball cap, and his stomach felt hollow. He scowled at the ocean of straw-hatted tourists and timeshare barkers and entered the Giggling Marlin at a near sprint. A row of elderly expatriates sat on stools at the weathered plankwood bar and stared at a corner-mounted television announcing the day's news via satellite. The symbol at the base of the screen read "CNN." A classic Van Halen song blared from the jukebox telling Weevil he might as well jump. Cigarette smoke hung in the air. A parrot balanced on the cross wires of a rusty cage, methodically working the skin from a *limón*.

"Shot of mescal," Weevil ordered from the Mexican barkeep, a middle-aged man with shiny black hair and a thick, sloping mustache. "And a bucket of Dos Equis." Weevil glanced around. "Maybe make it two shots, *por favor.*"

The row of old men at the bar telegraphed a knowing nod.

Weevil fished his wallet from the pocket of his board shorts and removed a twenty-dollar bill. He dropped the money to the counter, leaned over the time-beveled wood, and whispered, "*El baño?*"

"Bathroom's in the corner," the bartender said in perfect English. Then he added, "Say hello to Pez Gallo on your way by." He pointed a paring knife toward the birdcage.

Weevil blinked vacantly. "Pez Gallo?"

"Cabo's friendliest parrot. You don't stop, he gets mad."

Weevil glanced at the old men, who pretended not to notice. He walked to the parrot cage and paused, entranced by the bird's systematic stripping of the small lime. Weevil wavered slightly and reached out to steady himself on the wire mesh of the cage, its metal frame cool in his grip.

The parrot dipped its head in disbelief, dropped the lime, and released an earsplitting squawk. The high-pitched sound propelled Weevil backward. He released the cage, cupped his hands over his ringing ears, and stumbled over his flip-flopped feet and landed hard on the tile floor.

"Ooooh," came the collective slur from the barstools.

"I'm surprised you fell for that old trick," came a Mexican woman's voice. She reached down and retrieved his baseball cap from the floor. "The barman, his name is Juan Carlos. He knows the bird doesn't like gringos."

Weevil moved his gaze from the parrot to the hem of a black skirt resting carelessly on the knees of a light-skinned señorita. His eyes followed the skirt and stalled on the scorpion tattoo poking out from her scoop-necked blouse.

"Your cap," she said.

Weevil pushed himself from the floor and accepted the cap with an embarrassed grin. The woman sat back in her wicker chair beside a table covered in water-stained leather, stretched thin and sewn around the edges. A bright orange bowl of untouched tortilla chips sat at the center of the table. A clay bowl of salsa rested nearby.

She motioned to an empty chair. "Sit. I know Juan Carlos. He'll bring us your order."

Weevil rubbed his lower back and looked back at the parrot, his eyes drifting toward the restroom.

"*Caballeros* on the left," she said. "Just don't look the parrot in the eyes when you walk past." She tapped a forefinger beneath one of her heavily mascaraed eyes. "He doesn't like the baby blues." She gave a sultry smile and reached out a hand. "My name is Socorro. And blue is my favorite color."

Weevil scarecrowed to his feet. "Be right back."

The old men silently applauded. The parrot reclaimed its lime and resumed its peeling of the skin. Socorro watched Weevil enter the restroom, and then she opened her handbag. She removed a cellular telephone and pressed a key. She waited for the beep of the voice mail.

"Memo, it's me. I've got one of the gringos. The wiry one with greasy hair. I followed him to the Giggling Marlin. I'll have him ready for you. After midnight, *mi amor*."

Socorro closed her phone.

The bartender brought the shots of mescal and the bucket of beer and set it on the table.

"*Lo siento*," he said. "I did not know the American was your friend."

Socorro pulled an icy bottle free from the bucket. "He's not," she said, forcing a wedge of lime into the amber liquid. Inside, the shaft of beer bubbled. Socorro raised the bottle to her lips.

"To La Cucaracha," she toasted as she tilted the bottle upward.

CHAPTER 10

MAGDALENA BAY, BAJA CALIFORNIA, MEXICO

Atticus Fish stood in the kitchen of Cantina del Cielo carefully layering the stingray skins into a watery bin of borax and zinc phosphate to cure for twenty-four hours before washing them with acetone and stitching some non-slip boating shoes for the crew of the *Wahoo Rhapsody*. He felt guilty about canceling his plans to surprise Captain Winston, and he wondered about Skegs's true motives to keep him from flying south. Big dorado and a new fishing rod were powerful indicators of the salesman's priorities.

"That's a wrap, skinman," Skegs called out from the kitchen sink, where he stood cleaning his filet knife under the impatient gaze of ninety-year-old Mamacita, head cook and the town's most notorious tortilla maker.

Mamacita kept one eye on Skegs and one eye on her twice-baking corn tortillas. The tortillas were as legendary as her seven husbands, three of them brothers, all long buried in the local cemetery. Some said it was the tortillas. Mamacita said it was a series of weak hearts. Not that it mattered. Her tortillas sold so fast that Fish built her a larger kitchen and added a second flatiron stove.

"Mama's getting annoyed," Fish said, placing the final skinned stingray into the tanning solution.

"You think she really killed all them husbands?"

"I think she's about to kill a careless Indian if he doesn't quit wasting her hot water on that filet knife."

Skegs shut off the faucet and quickly dried the knife on his jeans. "I know how she killed 'em, man. Voodoo. She's a witch. A human chupacabra. Sucked away their souls and stole whatever time they had left. How else could she be a hundred and fifty years old?"

Fish snapped the lid over the bin of tanning solution. "Never met a bad witch yet."

"Yeah? Well it'll be too late when you do. Ready to roll?"

"How sure are you that I shouldn't buzz over to Cabo for a few hours? I can drop you and the dinghy offshore with the dodos, and if all goes well be back to get you before dark."

"If all goes well? Nothing can go well if you fly into that carnival. I'm not kidding, man. It makes Mardi Gras look a Sunday picnic."

"I don't know—"

"Listen, the only safe time for you to fly in there is daybreak. Before the booze starts flowing. By midmorning the place is a damn drunkfest. Trust me on this one, honcho."

Fish gave a disheartened nod. "Wait here while I ride to the bank and make the midday deposit. Shouldn't take long. You could help Mamacita kneed the masa while I'm gone."

"And have my soul sucked out of me? Not a chance." He whisked by Fish. "I'll load the new eye-opener into the seaplane and wait for you there."

"Eye-opener?"

"Waxwing fish slayer system. Vermilion red PowerPro line. Bleeding mackerel hydrodynamic jig. Trailing double hook, also red. UV reactive paint down the lateral line. Newest addition to my Shimano arsenal. Dorados don't have a chance, man."

"Uh-huh."

"You'll see."

Minutes later, Fish was on the back of Mephistopheles, a satchel of cash slung over his shoulder, moving slowly down the town's main dirt road. The swelter of midday kept most inhabitants indoors, enjoying a siesta or an omnipresent television soap opera. Everyone except the bleary-eyed man standing on the corner.

One thing about Baja, it was hard to stand out.

This guy stood out.

He looked to be in his late twenties, his neck covered in ink, the letters oversized and minacious. His head was a tightly whiskered ball. The pants were patent gangbanger-black and served mostly to buttress a pair of equally black boxer shorts. He wore a sweat-stained muscle shirt and mirrored sunglasses. His shoes were unlaced Nike Air Jordans, and he leaned against a telephone pole with the indifference of a career felon. Fish tipped his hat as he trotted by.

"*Yo, ese?*" the man called out, the click of the handgun ominous in the dead air.

Mephistopheles halted, and Fish turned.

"What you got in the bag, cowboy?"

"Donations. Kids need a clinic. Want to help build it?"

"Want to get shot?"

"Not so much."

"Toss the bag."

Fish shifted forward on the mule's back. "Where are you from?"

"Chula Vista Chicano." He touched the muzzle of the gun against the elongated letters covering his neck. A long V down his esophagus. A tall C down each carotid artery. "Now throw me the bag."

"City just south of San Diego, right?"

"You some kind of travel agent? Toss the bag before I empty six into you and that ugly horse."

"Mule."

"Gonna be a dead mule in a second."

Fish let the bag slide down his arm. He caught the strap in his hand, swung it in a swift arc, and released it with the speed of a Nolan Ryan fastball. The satchel knocked the pistol to the dirt, where it bounced in a cloud of dust, the hammer snapping harmlessly on an empty cartridge.

The robber glanced at the fallen weapon and then lunged for the satchel of money. As his hand grasped the strap, a calloused bare foot pinned it to the ground.

"*Oye!*" he blurted. "How'd you do that?"

"Lucky shot."

"No, how'd you get off your mule so fast?"

"Time travel. What's your name?"

"Alfredo."

"Well, Alfredo, seems you've got a choice to make. I'll let you go if you promise to help paint the community center—"

Alfredo windmilled his free arm. Fish hopped effortlessly and came down hard, both knees on Alfredo's back. "Wrong choice."

Air escaped Alfredo's lungs like smoke from a fire. Fish worked quickly. He unsheathed the filet knife still belted to his dungarees and slit the back of Alfredo's T-shirt. He tore the cloth

SHAUN MOREY

into two long strips and yoked the man's arms and feet. As he slung the failed gangbanger over Mephistopheles, he thought about Cabo San Lucas and the *Wahoo Rhapsody*. Maybe he should have risked the landing. Surprised the captain like he'd planned. Who couldn't manage a few drunken Jet Skiers? A couple of para-sailers? Captain Winston only turned forty once, and Fish wanted to be there for him.

Fish glanced up at the sky. Almost two o'clock. He could still get back in time to drop Skegs on the dorado and make Cabo by sunset. Just as the *Wahoo Rhapsody* was motoring out.

As soon as he saw the banker.

And the jailer.

CHAPTER 11

SAN DIEGO, CALIFORNIA

At a few minutes before noon, Edwin Sparks locked the door to his office on the second floor of Topwater Tuna and trudged across the parking lot to his reserved space beneath a large California pepper tree. The tree was covered in soot and sticky tuna smoke. Small peppercorns blackened on the branch and dropped to the ground like decayed teeth. But the shade it offered was the second of the two perks bestowed on Edwin by Mrs. Dockweiler. The first, of course, was all the canned tuna he could eat.

Edwin pulled the canvas cover from his 1986 Toyota Celica and shook free the peppercorns. He folded the canvas neatly into a square, placed it in the hatchback, and squeezed into the driver's seat. He slipped on a pair of imitation lambskin gloves and slowly backed from the space, sneezing at the sudden influx of freshly ground pepper wafting though the car's vents.

The blaring of horns broadcast his entry onto the freeway, where even at noon the summertime traffic trickled like migrating sloth. In the distance, SeaWorld's blue tower rose like a caricature, and beyond that the San Diego International Airport. The five-mile drive took thirty-five minutes, and at one o'clock sharp

Edwin's Celica coasted up the driveway of his stuccoed condominium. The two-story rectangular structure was perched at a ridgeline just beyond the airport's main runway, and its view of the San Diego skyline was as dazzling as the jumbo jets were deafening.

Edwin hadn't worried about the noise when he bought the discounted condo six years earlier. Back then he'd been confident of his investment. Alternative fuel was no longer a fringe concept, and global warming was about to transform the airline industry. Hybrid cars had become mainstream. Electric vehicles were more and more commonplace. It was only logical that quieter, eco-friendly planes would soon follow.

But within months of Edwin's purchase, San Diego's popularity skyrocketed. New residents flooded the southland, and airline traffic soared. Hybrid jet technology, while good for the environment, was bad for corporate profits. New engines were expensive, old planes difficult to retrofit, and all of it time-consuming.

So as airline traffic quadrupled so did the noise, the poisonous exhaust, and the earthshaking takeoffs. Edwin's condo sprouted new cracks weekly. The stucco peeled away like eczema. The foundation formed soft spots beneath the carpet where miniature sinkholes expanded monthly. Edwin's sure bet now looked to be a bust. All he could do was hope for airport expansion or government condemnation to save him from a total loss.

Edwin set the emergency brake on the Celica and stepped from the car. He ignored the newest fissures in his driveway, extinguished his sweet-smelling cigar, and in the span of two ground-rattling takeoffs, unloaded a week's supply of free tuna: four cases of canned Tuna Tenderloin. Edwin knew the name was a misnomer, that the only thing tenderloin about the blend of oily skipjack filets and mackerel steaks was the name. But he also knew that eating the more expensive canned tuna would affect the company's bottom line, and *that* would affect the mood of Mrs. Dockweiler.

As he set the cases on the kitchen counter, his cell phone began to vibrate. He wiped sweat from his brow and opened the phone.

"Yes," he said loudly, the noise of another jet fading behind the double-paned windows.

"Señor Sparks? This is Memo."

Edwin felt his Adam's apple seize in his throat.

"Señor?" the man asked a second time.

"Yes," Edwin croaked.

"The fish totals are smaller than expected."

"Smaller?"

"By twenty-five percent. Very unfortunate. What is left will arrive as scheduled."

"And the fee for processing?" Edwin squeaked.

"La Cucaracha expects your cooperation."

"But we had an agreement."

"The agreement has changed."

"What are you saying?"

"I am saying you can expect—"

The last words were smothered by a heavy rumbling. Edwin jammed a fat finger into his ear. "I can expect what!"

The phone fell silent, and the windows began to quake.

"Expect what!" Edwin screamed again into the phone. The only response was a dial tone.

Edwin slumped to the couch and checked for a return number. The screen showed a blocked international call. He dropped the phone to the Formica coffee table and slouched to the couch.

Thirty seconds later the phone began to quiver. Edwin sat upright and snatched it from the table.

"Memo?"

Nothing.

"Hello?"

Still nothing.

He checked the caller ID and saw no incoming call. Then the coffee table began to tremble. The windows began to shudder. The room filled with thunder, and Edwin flung the phone to the floor.

He barreled into the kitchen, opened the refrigerator door, found a half-empty glass of wine, and drank it in a single gulp. Next he reached into an adjacent drawer, liberated a prescription bottle of muscle relaxants, and poured a handful into his mouth. He opened a can of beer and washed down the pills. Minutes later, a ripple of courage descended his spine.

Cooperation is a two-way street, Edwin realized. Without a cannery man, La Cucaracha's smuggling operation was doomed. If the drug dealer wanted to reduce Edwin's fee, Edwin would make up for the loss. A quarter-size bud from every can of pot would add up quickly.

Edwin opened another can of beer. *Then again*, he thought, *why cull a little when you can take it all?* A few thousand cans of primo cannabis sold retail would pad his retirement nicely. Even if he did have to split the money with his cousin. A heist like that could jump-start a new life.

The more Edwin considered the plan, the more he liked it. He could buy an old trailer and load it with a lifetime supply of free tuna. Head north, away from the city and its incessant planes. Away from the Mexican border and Memo. Away from Mission Bay and the truckloads of stinking fish.

Someplace where it snowed when it was supposed to snow, where the leaves changed in the fall, where summers didn't make you sweat. People who didn't make you rush. Someplace rugged and eccentric. A place whose populace appreciated good pot.

A place like Alaska.

First, though, he needed a stronger cocktail.

CHAPTER 12

MAGDALENA BAY, BAJA CALIFORNIA, MEXICO

Skegs paddled the ten-foot inflatable dinghy toward the promise of schooling dorados. Atticus Fish sat on the forward thwart lamenting his lost opportunity to make a sunset landing in Cabo San Lucas. His plans to fly had been dashed against the rocky shores of circumstance: first it was the Chula Vista gangbanger, then a one-cop town with a pig emergency, and finally a banking siesta. By the time Fish had returned to his seaplane, Skegs was unloading the fishing gear and threatening to paddle the dinghy across the bay without him.

Now, as Fish checked the drag on his rusty Penn Senator, the sun was low on the horizon.

"That thing's as old as your damn mule," Skegs scoffed.

"At least it isn't red."

"When's the last time you changed the line?"

"Line's just fine."

"Please tell me you're kidding about that bucket of stingray guts."

"You've got your ultraviolet red chrome bleeding mackerel contraption. I've got the real thing."

"Man, I'm just glad there's no one out here to see you embarrass yourself like this."

Fish reached into the bucket and removed a hunk of bloody stingray. He folded it twice over the 6/0 circle hook and dropped the offering into the water. He played out a hundred feet of line and pressed his thumb over the spool.

Skegs suppressed a laugh. "I've got extra trolling lures, you know."

"I know."

"They swim like real fish."

"Chunk bait works better."

"For 'cudas maybe, but not big bulls."

"Uh-huh."

"We're not even to the spot yet."

Fish stared up at the sky. "Doesn't matter."

"But—"

The water erupted with the maw of a sleek turquoise predator. Fish eased his thumb from the spool and counted to five. He engaged the drag and reared back and watched a big bull dorado rocket from the surface. It shook its massive flat head, tail-walked across the horizon, and sounded.

"Holy shit!" Skegs yelled and dropped the oars. He fumbled with the Waxwing fishing rod and clumsily snapped a red lure onto an equally red swivel.

"Dorados swim in pairs, dude!" he sang out and pitched the lure toward the spot of the sounding game fish. He cranked the ergonomic power handle on the gold Trinidad reel and awaited the strike. Moments later the shiny lure clanked against the hull of the dinghy.

"Must be the wrong color," he mumbled to himself. He snatched an iridescent chrome sand eel from his lure box and replaced the bleeding mackerel. Minutes later it too clanked against the hull.

Skegs reached over to inspect the untouched lure, a look of confusion on his face.

"Hand me the gaff," Fish called out from the bow.

"No way, man. Keep it in the water. Quick change of lure and I'll get the other one."

"What other one?"

"The dorado that ignored my last cast."

"Two casts."

"It'll only take a second."

"Gaff!"

Skegs reluctantly set his rod against the gunwale with the lure dangling off the side. He rummaged for the small hand gaff and handed it to Fish.

"I also need the spray bottle wedged in the corner."

"You're going to brain it with a spray bottle?"

"It's filled with vodka."

"Something wrong with my mescal? Man, this is the worst fishing day of my life."

Fish leaned forward and gently pried open the dorado's mouth with the side of the gaff. "Spray bottle!"

Skegs passed the spray bottle forward. Fish buried the nozzle into the cavernous throat and squeezed the trigger. He angled the spray of vodka back and forth between the dorado's gills and seconds later hauled a forty-pound drunken game fish into the boat. As it lay motionless on the floorboards, Fish opened its gill plates and coated the red filaments with booze.

"That ought to do it," he said and freed the circle hook from the dorado's jaw. He reached into the bucket for another lump of stingray. "Row us a hundred yards that way." He pointed toward a frigate bird flying in a tight circle above the water.

"Not until you explain what just happened."

"First you need an old Penn reel—"

"The vodka, not the lucky strike."

"Oh that. Alcohol poisoning. Old Hawaiian outrigger trick. A big fish flopping in a small boat can get dangerous. Cheap vodka seems to work best. No violent clubbing. No blood splatter. It's humane and quick. And guaranteed to subdue a fish of any size."

Skegs's face brightened. "I'm starting to see a whole new market for my mescal."

Fish saw a flash of silver near the side of the dinghy and watched in disbelief as a small barracuda porpoised from the water and snared the chrome sand eel dangling just above the waterline. Before either man could move, the bright red Waxwing rod with its gold reel catapulted from the gunwale and plunged into the depths.

"Tell me that wasn't what I thought it was," Skegs implored.

Fish slowly nodded. "Yep. 'Cuda. Cute little one. Two-pounder maybe."

CHAPTER 13

CABO SAN LUCAS, BAJA CALIFORNIA, MEXICO

After delivering Pike to the hospital, Captain Winston returned to the *Wahoo Rhapsody* and by late afternoon readied for their departure. He'd sent Big Joe in search of Weevil, who had not returned as promised, and was making a fresh pot of coffee in the galley when a Mexican man stormed aboard demanding to see the thieving gringos who dared double-cross La Cucaracha. When Winston suggested he try another boat, the man revealed a large switchblade knife and led him to the back deck and told him to open the hatch to the twenty-ton fish hold.

Now, inside the fish hold, Winston stared sullenly at the aggressor who called himself Memo.

"There, you see?" Winston explained, pointing a flashlight across Weevil's workstation. "Just a freezer full of fish."

"No, *Capitán*. La Cucaracha's drugs are here. Most of them, anyway."

"Impossible."

Memo wagged the knife toward the workbench. "You see the burner, the jelly, the diapers?"

Winston shrugged his wide shoulders. "Weevil's an eccentric."

"And the jar of cockroaches?"

"Like I said—"

Memo moved within inches of the pony-tailed captain. "This is your ship. You are responsible for your crew's action. *Verdad?*"

"Of course."

"If your crew is smuggling drugs, then you are smuggling drugs. And if they steal those drugs—"

Winston shook his head angrily. "No! I—"

The deck gave way so suddenly that for an instant Winston thought the boat had been broadsided by a rogue wave. Cold air rushed across his face. The stainless steel floor landed solidly against his cheek, shattering the bone above his eye. Then all went black.

When he awoke, his eye was held shut by a blackened pillow of skin. He was on his back between the bench seats of a *panga*. His arms were trussed behind him. Above, through his good eye, he could see the big dipper overhead.

"*Hola, Capitán.* I thought we'd go for a ride. Do some night trolling. See what bites."

Winston inched upward and sat heavily on the thwart across from Memo. His head ached, and his mustache was matted with blood. "I know nothing about any drugs."

"So you said."

Memo rounded Cabo San Lucas's famed rock arch and ten minutes later slowed the *panga* a mile off Finisterra's Deadman's Beach. As the engine idled slowly forward, he raised a tuna rod rigged with a 9/0 short-shank hook. Memo scratched it against his neck. He brought the bloodied tip of steel to his tongue and smiled.

"Your bait hooks are very sharp, señor."

"Yes."

"A bale is missing. Your man, Joe, says it was lost at sea."

"It's a big ocean."

Memo motioned with the hook. "Stand, señor."

Winston stood.

"There are sharks in these waters, no?"

"Of course."

"And when you fish live bait, you thread the hook between the eyes."

"Sometimes."

"This is a large hook. It needs a large bait."

"A small skipjack or a king mackerel."

Memo reached out and grabbed Winston by the base of his ponytail. He stepped onto the thwart and brought the hook down toward the captain's bruised eye.

"I was thinking of something bigger."

Winston felt an ocean swell lift the side of the *panga*. Memo widened his stance and spread his elbows for balance. The swell passed, and as Memo leaned in close, Winston lunged upward, driving the top of his head into Memo's chin.

Memo's jaw snapped shut. He stumbled backward into the motor cowling and snagged his hand on the hook. The switchblade pinged off the plastic covering and dropped into the water. He clawed for balance and unwittingly twisted the throttle. The *panga* lurched forward, and Winston toppled over the gunwale and splashed into the sea.

"*Chingada!*" Memo cursed, a chip of tooth and blood spraying from his mouth.

He spun the throttle and cursed again when the engine reversed and water sloshed over his cowboy boots. He yanked the throttle into neutral and plucked the hook from his hand.

"I was only trying to frighten you, señor!" Memo called out. "It is safer with me than with the sharks."

Winston surfaced thirty feet away, his head bobbing just beneath the surface, his hands hogtied tightly behind his back. Without warning, the boat surged toward him. Winston jack-knifed his body and kicked. As he did, he felt the propeller cleave his calf, the sharp blade slicing the muscle like a scythe through a stalk.

He exhaled and drifted downward when he heard the engine pick up speed. It circled once and then sped off into the distance. Winston kicked his good leg and surged for the surface. He burst into the night air, sucking at the darkness. As his lungs filled with air, he could just make out the wake of Memo's *panga*, and beyond that the lights of the Finisterra Hotel.

He floated to his back and took a series of deep breaths. The saltwater helped loosen his binds slightly, but his legs were weakening, and he was losing blood fast. He moved his arms to one side and grasped the pair of fisherman's pliers strapped to his belt. He slowly shuttled the pliers free and worked them around his wrists and over the monofilament line. The angle was awkward, and the swells jostled his efforts, but on the third attempt the clippers caught line. He squeezed and felt his wrists separate. Quickly he tore open his button-down shirt. He twisted the fabric into a tourniquet and knotted it above his torn calf.

He had been truthful about the sharks. They had made a comeback in recent years. Especially the hammerheads.

To survive he had to swim.

CHAPTER 14

SAN DIEGO, CALIFORNIA

After the frightening phone call from Memo, Edwin hurried back to the tuna cannery and closed early. He stopped at the drugstore to refill his prescription of painkillers and by late afternoon was in downtown San Diego approaching a favorite happy hour destination. Edwin usually avoided paying barroom prices for booze, but this was a special occasion. Time to toast his decision to steal from La Cucaracha, his move to Alaska, and his soon-to-be status of *outlaw*.

He turned off Harbor Drive and pulled into the parking lot of San Diego's most unlikely tourist destinations. Once known as Punta de los Muertos, Seaport Village was the final resting place for Spanish sailors who had died of scurvy in 1782. By the time Edwin parked his Celica beneath a towering acacia tree, Point of the Dead had long been forgotten. The buried bodies had been bulldozed with landfill, and the sloping shoreline of the graveyard had been fortified with seawalls.

Next came the requisite marina, the landscaped boardwalk, the deluge of storefronts and eateries—and one very unique tavern. Renowned for its aquarium bartop and well drinks poured over patented salmon-egg ice cubes that were guaranteed to raise one's libido, the Fish Market was the envy of bar owners everywhere. Nowhere else were patrons as eager to guzzle their aphrodisiacal cocktails with such fervor.

Edwin, however, could do without the eggs. His libido was far from his mind when he took a seat at the thickly glassed bar. A blowfish the size of a walnut was hiding near a fake forest of kelp. Harsh white lights illuminated its tiny fins and oversized eyes. Edwin tapped on the glass and watched in horror as the blowfish puffed into a spiky ball and began to roll uncontrollably into a miniature whirlpool. The spinning fish flapped its fins furiously, caught a current, and whisked down the bar.

Edwin raised his flabby arms triumphantly and ordered a dry martini. He placed an unlit Swisher Sweets in his mouth and rolled his tongue across the sweetened tobacco. For the first time all day, he felt at peace.

"Sparks, old boy!" a voice exploded across the bar like a freeway blowout. "Who the hell let you out of the fish factory?" Derek Moneymaker slapped Edwin on a soft slab of shoulder. "I can't believe you'd patronize an establishment like this. A steakhouse maybe. Or a hotdog stand. Something less fishy, eh?" Moneymaker let out a boisterous laugh.

Edwin scowled.

"Just making a little joke, old buddy. You're not still holding a grudge about the lawsuit? Guy's got to make a living, right? It wasn't personal. You know my rule. People matter, corporations don't."

"Go screw yourself, Derek."

"Sometimes I wish I could. Have you seen the broads in here? Middle age has bottomed out on most of these gals." He slapped Edwin a second time and banged out another belly laugh.

The bartender whisked by and placed Edwin's martini on the glass above a miniature seahorse drifting dangerously close to the whirlpool. Edwin clapped the top of the bar and sent the seahorse skittering.

"Shouldn't you be working?" Edwin asked after downing half his martini.

Moneymaker flashed a set of blinding porcelains. He was one of San Diego's most prolific plaintiff's attorneys, and his airbrushed face appeared on every mode of advertisement: billboards, bus stops, buses, and taxis. Even the bathroom stalls at Petco Park broadcast his image. Then there was the Saturday morning radio talk show and the television commercials. In fact, everything Moneymaker did had been carefully crafted to garner attention—including his name.

Born Derek Doolittle, the once struggling law student knew he needed a gimmick to succeed. So he started with his surname. The idea came to him one night during his third year of law school when he happened upon the World Poker Championship. Mesmerized by the champion with the championship name, he marched down to the courthouse the next morning and filed the name-changing papers. And just like that Derek Doolittle became Derek Moneymaker.

A few years later, after graduating near the bottom of his class, Moneymaker emptied his small bank account and bought his first late-night slip-and-fall television commercial. The local call center was overloaded with inquiries. It seemed as if every San Diego County insomniac had slipped or tripped on something in their clumsy lives.

"Moneymaker makes 'em pay," he told the clients. The slogan stuck, and the cases continued to roll in.

From Coronado Island to Oceanside, if you felt even slightly broken Moneymaker promised a cash fix. Much of his success resulted from a persistence that bordered on harassment. Three years earlier he had sued Topwater Tuna for misleading the public about the quantity of fish contained in their tuna cans. He had taken out full-page ads in all the local print media demanding that Topwater Tuna stop overloading their tuna with springwater. Thousands of consumers agreed, all of them claiming to have squeezed copious amounts of water from their canned tuna. And not just Topwater Tuna was at fault, but other tuna companies as well.

Moneymaker quickly hired experts to conduct tests. Teams of highly paid scientists squeezed tuna cans like sponges, spinning them centrifugally and mopping them with sterilized wipes in order to weigh every molecule of liquid to the thousandth of an ounce. But instead of finding tuna diluted with springwater, they found tuna swimming in tap water.

Moneymaker was overjoyed. Within weeks he filed a class-action lawsuit on behalf of the tens of thousands of consumers duped into buying *springwater*-packed tuna from the country's top tuna companies. He upped his demand by millions of dollars, claiming the fraud was worse than illegal. It was deadly. Tap water contained carcinogens, he argued, and when added to the high content of mercury in the tuna could exacerbate the health hazards of the fish.

After endless paperwork, countless depositions, senseless negotiations, and a two-week trial, the judge made her ruling: canned tap water was far from deadly. In fact, the abundance of chlorine made the tap water useful in leeching away some of the deadly mercury, thus making the tuna safer for the consumer— albeit not safe enough to ignore governmental mercury warnings.

Nonetheless, the various tuna companies' claims of "springwater" tuna were misleading.

"False advertising must not be tolerated," she wrote.

Damages were awarded in the amount of two cans of tuna per week per claimant for an entire year, a formula mimicking the government's recommended safe consumption of canned tuna fish. The payout resulted in two hundred dollars per plaintiff—a total verdict of nearly twenty million dollars. Moneymaker took his ten-million-dollar fee, plastered his success on freeway billboards across America, re-veneered his smile, and hired a public relations firm.

"Moneymaker Makes 'Em Pay" became a national phenomenon.

"Funny you should mention working," Moneymaker said as Edwin finished his martini and ordered another. "I've got a big case brewing. Class-action product liability case." He leaned in close to the cannery man. "And there's still time to join in."

"Yeah?" Edwin feigned interest.

"Toothpicks, Edwin. Dangerously sharp slivers of wood killing and maiming the innocent. Worse than choking on a chicken bone. And what's even better is the toothpick companies *know* their product is dangerous. They thin down and sharpen those suckers so they can squeeze more and more picks from smaller and smaller trees."

"Sounds like smart business practice."

"Smart my ass. Hurts like hell when you get poked. Pain and suffering's a slam dunk, buddy." He slapped the top of the glass bar, startling a baby moray eel.

"Slam dunk!"

CHAPTER 15

MAGDALENA BAY, BAJA CALIFORNIA, MEXICO

After losing his expensive fishing gear to the baby barracuda, Skegs rowed Fish to a large kelp paddy where the barefoot expatriate landed a half dozen more bull dorados before calling it quits. They returned to the island at dusk, and as Skegs filleted their catch, Fish hurried to his rooftop radio tower. Lacking cell service at the sand dune, Fish had installed the VHF transceiver so that Isabela, his bar manager, could contact him from across the bay. He'd also installed solar-powered base stations throughout southern Baja so she could communicate with him while he flew. In case the crazies closed in.

He tried to raise the *Wahoo Rhapsody* but got no reply. He even toggled emergency channel sixteen without luck. He hung the mic from its metal clip and dialed the captain's mobile telephone from a satellite handheld. The recorded voice of his old friend was little consolation. Fish belted out a bad version of *"Feliz Cumpleaños"* followed by an equally bad translation of "Happy Birthday." He wished the captain another forty years of good fishing and asked him to call back as soon as possible. Said it was urgent. Said he had a surprise. Then Fish disconnected the call and joined Skegs on the back patio, contemplating a night-time flight to Cabo San Lucas.

"Cabo now?" Skegs sputtered as he stripped the skin from a half-filleted dorado. "You must be smoking the sea grass out here, sandman. Half the yachties down there don't even use anchor lights. And those are the sober ones." He dropped the skin into a plastic bin of borax and zinc phosphate. "That kind of desperation's going to get you scalped. Got to think ahead, hombre."

"Scalped?"

"It's a metaphor, man. Cabo's deadlier than ever after dark. Do you know how much mescal I sell down there? Tourists drink it like Kool-Aid. No way, man. I'll tie myself to the propeller before I let you attempt suicide."

Fish stared out at the dark sea, his calloused fingers twirling the crimp dangling from his chin. "I'm worried, Skegs. Winston never goes incommunicado when he's working."

"Radios conk out. Cell phones fall overboard. *Mañana* things be looking better."

Fish didn't answer.

"Listen, amigo, I'm heading that way tomorrow afternoon. I'll check around. And when I find him, I'll have him call you at the bar from my cell phone." He winked knowingly. "I did a little PI work on the reservation. Was known as Sherlock Skegs for a while. Has a nice ring to it, don't you think?"

Two hours later as Skegs snored in the porchside hammock, Fish dialed a stateside number on his satellite telephone.

"McGill detective agency," came a woman's familiar voice.

"Toozie?" Fish asked.

"Francis?"

"Alive and well."

"Alive seems evident," Toozie said. "The well remains to be seen. I was beginning to think you were dead."

"Has it been that long?"

"Eight years."

"Seems like yesterday."

"I sent letters to your PO box, but never heard back."

Fish sighed. "I abandoned everything after those death threats. Flew south and bought an island. Off Magdalena Bay. Even changed my name."

"Something catchy I hope."

"Atticus Fish."

"You're kidding?"

"No one reads *To Kill a Mockingbird* anymore."

"You're demented."

"No argument there," Fish said with a laugh. Then he added, "I need your help, Toozie. Think of it as a favor for your old brother-in-law. I'll pay double the usual fee and all of it upfront in cash."

"Cash is good, but you can drop the brother-in-law crap. We're ex-in-laws. My sister's been dead ten years."

Fish cleared his throat and said, "Ex sounds so—"

"Liberating?"

"I was thinking terminal."

"Don't be so dramatic, Francis—sorry, Atticus."

Fish waited for her to stop laughing and said, "An old friend's gone missing. You remember Captain Winston?"

"The man who saved your life?"

"He's supposed to be docked in Cabo San Lucas, but he's not answering my radio calls, and his cell phone goes straight to message."

"Maybe his radio's down or the boat's running late."

"He doesn't run late."

"Weather?"

"I checked."

"How long's it been?"

"Since early morning."

"Today?" Her tone was dismissive.

"Winston's not the type to go dark," Fish explained. "Not when he's working."

"Give it another day. If he still hasn't responded, call me."

Fish let out a long breath. "My instincts are screaming at me, Toozie. I've learned to listen to them these last few years."

"You have an inner voice that doesn't slur?"

"I gave up the booze when I bought the bar."

"You bought a bar?"

"Keeps me sober."

"Interesting recovery program."

"You should come down sometime. Free room and board. Guaranteed ocean view. Stay as long as you like. The fishing's phenomenal."

"Tempting. But listen, if the captain's still missing tomorrow afternoon, call me. We call it the rule of twenty-four. Twenty-four hours. Nine out of ten times the person turns up."

"And the one out of ten?"

"Pays the mortgage."

Fish heard the phone disconnect. He walked to the driftwood railing and stared up at the powder of stars. Then he turned and hurried inside.

If he hoped to make Cabo by dawn, he'd need to be airborne soon.

CHAPTER 16

CABO SAN LUCAS, BAJA CALIFORNIA, MEXICO

Weevil awoke with a hammering headache and blurred vision. He blinked his eyes and searched for Socorro. He had a vague memory of her offering to take him from the Giggling Marlin to a popular taco stand for what she promised would be the world's best fish tacos. Weevil didn't remember eating.

Now, as his eyes came into focus, he saw the silhouette of tree branches. His confusion was compounded by the binds at his wrists and ankles. Lying on his back, he wondered why he saw handlebars in his peripheral vision, and beyond that the night sky with its astral grove of stars. Each twinkle of light bored into him like a welder's torch. His tongue felt warped, his lips deflated and cracked.

"Socorro?"

"I'm here, honey," came Socorro's voice from far below.

"Where am I?"

A Mexican man's heavy tone vectored through Weevil's brain. "On a Jet Ski, in a dead tree, in the courtyard of Squid Roe. Free Jell-O shots after midnight. You don't remember?" Memo's wet cowboy boots made squishing sounds as he moved into Weevil's sight.

"I think I passed out," Weevil said, his mind moving in gaps and static like a badly spliced movie.

"Socorro's cousin owns the place," Memo continued. "We have after-hours privileges."

"A Jet Ski in a tree?"

Memo gave a throaty laugh. "Tourists love it. A drunk gringo climbed up last year and tried to drive it away. He fell off and broke his neck."

"Socorro?"

"Yes," she called up.

"What's going on?"

Weevil felt the tree sway and saw a large shadow swing to the branch beside him.

"You drank a spiked beer and woke up in a tree next to me."

Memo's smile was oddly simian, and Weevil wondered if the man might tear a limb from the tree and beat it against his bulging chest. Memo fingered his sore chin and said, "I work for La Cucaracha. So does Socorro. And you, unfortunately, have taken something from our boss."

"Shit."

"*Mande?*"

Weevil could smell the man's sour breath, could see the dark bruise beneath his chin. "The other bale wasn't out there. I looked. But we had to go. We couldn't spend all night trying to find it. The captain only takes a short break to sleep. I think the signal must have malfunctioned."

"Your captain seemed surprised by my visit."

"You saw Captain Winston?"

"The two of us went fishing."

"But he doesn't know anything about the drugs," Weevil stammered.

"*Didn't* know."

Weevil felt a rush of anger. "What's that supposed to mean?"

"It means I fed your captain to the sharks."

"Not with Big Joe around. Nobody gets by Big Joe."

"Big Joe?" Memo clamped his hands around Weevil's neck. "Is lucky he wasn't there. Maybe he was hiding. Maybe he was looking for you."

Weevil's face reddened, and his eyes bulged. "We don't have the other bale. I swear. Take me to the boat. I can show you."

"I searched the boat, and I think you know more than you say." Memo's hand fell to his waist and dug through the pockets of his jeans. "*Híjole!*" He peered down through the branches. "Socorro, I lost my knife. Give me something to torture him with."

"*Un momento, mi amor,*" she called up. A few moments later she reappeared beneath the tree. "Here." She lobbed a chrome tool up to Memo. "I found it behind the bar."

"What's this?" Memo growled, inspecting the pliers-like tool.

"A hole punch."

"Hole punch?"

"They use it to validate frequent drink cards."

"You don't have a nail file? Something sharp?"

"I go to the salon."

"Every time you break a nail?"

"They're fake, baby. They don't really break—"

"Excuse me," Weevil said with a tremulous smile.

"*Qué va!*" Memo snapped his head around and glared into Weevil's face.

"There's really no need to torture me. I'm telling the truth. I swear. Fisherman's honor."

"Fisherman's honor?" Memo glanced down at Socorro. "What is fisherman's honor?"

"It's like Scout's honor," she called up.

"See," Weevil said. "I'm telling the truth."

"Both of you, *cállensen!*"

"But—"

For a large man, Memo moved effortlessly among the branches. He straddled Weevil's chest, pinning the boatman's face between his knees.

"Okay, okay," Weevil gasped. "That makes it really hard to breathe. I—"

Memo thrust the hole punch far up Weevil's right nostril and squeezed. A tab of symmetrical skin fell through the air and bounced among the branches like a BB in a pachinko game.

Weevil yelped.

Memo smothered Weevil's face and pinched back one of his eyelids.

Weevil stiffened. "Whoa! Whoa! Not the eyes. I swear I can find the missing bale. Tonight. Right now. Scout's honor."

"Guillermo!" Socorro's voice cut sharply through the air. "Enough!"

Memo hesitated. "Just one eye, *mi amor*? So he can replay his foolishness each time he blinks." Memo slipped the tool into place. "The skin is thin, Socorro. It will cut easily. Then we can go."

Socorro placed her hands on her hips. "I said no!"

Weevil felt the pinch of metal. Then his vision blurred and a swirl of darkness descended over him. When he awoke, a young Mexican nurse stood beside him, her white smock blurry through the lens of his one unbandaged eye.

Captain Winston sat uncomfortably against a stack of thin pillows at the head of the hospital bed. It was four in the morning, two hours since he'd washed ashore in front of the Finisterra Hotel. A young couple in the throes of a tequila-induced skinny-dip had quickly re-suited and carried him to the front lobby of their hotel, where a taxi rushed him to the nearby hospital.

Now, as he lay in the bare-walled recovery room, his calf repaired and his eyebrow stitched, he overheard the doctor talking in the hallway with one of the nurses. The Spanish was swift, but there was no mistaking the words *policía* and *Wahoo Rhapsody*. Or the names that quickly followed: Wendell Ott and Willie Pike. The captain knew Pike was here. He'd come to check on the intern's injuries before returning to the boat and his unfortunate meeting with Memo.

But Weevil?

Winston waited for the doctor and nurse to enter the adjacent room before hobbling to the door. He peered into the vacant hallway. It was quiet and dimly lit. He moved into the corridor, his calf aching with each step. The recovery wing of the hospital was small, and he soon found Weevil on his back snoring awkwardly through a cone-shaped bandage. A second oval-shaped bandage covered Weevil's left eye.

Winston limped to the bed. He leaned close to Weevil's ear and growled, "You ever bring drugs aboard my boat again, I'll gut you like a goddamned ballyhoo."

"Captain!" Weevil blurted in a nasally whistle. He tried to sit up, but Winston placed a hand on his chest. "You're not dead?" Weevil asked, blinking his undamaged eye.

"Not yet."

"I knew it. Nobody gets by Big Joe."

"Except when he's off looking for you." Winston pointed at his bruised and swollen eye.

76

Weevil lowered his head shamefully.

"Damn it, Weevil. What the hell were you thinking?"

"I owe a lot of money to someone. It was supposed to be an easy one-time gig. I guess I got greedy."

"Some thug showed up asking for you and Joe. Made me take him into the fish hold where you've been keeping your secret. He took a cheap shot and then ran me over with his *panga*. Not the best way to spend my birthday."

Weevil hung his head again. "I told him we didn't steal the drugs, Captain. He didn't believe me."

"All these years and you risk everything on a load of dope?"

Weevil's voice quivered, the nose whistle barely audible. "I was gambling during the off-season. Got in over my head. Big Joe was just helping me out."

"You could have come to me."

"And ask you for a hundred grand? I'd never do that."

"So instead you risk our lives and careers?"

Weevil swung his head back and forth. "It wasn't supposed to be this way."

"Did Pike find out about it? Is that why—"

Weevil's head snapped up. "He was snooping around a lot. I was trying to scare him off the boat."

"You nearly killed him."

"I might have overreacted."

"Overreacted? Jesus, Weevil. This could end up costing me my license, the boat, even my freedom. Not to mention I was almost killed." He showed Weevil his bandaged calf. "Boat propeller."

Weevil wiped at his eye.

Winston sat at the edge of the bed. "As much as you deserve it, I'm not going to fire you *or* turn you in. Not yet, anyway.

I overheard the doctor and his nurse talking. They mentioned the boat and your name. The police have been notified. I'd rather we not be here when they show up." He paused. "And Pike's coming with us."

"Pike?" Weevil blurted, the whistle amplified by his nose cone.

Winston clamped a hand over Weevil's mouth. "Like it or not, Pike's a member of the crew. That makes me responsible for him. And thanks to you and Big Joe, I'm now a drug trafficker. We'll all be arrested and tossed in jail."

"But you and Pike are innocent. So's Big Joe, really."

"Not under Mexican law. Here you have to prove innocence. They'll confiscate the boat—if they haven't already—and wait for us to build our case. Our only chance is to get out of the country. I'll worry about the *Rhapsody* after that."

Weevil's eye filled with tears. "I'm sorry, Captain," he said in a quavering voice.

Winston stood on his good leg. "I know someone. An American who lives north of here. A few hundred miles up the Pacific. You'll remember him. The lawyer who fell off the boat."

"Francis the billionaire boozer?"

"He's sober now. A while back he bought the *Rhapsody*."

Weevil eyed the captain quizzically.

"He's a silent partner. Mostly I think he was paying me back for saving his life."

"You took his money?"

"He didn't take no for an answer. He went to the bank and made an offer on the loan they couldn't refuse. Then he sent me a partnership contract. It listed him as the sole creditor. It also required my monthly boat payment be sent to the Nature Conservancy—the group that buys islands and wetlands around the world to keep them from developers. They bought Espíritu Santo. Cerralvo might be next."

"Persuasive guy."

"And a good friend. He now lives on an island and flies around in a seaplane. He's off the grid, but he's got a marine radio. I always check in when we pass by. He'll know how to get us out of this mess."

Weevil slid to the edge of the bed. "My wallet's gone, and we can't go back to the boat and get money. Halfway up the Pacific is a long walk."

"We're not walking."

"Then how—"

"You've hotwired cars before. Normally I'd never ask. But under the circumstances, I'd say you owe me a favor."

"It's the least I can do."

"Get dressed and meet me outside the hospital in five minutes."

JJJ

"You're so dead," Pike said, his head bandaged mummy-like, his arms and legs covered with white Xs of surgical tape. He wore beige boating shorts, a short-sleeve button-down, and white Sperry Topsiders without socks. In the drab yellow streetlight he resembled an accident victim in a straight-to-video horror movie.

"I said I was sorry," Weevil offered in a tinny whistle. He had on the same board shorts and T-shirt from the night before. The baseball cap, however, was missing, and the T-shirt was stained with dried blood. He glanced back toward Winston, who hobbled on his borrowed hospital crutch. He was barefoot and wore his pair of damp zip-off pant-shorts from earlier that evening. His shirt had been ruined as a tourniquet, so he'd tucked the hospital gown into his waistband and rolled the loose sleeves up to his shoulders. Loud music filled the balmy night air.

"Doesn't matter," Pike answered. "And what the hell's wrong with your voice?"

"Nothing's wrong with my voice," Weevil whistled. "It's my nose."

"It's annoying."

"You're annoying."

Pike spun to face Weevil. "You're kidding, right? After a week of tangled lines and clogged toilets and staying up all night so you could play with your dead fish, I get thanked with a bed full of hooks. I ought to have you arrested."

"It was a joke."

"Some joke."

"You sound more like a drama major than a marine biologist." Weevil turned away and pinched his nose cone, trying to smother the whistle.

"What?"

"You heard me."

Pike grabbed Weevil by the arm and threw him to the ground. "You want drama?" Pike kicked Weevil in the rib cage. "How about a Shakespearean wallop?" He stomped on Weevil's chest. "Maybe some Broadway sole." He raised both fists and brought them down onto Weevil's back. "A little Laurel and Hardy two-punch."

"Enough!" Winston hollered. He struggled across the broken tarmac on his crutch. "This isn't the time for settling the score."

"Seems like a good enough time for me," Pike said and kicked Weevil again.

Weevil groaned and logrolled into the middle of the dirt street holding his side. Pike followed, kicking with each step. "How's it feel, fish-man?"

A taxicab appeared in a plume of dust, and the driver leaned out the window.

"Twenty dollars, *amigo*," he said in practiced English. He wore a Dodgers baseball cap and a Padres jersey shirt. "But hurry before Frankenstein kicks you in the *cajones*."

Pike's foot glanced over Weevil's thigh.

Weevil rose to his knees. "Will you take an IOU?" The last three letters ascended into a whistly trill. "My wallet was—ahhh!"

Pike's foot caught Weevil in the solar plexus.

"Fifteen," the taxi driver called out. "*No mas*, no less."

Weevil rolled to his back and tried to catch his breath. He flashed an okay sign at the taxi driver when he heard Pike grunt. He looked up and saw Winston holding his crutch in the air.

"I said enough!"

"Fight!" came a collective cry of unfamiliar voices. Weevil turned his head and saw a pack of drunken college students in Texas A&M shirts and oversized sombreros hurrying toward him.

"*Buena suerte, amigo!*" the taxi driver yelled and sped away, covering Weevil in a fresh cloud of dust.

"Ten bucks on the guy with the crutch!" one of the drunks hollered. "Hit him hard, old man!"

"Twenty bucks says the asshole in the turban takes them both."

Pike glanced quizzically at the captain, who motioned toward Pike's head bandage.

Another voice in the crowd spoke up. "Hey, my dad's Indian!"

"That's not a turban," another said. "It's a gauze wrapping, you idiot. Can't you see they just left the hospital?"

"Who are you calling an idiot?"

The drunk in the sombrero hat swung his fist.

"Fight!" the crowd hollered, and they turned their attention away from the hospital evacuees.

As bodies merged, Weevil scrambled to his feet and followed Pike and the captain up the street and around the corner. Ten minutes later they stood beside an old rusted pickup truck near a dirt lot cluttered with trash.

"I think you broke one of my ribs," Weevil panted in a high-pitched whistle.

"Good."

"It hurts to breathe."

"Even better."

"What if you punctured one of my lungs?"

Pike winced. "Don't say puncture."

Weevil let out a short laugh and then doubled over in pain. When he caught his breath he said, "Okay, I think we're even. My ribs hurt bad."

"Try having your hand treble-hooked to your ass."

"I guess you could say you had it handed to you." Weevil crumpled to the ground in a fit of laughter.

"Help him up, Willie," Winston said. "Let's get this over with."

Pike reached down and yanked hard on Weevil's outstretched hand. Weevil let out a wail.

"Sorry," he said flatly, and he watched Weevil limp to the driver's side of the pickup and open the door.

CHAPTER 17

MAGDALENA BAY, BAJA CALIFORNIA, MEXICO

After leaving a note for Skegs, who still lay sleeping on the porch-side hammock, Fish taxied his seaplane across the shallow inlet to clear the water of any birds and then turned into the breeze and lifted into the predawn sky. The first hour took him east across the narrow Baja peninsula and down the Sea of Cortez south toward La Paz with its magnificent islands and world-famous seamount. He spotted finned whales feeding off Isla San José, and dolphins off Las Animas. There were mantas half the size of his plane, marlin crashing bait, and enough blue-footed boobies to fill an aviary. Then came Isla San Francisco and the blue-eyed bays of Espíritu Santo rimmed by acres of bone-white beach and sloping cliffs crowded with cardón and cholla.

La Paz appeared on the horizon, and Fish's sentiment soured. Bulldozers had flattened the hills above Tecolote, one of Baja's most spectacular beaches. Swaths of desert had been cut into fairways. Homesites clung to the terrain where freshly tarred roads displayed colorful promotions snapping in the wind. A guardhouse stood at the entrance where a man-made lake glistened like a canker. Fish considered a splashdown in protest and then remembered the missing captain and banked hard up the coast.

He flew past bays mushrooming with yachts and beaches molested by umbrellas. Mansions and swimming pools lay stacked along the coast. Beyond San José del Cabo came the mini malls and parking lots and rich American ladies in hats. Humvees and Cadillacs and fat men in Bermuda shorts. Fish hadn't flown this corridor in years, not since he'd bought the island. Back when much of the coastline was still colonized by sand dollars and cactus wrens.

Fish increased speed and thirty minutes later descended over Cabo San Lucas Bay. He abruptly leveled the plane and gawked. Not a square foot of Médano Beach was unclaimed. Monolithic resorts stood wall-to-wall with roped-off sand and color-coordinated lounge chairs. Matching ropes and color-coordinated buoys marked small squares of designated swimming areas where crowds of tourists washed away hangovers. Beyond the buoys were dozens of ski boats hosting parasailers and dozens more towing water-skiers. There were wakeboarders slaloming between million-dollar yachts and waverunners maneuvering a ski jump course. Glass-bottomed boats bravely jockeyed for clarity, and a wayward kayaker paddled furiously for shore.

And all of it before seven in the morning.

Fish circled the marina hoping to sight the *Wahoo Rhapsody* from above, and then he angled offshore for a thin runway of water. He splashed down and taxied toward a far-off anchorage when two souped-up Sea-Doos turned into his path. Each machine was painted candy apple red with hot rod flames. Each driver wore wraparound sunglasses. They were husky males, deeply tanned, with tightly cropped hair and wearing nothing but Speedos. Each had a bikinied blonde at his back.

Fish waved them off.

The drivers grinned and increased their speed.

"Propellers!" Fish yelled.

The drivers kept coming.

Fish slid open the window and pointed at the blades spinning beneath the wing. The racers widened their grins. They crouched motocross-style and turned the volume up on their waterproof stereos. The chorus to Nazareth's "Hair of the Dog" crashed over the water and into the cockpit: *Now you're messing with a…a son of a bitch!*

Fish wondered if the drivers were drunk. He waved his arms and yelled again. He cranked the tail rudder in an attempt to throw them off. The Sea-Doos closed in. Fish shut down the engines and held his breath.

"Righteous!" came a man's voice rocketing over the music.

Fish watched the driver thread the narrow space between the slowing propeller and the cargo door. Then he turned and saw the other driver breeze by the second propeller. Both avoided catastrophe by inches.

Fish released a heavy sigh. He stroked his braided goatee with thumb and forefinger when the Sea-Doo drivers reappeared. They sped toward him again, spun hard, and sprayed twin sheets of water over the plane's windshield. Laughing, they raced across the bay and stopped at a large anchored yacht with the name *Miss Beehaven* painted across the stern. The girls stepped onto the boat and blew kisses as their boyfriends turned and headed for the marina.

Fish shook his head in disgust. He opened the cargo door, dropped anchor, and deployed his inflatable dinghy. As he rowed toward the marina office to inquire about the *Rhapsody*, a wolfish grin crossed his face. Sea-Doos were easily disabled, throttle wires simple to cut. A sure way to add a few hours to the boys' return.

Plenty of time to remove the props from their yacht.

CHAPTER 18

CABO SAN LUCAS, BAJA CALIFORNIA, MEXICO

Big Joe stood outside the Giggling Marlin, hands stuffed into his pockets, staring hopelessly at a pay phone. He had come into town the night before to roust Weevil from his barstool. He searched Cabo Wabo, the Giggling Marlin, and Squid Roe. He even traipsed out to the locally renowned Latitude 22. But Weevil was nowhere to be found. Big Joe returned to the marina near midnight, sure that Weevil would be on deck. Instead he found an empty boat slip.

The *Wahoo Rhapsody* had vanished.

For a moment he considered notifying the port captain, but a freezer-full of pot-stuffed fish changed his mind. La Cucaracha had lied about letting Weevil recover the lost bale of pot. There would be no second chances. The *Wahoo Rhapsody*—and most likely the captain and Weevil—were now collateral for the missing drugs.

Or worse.

As Big Joe stepped toward the pay phone, he considered his lack of options. His wallet remained on board the boat with his personal belongings. He had no money in his pockets and no identification. His best friends were kidnapped or dead, and hitchhiking the thousand miles north without a centavo for shared gas would be futile. It would also be an abandonment of his fishing family. Big Joe picked up the pay phone.

His ex-girlfriend would understand. She used to be a crew-member on a rival fishing boat, and she allowed him to sleep on her couch when the *Wahoo Rhapsody* dry-docked for repairs. She knew about the lockbox in the trunk of his restored 1940s woody parked in the back of Weevil's studio apartment in El Cajon, the hide-a-key secured above the rear passenger wheel. Inside the lockbox was four hundred bucks cash. He'd need it wired to the marina office as soon as it opened. He glanced at his watch. Two hours. Then he could hire a local pilot to fly a search grid for the boat. Find the *Rhapsody* before it was too late.

Big Joe picked up the phone and began to dial when three middle-aged American women in high heels stumbled from the Giggling Marlin. One held a partially eaten breakfast burrito in her hand. Another sipped a Bloody Mary from a plastic cup. All three squinted into the punishing light of dawn.

"Hey, big man on the phone," the tallest of the trio slurred. "We're headed to the beach for a skinny-dip. Want to play life-guard?"

Big Joe smiled and then returned to his dialing.

The tall woman cantered on stiletto heels to the phone and pressed her finger over the cradle. Leaning close she said in a seductive slur, "These babies are brand new." She hooked a finger over her halter top and exposed a silicone beauty. "Brought 'em to Cabo for their big debut. Squeeze one and tell me what you think."

Big Joe let the phone drop from his hand. He eyed the nippled cue ball and said, "You wouldn't happen to have a few hundred bucks you could lend me?"

The woman yanked up her top. "What are you gay or something?"

Her two friends stumbled to the pay phone. One draped her arm over Big Joe's shoulder and kissed his neck. The other grabbed at the seat of his pants.

"I think he's gay," the tall woman said.

"Let's find out," the other two cooed.

"He asked me for money."

The two sized him up.

"I'm in," one said.

"Me too," said the other before returning to her neck nibbling.

"Then it's settled. A foursome on the beach," the tall woman offered.

Big Joe put up his hands. "Sun's coming up. I'd rather not get arrested. How about a hotel room?"

"We're sharing a suite at the Solmar."

"Perfect," Big Joe said and hailed a cab.

An hour later he sat exhausted on a sofa chair, his body covered in hickeys. Beer bottles and unopened condoms spilled across the floor. Women's clothing lay crumpled everywhere. The two shorter women snored from the king-size bed where they'd passed out after failing to liberate a single condom from its package. The tall woman fared better only to vomit upon tearing open a foil wrapper with her teeth. Big Joe helped her to the bathroom and then to the pullout couch, where she lay on her back, her breasts propped on her chest like a pair of emu eggs.

Big Joe dressed. He went to the desk near the window and jotted a quick thank-you note. Then he rummaged through the women's purses and extracted three hundred dollars and a handful of pesos. Halfway out the door he paused. He returned to the note and added his stateside telephone number.

In case they wanted their money back. Or a rain check on the four-way.

CHAPTER 19

CABO SAN LUCAS, BAJA CALIFORNIA, MEXICO

Seconds after entering the truck, Weevil lay on the footwell staring beneath the dashboard.

"A little light sure would help," he complained in a muffled whistle.

"I can't believe you're stealing a piece-of-shit truck," Pike said. "I hope you get arrested."

"Ever heard of conspiracy, dickwad?" Weevil said as the truck fired. He scrambled to the driver's seat. Captain Winston hobbled to the passenger door and pulled himself inside.

"Hurry up, Willie," he said in a loud whisper.

Pike ambled unenthusiastically to the open passenger door and hesitated, but then a gunshot sent him bounding inside.

"Drive!" he hollered and slammed the door closed.

Another shot rang out before Weevil floored the gas pedal. Dust and gravel sprayed into the night air. He turned left at the first intersection and checked the rearview mirror.

"Shit!"

Pike turned and stared through the rear window. "They must really like this truck."

Winston pointed at a curve in the road. "Around that bend is a split. Take the road to the right and then a quick left. It leads to an old rancho outside of town. I think we can lose them in the coconut groves."

Pike yanked open the glove compartment. He found a nearly empty roll of duct tape, a half-finished pint of mescal, and a baggie of marijuana. Pike removed the drugs and slammed the compartment shut.

"Jackpot," he said and held up the pot. "Slow down and I'll toss it out so they can see it."

Weevil slowed. The pursuers neared, and Pike heaved the baggie into the glare of headlights. Bullets pinged off the truck in response.

Pike ducked. "These guys are seriously pissed about their truck!"

Weevil gunned the engine.

"Tell me again, Captain, why the hell we aren't just going to the cops?" Pike asked.

Weevil glanced at the captain. "You didn't tell him."

"I thought I'd let you have the honors."

"Tell me what?"

Winston motioned for Weevil to answer.

"The guy that hole-punched my face tried to kill the captain. His name's Memo, and he works for a drug dealer named La Cucaracha."

"Like the song?"

"Sort of."

Pike looked over at Winston. "You're a drug smuggler?"

Winston frowned. "Of course not. I found out about the drugs when I was attacked last night."

"Weevil's a drug runner?"

"Apparently."

Pike turned to Weevil. "But why would La Cucaracha want to kill you?"

"He thinks I stole his drugs," Weevil said, the whistle less evident over the engine noise.

"You stole from a drug lord?"

"Not exactly."

"Either you did or you didn't."

"I re-marked the pot for later retrieval."

"You're kidding, right?"

Weevil skidded along the curved dirt road and took a sharp right into a coconut grove. "At least I didn't run off in my underwear screaming about scorpions in my bunk."

Pike turned to Winston and said, "I'm calling this in as soon as we stop."

"Once we cross the border, Willie, you can do whatever you want. Until then, no cops."

"But—"

"My friend who lives in Magdalena Bay owns a seaplane. You'll be back in the States sooner than you think."

Pike sighed. "A seaplane?"

"Beats a stolen truck."

A bullet whizzed off of the passenger side mirror.

Pike ducked again.

Weevil turned and bounced over a low rise in the road, just missing a wild turkey that had crossed the road. Seconds later headlights revealed a dozen more clucking and putting across the dirt road.

"Do turkeys fly?" Weevil asked, eyeing the rearview mirror.

Pike ignored the question. "You guys smell something?" He bent forward and inspected a ragged bullet hole in the door paneling. He knocked his fist around the hole and sniffed loudly.

"They're drug runners!"

"Not for long," Weevil commented and motioned behind them with his head.

The headlights suddenly fishtailed, and feathers filled the air. The headlights rolled, and a crashing sound was followed by flames climbing the trunk of a coconut tree.

Pike glared at Weevil. "You're a fucking menace. Everything you touch turns to shit."

Weevil narrowed his one-eyed gaze. He reached across Winston and touched Pike on the arm. "Looks like you're right for a change."

"Get me out of here, deckboy, or I swear to God you'll regret it for the rest of your lousy life."

Weevil shrugged. "We're in this together, douche bag."

Pike's face parted affably as an eel's. "Careful what you wish for."

CHAPTER 20

CABO SAN LUCAS, BAJA CALIFORNIA, MEXICO

Fish tied the dinghy to the public dock and stepped ashore. His light cotton shirt was opened to the waist, and the cuffs of his dungarees were wet with saltwater from the long row in. He pushed back his fishskin cap, ran a hand along his goatee, and scanned the personal watercraft lining the dock. Dozens of Sea-Doos in flaming racing stripes bobbed against the pilings. Fish sighed and moved toward the first Sea-Doo for a closer look when a sudden commotion caught his attention.

A long line of pickup trucks were pulling into the parking lot, their rusted beds piled with knickknacks. Drivers began to unload portable tables and covered them with varnished frogs, cow-hoof tequila bottles, and stacks of cartoon T-shirts. Next came baseball caps stitched with colorful game fish, glass turtles, and porcelain whales. There were boxes of ironwood carvings and hand-painted shells. Columns of pirated movies and knock-off handbags, faux Rolexes, and felt paintings of the Last Supper. But mostly it was silver. Mountains of trinkets and rings, bracelets and earrings, necklaces and pendants, and all of it stamped in sterling certification—.925, the international symbol for sucker.

Shoppers appeared as suddenly as the vendors, and within minutes the makeshift market was bustling. Fish dreaded crowds almost as much as philistine tourists. He dropped his plan to disable the Sea-Doos, spun on his bare heels, and hurried along the marina in search of the *Wahoo Rhapsody*. He gawked at the huge private yachts, the slick jet boats, and an enormous turn-of-the-century sloop restored to mint condition. What he didn't see was an eighty-two-foot long-range fishing boat, its hull painted kelly green, its stern stenciled with a school of leaping wahoos. Worried more than ever that Winston was broken down at sea or stuck at the islands without radio power, Fish headed to the marina office to file a report and check for any updates.

He'd taken only a few steps when he was confronted with offers to parasail, Jet Ski, sportfish, snorkel, or for the discounted price of fifty dollars, paddleboat the marina with a map of the yacht stars. This last offer was a Cabo San Lucas novelty created in response to the multitude of rich and famous descending en masse to the famed party port. And the current highlight was the 120-foot *Snicker's Delight*, owned by the heir to the Mars Bar fortune. The paddleboat salesman promised a clear view of the mammoth candy bar painted on the yacht's transom. "*Cacahuetes* as big as a burro," he proudly announced as Fish ducked through a breezeway and onto Cabo's main thoroughfare.

He'd hoped for some respite from the hordes of salesmen before circling back to the marina office. Instead he was confronted by commercial chaos. Storefronts had spawned like plankton. Stoplights now backed up thick lines of traffic. Volkswagens mostly, and Jeeps advertising Budget or Avis. Taxi vans veered over sidewalks, their drivers honking with impatience. The air swirled with exhaust. Music blared from the all-night discos and off-track betting parlors. Dueling mariachi bands stalked tourists while a man with a dancing iguana posed for pictures.

Fish sprinted past a Ronald McDonald statue holding a banner offering jalapeño fries and ninety-nine-cent margaritas. He glanced at a Baskin-Robbins sign advertising tequila-flavored ice cream and *chicharrón* malts. He couldn't help but notice the bright pink billboard flashing above with arrows directing tourists to Cabo's newest topless bar. Fish felt sick to his stomach. He tried to envision the sleepy fishing village with its dirt streets and corner taco vendors, but a taxi hopped the curb and nearly ran him down.

He ducked into an alleyway where a sign read *"Oficina de la Marina."* Aquamarine sharks arced over the words. He could see sailboat masts in the distance, and he began to relax when the shrill of timeshare hawkers stopped his progress.

The center of the alleyway had been converted to a gauntlet of plywood stalls, each beaming with a youthful sales clerk: women with centerfold smiles, colored contact lenses, and highlighted hair; men plucked from Calvin Klein ads with low-slung jeans, skintight shirts, and chiseled chins. They too wore colorful contact lenses, and all spoke flawless English.

Fish felt both disgust and fascination, as though he'd turned down a rabbit hole instead of an alleyway. He reset his fishskin cap and resumed his jog, dodging the volley of teasers: free lobster dinners, unlimited margaritas, parasailing, Jet Skiing, even a half day of fishing if he would agree to a spectacular two-hour presentation.

No obligation, amigo.

Fish hurried on. The offers grew louder, the vendors more aggressive. One especially fit young man offered him a ride to

Cabo's hidden nude beach. Fish waved him off, and as he neared the end of the alleyway, a muscled young man leaped the counter of the final stall and blocked his way.

"Beautiful morning," the man said, his Hollywood smile stretching from ear to ear. He reached out and gripped Fish's hand. "I see my associates have failed to interest you in our products. Maybe I can do better."

"I doubt it."

"Señoritas?" he asked, still gripping Fish's hand.

Fish tried to sidestep the salesman, but the agent mirrored the move with the grace of a salsa instructor. Fish squeezed the man's hand with bone-shattering force. The manicured fingers held firm. The guy was a pro.

"Here's the thing," the salesman said, casually releasing Fish's hand. "I live or die in this alley. If I don't fill the presentation room, I don't eat. Just a few quick hours, my friend, and I'll throw in everything we've got. The fishing *and* the parasailing *and* all the margaritas you can drink in an hour. What do you say, partner? Help out a friend?"

"No thanks."

"Don't forget the señoritas. I can get you a front-row seat at Cabo's newest titty bar." He winked. "Girls will dig the long goatee, man."

"Get out of my way."

"But—"

Fish snatched the man's opposite hand and bore down with shell-cracker force.

The man yelped.

"*Comprende?*" Fish asked, ratcheting up the southpaw handshake.

The man's head nodded rapidly.

"Those spring-loaded grip strengtheners are great, but you might want to switch hands once in a while."

The head nodded again.

"I'm walking away."

"Okay," he squeaked.

Minutes later Fish stood inside the marina office listening to the clerk explain that the *Wahoo Rhapsody* had arrived as scheduled. Captain Winston had paid the dock fees upon arrival. He'd reported no radio problems, and the boat had departed in the middle of the night, which the clerk assured him wasn't unusual for a charter boat heading to San Diego.

Fish made it back to his dinghy in record time. He untied the inflatable and began rowing, the ulcer of doubt burning wider with every stroke. It wasn't like the captain to sail without a working radio. Especially in the middle of the night in foreign waters.

Fish rowed from the marina into the mouth of the bay and stopped. It was barely nine in the morning, and the water was pandemonium. Catamarans towed floating amusement parks packed with people. Huge inflatable trampolines advertised ten-dollar tequila jumps. Cuervo Gold banners read "Belly-flop for a Shot." Speedboaters with bullhorns offered parasailing by the minute. Sea-Doos swarmed like ants. Water-skiers and wakeboarders seemed to have procreated into every gap of the bay. Skegs was right. It would have been deadly to land a seaplane after breakfast.

Fish plotted a semi-safe course through the mayhem when a pair of hot rod red Sea-Doos roared from the marina. The familiar drivers were shirtless and wore wraparound sunglasses. Each held a Domino's Pizza box on his lap. They closed in on Fish and then cut away sharply just before impact.

Twin wakes slammed into the dinghy. The inflatable bucked. Water sloshed over the rubber gunwales, drenching Fish. He dropped the oars and bailed frantically with his cap. The drivers flashed twin birds and raced to their yacht at the far end of the bay. Fish could just make out the name stenciled across the stern: *Miss Beehaven.*

As Fish scooped seawater, he thought of those two large pizzas. The concomitant beers. The bikinied girlfriends. A lunch like that could last hours. To hell with removing the props.

Time to get airborne and teach the boys a real lesson in waterborne courtesy.

CHAPTER 21

SAN DIEGO, CALIFORNIA

Edwin was rarely late for work. He couldn't be. He was the only one Mrs. Dockweiler trusted with a key. But on this Friday morning he was not only late, he was languid with a hangover, and as he parked beneath Topwater Tuna's towering pepper tree, the group of Hispanic cannery workers eyed him like an alien life form.

"*Buenos días,*" Edwin said, elbowing clumsily from the car. "Sorry I'm late. *El tráfico.*"

The men shrugged. None of them owned a car.

Edwin opened the trunk and hastily covered the Celica with its canvas cover, a job made nearly impossible by the mounting pressure at his temples. Five double martinis in the presence of the pushy plaintiff's attorney had soured his plans for a good buzz. Especially when Moneymaker had shown him the photos of toothpicks lodged in clients' throats, buried in tongues, and plunged through cheeks and lips. Edwin was doubly horrified by the unlucky patron who'd fallen while scratching his inner nostril with a plastic olive spear. The man's pierced septum reminded Edwin of a native with a miniature nose bone.

Edwin had been so mortified, and so drunk, that he waited for the lawyer to use the restroom and then weaved from the bar, taking special care to leave all toothpicks behind. He also left Moneymaker the bill.

Now, after opening the factory and lighting a Swisher Sweets cigar, Edwin scanned the morning paper. He thought of the upcoming delivery of pot-stuffed fish and his impending getaway and gasped. Buried near the back of the regional section under the heading "Mexico" subheading "Baja Beat" was an article about a recent drug bust at the Arizona/Mexico border. The headline read "Arizona Federal Prosecutor Traps Notorious Drug Bug La Cucaracha."

Edwin felt faint. The cigar dropped from his mouth and landed on the newspaper. His vision blurred. The news began to smolder, and Edwin lost consciousness. His head bounced to the desktop, extinguishing the sweet-smelling cigar in a flab of neck skin.

Edwin awoke moments later to the smell of singed flesh.

And the sound of his cell phone ringing.

CHAPTER 22

BAJA CALIFORNIA, MEXICO

Five hours after escaping the car chase in the coconut grove, Winston directed Weevil to turn off Highway 1. They were outside Ciudad Constitución, a flat, windblown town on the Magdalena Plain.

"It's going to be thirty miles of the baddest washboard in Baja," Winston said, motioning for Weevil to stop at the side of the road to Puerto San Carlos. "We need to lower the tire pressure to eighteen psi. Maybe less if we want to keep this old truck from rattling to pieces."

"Yeah, we'd hate to lose our load of stolen pot," Pike grumbled, stepping from the truck.

Minutes later Winston drove while Weevil slumped into the corner, his head propped against the passenger window. Pike sat hunched in the middle. The truck's springy seat absorbed the vibrato of the road as the three boatmen watched the desert whiz by in a cloak of dust. Mostly a blur of creosote bush and greasewood and creeping devil cacti.

"The faster you drive, the smoother the ride!" Winston called out over the creaking truck. He drew his eyelids against a wind drift of dust and continued, "There's a cantina on the bay owned by Atticus Fish. It's very popular these days."

"Like the lawyer in *To Kill a Mocking Bird*?" Pike asked.

"Sort of."

"What's the name of the bar? Hoppy Lee?" Pike slapped his thigh in laughter. "Get it? Harper Lee...Hoppy Lee...?"

After a long pause, Winston said, "Cantina del Cielo."

"Heaven's Bar?"

"Yep."

"Sounds blasphemous."

"I'm sure he'd agree."

"I'm feeling sick," Weevil muttered. He lowered the passenger side window and sucked at the dusty air.

The truck hit a pothole, and the back end bounced into a jaw-shuddering fishtail. Winston regained control of the steering wheel and redoubled their speed.

"Hydroplaning!" Winston yelled over the vibrations. "Keep an eye out for large rocks!"

Pike turned to Weevil. "I can't breathe with all the dust in here! Roll up your window before I choke to death!"

"I told you I get carsick!" Weevil whistled loudly.

"You live on a boat! How can you get motion sickness?"

"You go to college! How can you be stupid?"

Pike jabbed a finger at Weevil, who bullwhipped it away. Pike shoved the first mate farther out the window.

"You must have a fucking death wish," he said, watching Weevil jut his head to the side and wretch.

"Look out!" Winston hollered.

He spun the wheel and jammed the brake pedal to the floor. The truck's back end spun counterclockwise over the uneven road. Weevil, discombobulated by detox, carsickness, and a partial lack of peripheral vision, froze in the open window, his head protruding like a human dart. He squeezed his working eye shut. The centrifugal force of the sliding truck thrust the first mate farther out the window until both of his bony shoulders hung precariously from the doorframe.

The truck slowed, and Weevil opened his eye. He peered into the whirling dust, and like an apparition from a dream, one-eyed the hazy outline of an immense animal. It stood at the side of the road, its head the size of an engine block with two exceptionally sharp horns.

Weevil windmilled his arms and screamed. He backpedaled like a televangelist caught in the tabloids. A rank smell rushed into his exposed nostril. An enraged snort surged into his ears. Weevil twisted his upper body and felt himself accordion into the head of the beast and then rebound into the truck, an uncomfortable ache ascending through his right shoulder. He landed prone over Pike, who fell against Winston. The truck came to an abrupt stop and began to quake.

"Bull!" Pike shouted. "In the window!"

CHAPTER 23

CABO SAN LUCAS, BAJA CALIFORNIA, MEXICO

Fish paddled through the gauntlet of crazed waterborne tourists, ignoring the droves of watercraft vying for position at the edge of a floating trampoline. He ignored the pontoon bars selling cans of Tecate and multicolored Jell-O shots. He ignored the couple Jet Skiing naked, the parasailing dog, and the Elvis impersonator on a wakeboard.

He even tried to ignore the sudden cheer that reverberated across the water. But the cheering increased as the crowd at the beachfront Office Bar leapt from their chairs and jammed the waterline. Shirtless college boys swam fervidly into the bay.

A florescent pink catamaran had appeared and was approaching the floating trampoline, its deck brimming with bikinied sorority girls. A banner strung from the masthead read "Bouncing Bikini Contest."

Fish stared in wonderment as an inebriated blonde bounded to the center of the trampoline, where she was pelted by Jell-O shots. She tried to duck and slipped to her knees. The waterborne crowd erupted.

The girl wobbled to her feet, and the crowd yelled, *"Uno!"*

She bounced.

"Dos!"

She bounced higher.

"Tres!"

She blinked at the crowd, unaware of the sudden barrage of Jell-O shots. The marshmallow-size gelatin bombs raked her body as she braced for another high-flying bounce. Her feet touched down into a puddle of melting Jell-O, and as her breakfast buffet of blended margaritas and Jägermeister chasers emboldened her courage, the trampoline tilted with an incoming swell. Syrupy goo ebbed between her toes, and she crashed to her back, losing her top. The trampoline launched her sideways into the jib of a nearby sailboat, where the blanket of canvas cradled her briefly. She rolled free, toppled to the deck, and barfed. The crowd roared appreciatively.

Fish frowned and began to paddle more furiously when a bevy of speedboats zoomed past him—*away* from the bouncing bikini contest. Dozens of the parasailing boats were headed out to sea, their drivers deploying enormous advertising banners. Fish stared into the distance and felt his heart begin to race. Not one, but two cruise ship were anchoring outside the bay. Both were deploying tugboat-size tenders loaded with tourists. Fish knifed the oars into the sea. He hauled against the water with newfound urgency. Cabo was imploding. He had to get out.

And soon.

Fish made it to the seaplane just as the first tender of middle-aged couples approached. Forty smiling faces aimed cameras and called out ahoys. Fish ignored them. He opened the seaplane's cargo door and hauled the dinghy inside. The tourists offered *holas* and *como estás*. Fish still didn't respond. He leaned down to hoist the anchor when a woman excitedly inquired if he was the real Indiana Jones. Fish double-hauled the rope.

A second tender of tourists arrived, and a woman squealed, "It's George Clooney with a goatee!"

More cameras took aim.

"Naw, he's too tall."

"It's Richard Branson!"

"Too young," someone else shouted.

"Hey, didn't Howard Hughes spend millions searching for the fountain of youth?"

"I think he flew a plane just like that!"

"Look how young he is!"

"Hey, Howard!" came a collective cry.

Fish dropped the anchor rope. He lunged inside and grabbed the machete hanging from the doorjamb and then leapt back to the pontoon and brought the heavy blade across the rope. The crowd shrieked. One lady asked for his telephone number. Fish climbed inside and closed the door.

Time to fly.

He started the engines and lifted off in record time. The plane gained altitude and then banked sharply. The *Miss Beehaven* still lay at anchor at the far corner of the bay, its back deck littered with pizza boxes and beer bottles. Fish rummaged for a CD in the plane's center console and placed *Live Rust* into the portable player. He pressed play, took aim, and dropped altitude.

His first flyover scattered the pizza boxes and toppled the beer bottles. It also brought the muscle-bound show-offs to the deck. Each was red-faced and shirtless with towels wrapped around their waists. One held a bottle of tequila by its neck. Fish took a sweeping turn and to the chorus of "Hey Hey My My" bore down on the yacht's stern.

The boys waved angrily. Tequila sloshed from the open bottle. One of the girls poked her head from the salon and quickly ducked inside.

Fish increased his speed.

Seconds before impact both boys dropped to the deck, the tequila bottle shattering across the teak inlays. Fish yanked back on the wheel, and the plane swooped across the boat's stern, rattling the riggings.

"Lesson number one," Fish said aloud. "Never play chicken with a seaplane."

He circled around and trained the pontoons on the water just beyond the stern. He dropped the plane's nose and dive-bombed. Both boys were on their feet hurling obscenities into the air. Fish slid open the plexiglass window and flashed a thumbs-up. The boys turned and ran. Fish punched the throttle kamikaze-style, reared back, and porpoised the plane's pontoons hard off the water.

The yacht shook as a massive curtain of saltwater poured over the *Miss Beehaven*'s stern. Hundreds of gallons slammed into the cockpit and thundered across the deck. The wave shattered the bottles and swept both boys through the open salon door.

"Lesson number two," Fish said. "Never underestimate a guy in a dinghy."

Moments later both couples stumbled like soaked cats from the salon. Fish feigned a sharp turn, and all four scurried back inside, slamming the door shut.

Satisfied, Fish turned north and charted a course over the Pacific.

He had a boat to find and a captain to see.

CHAPTER 24

CABO SAN LUCAS, BAJA CALIFORNIA, MEXICO

By the time Big Joe made it to the Cabo San Lucas heliport, the midmorning heat was at triple digits. He stood in the shade of a faded awning eyeing the personal two-man ultralight gyrocopter. The teenage pilot checked the rotor blades and tail rudder.

"*Listo?*" he said and hailed Big Joe. "Three hundred bucks cash, señor. Before I start her up, no?"

"You sure you're old enough to fly this thing?"

"*Sí señor*. See?"

He dug through the pocket of his jeans and produced a photocopy of an AeroMexico pilot's license.

"It says José Hernandez *SENIOR*."

"I plan to have many children, señor," the pilot said with a wink, motioning at the hickeys covering Big Joe's neck.

Big Joe turned around to leave.

"Okay, I make you a deal. Two hundred bucks. We fly anywhere you want."

Big Joe frowned.

"Okay. Last offer. One fifty."

Big Joe pulled the pilfered money from the pocket of his jeans. "No hotdogging, *comprende*?"

"Of course, señor. Where to?"

"Over the Pacific. Todos Santo north to Magdalena Bay."

"*Muy bien.*"

An hour and a half later the gyrocopter buzzed the coastline between Todos Santo and Magdalena Bay. In the distance Big Joe could see the outline of the *Wahoo Rhapsody* angling toward the deepwater port of San Carlos.

"Drop me at the old port," Big Joe yelled over the engine noise.

The pilot nodded and upped their speed, dropping low over the beach when the engine coughed and the rotor slowed.

"Hang on!" the pilot yelled and jammed his foot on the rudder control. The gyrocopter bucked. He torqued the tail fin and spun the machine in a tight circle.

"*Listo?*"

He released the controls, and as the engine sputtered the cockpit stopped spinning, and the skids bounced gently across the sand. Big Joe opened his eyes and looked around.

"You okay, señor?"

"How'd you do that?" Big Joe stammered.

"No gas gauge. *Mucho practico.*"

"Where are we?"

"On the beach, señor. Beautiful, no? You want, you go for a swim? I go find *gasolina*."

Big Joe unbuckled and stumbled from the small craft. "I think I'll walk from here."

The pilot shrugged. "*No problema.* There is a fish camp maybe one mile ahead. We walk together."

Big Joe nodded.

"First time in a whirlybird, *amigo*?"

Big Joe nodded again.

"*Muy bien.* Maybe we fly again one day, huh? I give you big discount. Promise to fill the tank all the way next time."

Big Joe gave a boisterous laugh. He slipped free of his cotton shirt and tied it around his forehead as a sunshade. "Big discount, huh?"

"Oh yes, señor. The best."

"What you did back there was impressive," Big Joe said, his smile growing. "Thank you for saving my life. But from now on I think I'll stick to land-based travel."

"I rent dune buggies as well," José said, his face brightening with anticipation. "Same discount applies."

Big Joe patted him on the back. "I like you, kid. If I'm ever in need of a good dune buggy, I'll look you up."

"*Muy bien, amigo,*" José said cheerfully and hurried up the beach. "*Ándele pues.* Before the sun gets any higher and we die of thirst."

Big Joe laughed again and trotted up the sand.

CHAPTER 25

SAN DIEGO, CALIFORNIA

The sound of the cell phone clanged like a death knell inside Edwin's skull. He tugged it from his shirt pocket and flipped it open.

"Yes?" he grumbled, lightly touching the blister at his neck. His head throbbed from the collision with the desktop moments earlier, and his hangover was about to be exacerbated by the tenor of his cousin's voice.

"Eddie, it's me, the Angler."

Ever since meeting Socorro at the after-hours nightclub in Cabo San Lucas, Edwin's cousin had become paranoid about using his real name. Especially after he'd agreed to meet her partner, Memo, in Tijuana, to discuss cash payments for managing the new Cabo-to-San Diego smuggling route. The Angler refused to give Memo his real name, knowing that most drug dealers invented nicknames. He also avoided talking on landlines or using credit cards. Having spent considerable time smoking pot at some of San Diego's most prolific bass lakes, the man was also privy to the fact that more than sixty million anglers lived in the United States. When it came time to choose an undercover moniker, Edwin's cousin naturally became *The Angler*.

Edwin sighed and tried to remember the script for speaking on the telephone. "How's the fishing?" Edwin finally asked. It was the Angler's code for *no cops sniffing around.*

"Shitty. The fishing's real shitty, Eddie. Did you see the morning paper?"

"No," Edwin lied.

"It's over, man. The feds got the big fish locked down. Time to reel in the lines."

Edwin ignored his cousin's absurd use of metaphor and said, "Reel in the lines? What the hell does that one mean?"

"It means we're done fishing."

"What?"

"Fishing, bro. *Fishing!*"

Edwin fanned his blistered neck with a section of newspaper. "You still there, Eddie?"

"Just reeling in the lines."

"Is the shipment still en route?"

"I think so."

"Okay, then just because the big dog caught the big fish doesn't mean the minnows get caught too."

"Minnows?"

"Exactly. I'll go down to the dock this weekend in the refrigerated truck like always and pick up the product. Pretend like everything's normal. Then, instead of bringing the fattest bellies back to the factory, I'll drive out to Palm Springs and bury them in the desert. That'll cover the stink while they thaw out. I'll bring the skinnies back to your place so you can process them as usual. That way if you-know-who rats us out, there'll be nothing for the feds to find at the cannery. We'll be clean."

"And then what?"

"Then I'll go back to the desert in a different vehicle. You know, incognito, and dig up the mess, clean out the bellies, and can them up with one of those portable jobbies."

"Really?"

"No, I'm making all this up. Jesus, man. You all right?"

Edwin opened his desk drawer and rummaged for a bottle of prescription painkillers. He dropped two into his mouth and crushed them between his molars, hardly noticing the bitter taste. "I'm fine," Edwin said dryly. "It all sounds pretty risky. Seems like you're willing to do a lot of work by yourself."

"Whoa now, Eddie boy. We're family, man. No one cheats their own family."

"What I mean is the cops might already know. What if they're waiting for you at the dock?"

Edwin heard the Angler clap his hands. "That's the Edwin I love. Thinking ahead. Been doing the same thing myself. As soon as I hang up, I want you to send our couriers a fax. Tell them to switch docks. Make sure it's miles from Fisherman's Landing. They can tell their customers that the old dock is under repair."

"Switch docks?"

"Brilliant, huh?"

"But a boat that big can't just dock anywhere."

"Not my problem."

"You got a dock in mind?"

"That's up to you, Edster. You're the fishmonger."

"Can you narrow it down?"

The Angler didn't answer. The phone line had gone dead.

CHAPTER 26

BAJA CALIFORNIA, MEXICO

Minutes after banking away from the *Miss Beehaven*, Fish glanced at the fuel gage and felt his stomach drop. He'd arrived in Cabo with two mostly full tanks. Now both were nearly empty. He switched to the small auxiliary tank. It too was low. He ran a hand down his goatee and frowned. He hadn't noticed a fuel slick on the water, no alarm light to indicate a sudden loss of fuel pressure. That meant only one thing:

Sabotage.

A brazen siphoning of both tanks in broad daylight.

Fish tugged at his goatee, wagging his head at the irony. And the bad luck. He didn't use high-octane fuel. He'd converted the seaplane's engines to diesel and then modified the inner mechanisms to burn fish oil. Swapped the rubber hoses and seals with biodiesel hardware. Gasoline was inefficient, polluting, and government-owned. If there was one thing Fish hated worse than mollycoddled Americans it was inane bureaucracy of any kind.

So instead of participating in the Pemex monopoly, Fish filled his seaplane's tanks every few weeks at the local cannery. He had donated a fish oil filtering system along with non-slip floors for the workers and a weekly bonus for anyone refusing to process a growing list of endangered sharks and rays. And to alleviate the economic impact on the *pangeros* targeting sharks and manta rays, Fish purchased new outboard engines and turtle-friendly nets for the entire fleet. The effect was almost immediate. Baby sharks were sighted for the first time in decades, and manta rays were multiplying along the shoreline like locusts.

Unable to fly out over the Pacific and search for the *Rhapsody*, Fish leveled the seaplane to conserve what fish oil remained in the fuel tanks. He redirected the plane on a straight line to Magdalena Bay and was drifting off course toward the Pacific with a pair of binoculars in his hand when the radio crackled. It was Isabela, his bartender at Cantina del Cielo. Mephistopheles had chewed through her rope, crossed one of the island's sandbars at low tide, and was rooting through fish carcasses at the cannery. She said Skegs had tried to corral the mule, but a bruising kick to the calf sent him limping in for a free lunch.

"Maybe you could get here before Xavier returns from La Paz," she said. "He almost shot Juanita's pig yesterday," she reminded him.

Fish remembered. He set the binoculars on the seat and drifted back on course, splashing down an hour later in Puerto San Carlos near his bayside bar. He tied the seaplane to its mooring and paddled the dinghy to the short dock. As he tied the inflatable to a cleat, Skegs limped from the bar.

"*Machaca!*" Skegs spat. "That's what you should do with that oversized vermin. She's damn near rawhide anyway."

"Sorry to hear about the leg," Fish said, eyeing the bandage. "Kicked you, did she?"

"Would have killed me if I hadn't spun out of the way just in time."

"Must be those Indian reflexes."

"I'll skin her free of charge. Learned it in my village. Got to where I could flay a dead horse before the flies showed up."

"You skinned horses?"

"For the teepees, man. Canvas was hard to come by in the middle of the Sonoran desert."

"I would have expected cows, not horses."

"Hide's a hide."

"Mephistopheles isn't dead."

"Smells dead. Let's end the misery."

"How about you drive me to the cannery instead so I can pick her up."

Skegs shrugged. "Your loss, kemosabe." He limped toward the Buick. "Got to head south anyway. Cabo's in need of more world-famous mescal and some genuine hand-poured Indian ironwood." He paused. "Plus, I need a new set of fishing gear. Thinking of trying something new. A secret weapon guaranteed to catch anything that swims."

"As long as it isn't red." Fish climbed into the Buick. "Heard you got a free lunch out of Isabela."

"Free! This leg's probably gangrenous by now. I'll be lucky to ever surf fish without falling over. You should be offering me a *lifetime* of free lunches."

"Maybe I should take a look at that leg."

"Can't expose it to the air. Packed it with herbs. Medicine man stuff. Say, how was Cabo?"

"Like a hemorrhoid."

"Glad to hear it's improving."

Twenty minutes later Skegs pulled the Buick into the back lot of the fish plant built at the edge of the mangroves. The hard-packed dirt was damp with spilled seawater, and the marine layer had burned off. Stacks of empty fish crates were drying in the noonday heat. Desultory fish heads littered the ground.

"Looks like the mackerel are running," Fish commented.

Skegs reached down and plucked a decapitated head from the dirt. He motioned toward the muddy shoreline. "Looks like your ass found a friend."

Fish looked up and saw Mephistopheles standing in the mangroves munching leaves with a wild burro. He whistled. Mephistopheles raised her head, snorted once, and returned to her machinations.

"Stubborn as a bar owner," Skegs said and hurled the fish head at the mule. It missed and ricocheted off the head of the wild burro. The burro turned, its ears flattening.

"Uh-oh," Skegs said and sprinted for the Buick.

"Careful on that leg!" Fish called out as the burro gave chase.

Skegs leaped into the car and disappeared in a cloud of dust. Fish strolled to the shore by the mangroves, patted Mephistopheles on the back, and rode back along the bayshore toward Cantina del Cielo.

He needed to try raising the *Wahoo Rhapsody* again. Before fueling up for an afternoon flight over the Pacific.

CHAPTER 27

PACIFIC OCEAN, MEXICO

Big Joe and the young helicopter pilot paused in the late afternoon shade of a lone palo verde tree. An ocean breeze gave the heat a pleasant tang and ruffled the incoming tide with tufts of white foam. In the distance lay half a dozen shacks and a multilayered rack of cactus ribs. The ribs were covered with dead guitarfish and small horn sharks in various stages of dehydration.

"*Fish machaca*," the pilot said. "Same as regular *machaca*, only fishier."

Big Joe arched his eyebrows.

"*Comprende?*"

Big Joe just smiled and strolled into camp.

A group of sleepy *pangeros* eyed him warily until the young pilot caught up. The Spanish was rapid-fire, and after a torrid bout of haggling Big Joe found himself fifty dollars poorer and in the bow of a *panga* watching the shoreline slowly fade away. The *pangero*'s eyes were bloodshot, and the constant waft of cheap mescal hung on him like a remora.

"*Vaya con Dios!*" the young pilot hollered from the beach, waving fervently with his free hand, and his other holding a small gas can. "Remember the discount next time we meet!"

Big Joe returned the wave and then gripped the gunwale as the *pangero* gunned the outboard and sped across the light chop for Puerto San Carlos. Minutes later he reached under the thwart and liberated a fresh bottle of tequila.

"*Quieres?*" he asked and motioned with the bottle.

Big Joe declined. "*Cuantos tiempo para llegar a San Carlos?*"

The fisherman shrugged. "*Un hora más o menos.*"

An hour later, as they neared the small port of San Carlos, the *pangero* abruptly cut the engine. He scrounged between the thwarts and raised an empty two-liter soda bottle coiled with hundred-pound monofilament fishing line. At the end of the line were a steel leader and a fist-size hook. He plunged a hand into the bait tank and removed a rotting mackerel. In one fluid motion, he threaded the mackerel onto the fishhook and flung the offering into the sea.

"*Tiberón grande,*" he slurred. "*Mira!*"

Big Joe squinted into the glare of the setting sun and saw a large shadow rising from the depths. It was a hammerhead closing fast. Big Joe wanted to tell the man it was too big for a handline when the surface eddied and the hammerhead's huge tail crashed against the side of the *panga*.

"*Arriba! Arriba!*" the man cried out to Big Joe, a worried look on his leathery face.

Big Joe scrambled to the stern and took the throttle control. The fisherman snatched a rag from his overalls and gripped the heavy line.

"*Ahorita!*" The *pangero* leaned against the weight of the shark as Big Joe gave pursuit.

For thirty minutes they fought the mammoth shark, twice bringing it to the surface before it plunged back to the depths.

SHAUN MOREY

It had swum far out to sea, and as the sky darkened, Big Joe could just make out the distant lights of San Carlos.

Suddenly the line slackened, and the *pangero* hauled back with both hands.

"*La cuerda, amigo,*" he panted and pointed at a rope secured near the bait tank.

Big Joe freed the rope. He quickly tied a Honda knot, widened the lariat, and waited for the shark to surface.

The *pangero* glanced at the lasso and grinned. "*Muy bien, señor. Un momento sí?*"

Big Joe nodded. He'd lassoed big sharks before. Back when they were plentiful. Before the long-liners had taken their toll.

Big Joe moved into position beside the *pangero* and watched the shark surface like a small submarine. He leaned over the water and pitched the lasso over the tail. He let it sink into place and then gently tugged it tight. As the *pangero* cut the line, Big Joe fed out a few leagues of rope and tied the slack end at the stern. Then he turned the *panga* and headed back for San Carlos, towing the hammerhead slowly behind.

The *pangero* retrieved the tequila and took a long pull from the bottle. Then he reached into his coveralls and removed the fifty dollars Joe had given him earlier and held them out.

Big Joe waved off the money and instead pointed toward the bottle. "*Tequila por favor.*"

The *pangero* smiled. "*Bien, bien, amigo,*" he said and passed the bottle, his eyes suddenly bright as taillights against the starlit sea.

121

CHAPTER 28

SAN DIEGO, CALIFORNIA

After his lunch of sedatives, Edwin's hangover deflated like a pinpricked blister, finally freeing his mind of its anaconda-like squeeze. The painkillers gave his lips a pleasant numbness, and the cigar smoke covered the scent of boiling tuna. The bay breeze had begun to blow, and he almost felt happy as he faxed the *Wahoo Rhapsody* instructions to switch docks.

He had addressed the note generically to "The Captain," on plain white paper asking him to "unload all the stuffed fish at the pier in Imperial Beach due to an unexpected bug infestation at Mission Bay." He hoped the clue was both obvious and clandestine should someone other than the smugglers see the fax.

As he waited for the captain to confirm the new mandate, his thoughts meandered to his cousin's offer to hijack the drugged fish. The Angler had seemed too eager to do the job, too willing to risk his personal safety. It seemed out of character for a man so obsessed with security. The more Edwin considered it, the more he felt uncomfortable with his cousin's plan, and the more confident he became in his own. As Edwin dreamed of his pot-inspired Alaskan road trip and the fresh-aired freedom it would provide, the fax machine began to whir.

Edwin sucked a last lungful of cherry-flavored smoke and extinguished the cigar in the tin ashtray. He lifted the page from the machine.

TUNAMAN,
STEAL FROM LA CUCARACHA AND YOU DIE
MEMO Y SOCORRO
P.S. FISH DELIVERY CANCELLED
P.P.S. AWAIT FURTHER INSTRUCTIONS
P.P.P.S. MAYBE I GUT YOU LIKE A DEAD TUNA

Edwin felt dizzy. He leaned back to avoid colliding with the desk again. His heart mutinied and his stomach cowered. Sweat slalomed down his round cheeks. He wrenched open his desk drawer and poured a puddle of sedatives into his mouth. The placebo effect was immediate. He dabbed away the sweat and wandered to the window. Maybe Memo and Socorro were on board to meet with the captain. Or maybe they were escorting the drugs through Mexican waters. La Cucaracha couldn't know about his plans to steal the drugs. Only he and the Angler knew about that. Edwin jabbed a Swisher Sweets into his mouth, wishing he'd never gotten involved with the Angler's stupid venture.

Then he thought of Mrs. Dockweiler. *She* was the reason for his current predicament, his desperate financial state, his general state of unhappiness. Her penurious ways had forced him into crime. Did she really think he could retire on a lifetime supply of free tuna fish? Impossible. The old bat was deranged.

And obscenely wealthy.

Edwin had seen the mansion. First at the wake for Mr. Dockweiler—the self-described tuna king—and then at the quarterly management meetings where Edwin was forced to endure hours with the rich widow and her accountant. Formal meetings. Mrs. Dockweiler dressed to intimidate. Black dress, black stockings, jewels on every finger—diamonds, sapphires, rubies. Enormous pearls draped in gold and dangling from her pallid, pencil-thin neck.

Edwin had been summoned to the mansion four times in the last year to give his quarterly State of the Factory address. He'd always felt awkward and outnumbered. The accountant bombarded him with expense reduction strategies, revenue graphs, and tuna-catch projections. Mrs. Dockweiler frowned and fingered her fancy baubles. Just one of those precious necklaces was all Edwin needed. How hard could it be? After all, the eccentric millionairess lived alone. A distraction was all he needed. Something to send her fleeing from the mansion. Something to distract her from her precious stones *and* her state-of-the-art security system.

Edwin lit the cigar. As he blew the flame from the match and dropped it into the ashtray, the answer sparked in his mind. The room seemed to brighten and expand. Maybe it was the sedatives. Edwin didn't care. Laughter erupted from his jowls. He stared at the extinguished match, the tin ashtray, the newspaper fluttering on the desk. He glanced at the open window and smiled at the stiffening sea breeze.

Everyone knew he kept the office window open after work. It was the only way to dilute the stench of boiled tuna. They also knew he chain-smoked cigars and kept a stack of daily papers on his desk. He would tell fire officials that one of the cigars must have remained lit after he closed for the evening. That the wind had blown an ember from the ashtray. That the stack of daily newspapers caught fire.

As for Mrs. Dockweiler, she would be summoned from her mansion in a panic, angry that her late husband had been too cheap to install fire sprinklers. Angry that the Tuna King had pressured his cronies into granting him that fire code exception. Angry at herself for continuing the charade after his death. Surely all that anger would make her forget to set her house alarm. Maybe even forget to lock the doors. Certainly forget to put the jewels in the safe.

All that finery out in the open.

Simple as collecting shells from the beach.

Edwin couldn't stop grinning. He puffed forcefully on the cigar. The afternoon breeze was gathering speed. He held out the cigar and watched the tip flare at the incoming draft.

"Fire in the fish hole!" Edwin snickered, the smoke escaping his lungs like prisoners from a jailbreak.

CHAPTER 29

BAJA CALIFORNIA, MEXICO

The enraged beast shook the stolen truck. It bucked and snorted and tried to free its head from the passenger side window. Weevil was prostrate across Pike, groaning, his shoulder gored, staring into a set of black bovine eyes. The creature lunged and bucked, and the truck bounced like a low-rider at a gangbanger convention. It thrust its horns across the ceiling, gouging the rusted metal and yanking its head backward with a loud clank.

"It's stuck!" Pike yelled.

Winston slammed the gears into park, swung open the driver's door, and hopped carefully to the ground. Pike lunged toward freedom, hauling Weevil behind him. The recoil from the springy seat flung both through the door and onto the rocky ground.

"Weevil okay?" Winston asked breathlessly.

"Sort of," Pike answered.

The first mate writhed in the dirt, cradling his shoulder. He gave a low moan and rolled to his knees, staring disbelievingly into the truck. The trapped animal bellowed angrily, seesawing its horns and head-butting the wrecked ceiling. Its neck was immense and corked the open window with folds of skin pouring down the cracked paneling like a hirsute waterfall.

"Man, that had to hurt," Pike panted, staring at the crimson hole in Weevil's shoulder. "You reminded me of one of those rodeo clowns. Hanging onto the head of the bull like that. For once, I actually felt sorry for you."

Weevil felt the urge to steer-wrestle his rival across the road and pin his head to a cactus. Crucify the obnoxious jerk to the arms of a nearby saguaro. Maybe spear him with a yucca spike. Instead, Weevil coughed out another moan.

Pike meanwhile reentered the front of the truck. The beast eyed him warily, bits of frothy acacia pods hanging from its lower jaw. Its eyes glistened black as eight balls. Pike inched forward, waving his hand like a cape over the dashboard. The animal cocked its head, and Pike dove forward, slamming open the passenger door. It bucked, and the door swung open and snapped from its hinges.

"Drive!" Pike yelled, scrambling back out to the dirt and hauling Weevil into the truck.

Winston climbed into the driver's seat and rammed the truck into gear. The creature thrust its head up and down, pawing at the ground, the pot-stuffed door swinging wildly around its neck. The truck lurched forward, slid briefly, and then caught traction, spitting rocks and dirt into the air.

"You're an asshole," Weevil whistled from a fetal position on the footwell, his gored shoulder seeping blood.

Pike leaned down. "Say again?"

"You purposely yanked my bad arm pulling me into the truck."

"If you weren't so pitiful, I'd think you were ungrateful."

Winston glanced down at his first mate. "That wound needs to be disinfected, Willie. As soon as possible."

Pike's face brightened. He opened the glove compartment and retrieved the flask-size bottle of mescal.

"This ought to do the trick."

He swirled the tawny liquid with a look of satisfaction, watching the pickled worm rise from the bottom like an albino eyebrow.

"This might hurt," Pike said as he uncapped the bottle.

"Like hell."

Weevil grabbed for the bottle. Pike flinched, spilling mescal across Weevil's shoulder.

"Aghhh!"

"That was easy," Pike said, smiling.

Weevil threw an awkward punch and knuckled the bottle of mescal into the air. It shattered against the roof of the truck, raining mescal and broken glass across the first mate. Weevil shrieked in pain and then stared fixedly at the ceiling, his good eye widening. He carped his mouth and pulled back his lips. Pike gaped up in wonderment. Winston craned his neck and frowned.

A pothole jarred the truck, and Weevil licked his lips. The marinated worm slowly dislodged from the ceiling and tumbled head over tail through the air. Weevil widened his jelly-jar mouth.

"Bull's-eye," he muttered. Then his eye rolled into the back of his head and he fell limp.

"Impressive," Winston said.

"Abominable," Pike commented, and he plucked a shard of glass from Weevil's weedy chin.

⌁ ⌁ ⌁

By the time the old truck clanked into Magdalena Bay's small port town of San Carlos, Weevil was delirious. His bull-horned shoulder was wrapped in Pike's head gauze, and his face was flecked with dried blood. His exposed eye was rheumy with shock.

"Over there," Winston said, gesturing at a chile-green structure at the edge of the bay.

A weathered oar hung above the entrance with the words "Cantina del Cielo" burned in black across the paddle. Patrons lined the stools, staring out at the cerulean bay. A hodgepodge of old pickups filled the lot, fine particles of dust covering their rusted hulks like sullied shrink-wrap. There were mud-encrusted *norteamericano* four-by-fours loaded with driftwood, and an ancient VW bus topped with surfboards. A lone mule stood saddleless in the shade of a mesquite tree, its ears twitching at an onslaught of mangrove flies. A sign above its head read "Mephistopheles."

Winston turned into the parking lot and stopped near the front door. He laid on the horn, and moments later a towering barefoot man emerged, casually dressed, wearing a fishskin cap.

Atticus Fish squinted into the late afternoon sun. He slackened his tackle box jaw and let his fingers fall to the sun-washed goatee twisted into a tail and held tightly by a fisherman's crimp. He wore faded dungarees and a loose guayabera shirt. From his belt hung a machete tied to his thigh with a dogbane rope. He removed his hat and pushed back sprigs of light-colored hair.

"I'll be goddamned," he said with relief.

Winston hopped awkwardly from the truck. "Five years in Baja have been good to you, my friend."

"Five years at sea and you look like hell." Fish wrapped his reef-hard arms around the captain and capped him lovingly on the back. "I was getting worried. What the hell happened?"

"Long story. You got a doctor in town?"

"Finest in Baja's sitting at the bar nursing a shrimp cocktail."

Winston missed the satire and said, "Weevil's hurt bad."

Fish hurried to the missing door and ladled Weevil into his arms. As he turned he watched a policeman exit the bar trailing two red-faced middle-aged Americans restrained by plastic flex-cuffs. Their flowery shirts were unbuttoned, and twin porcine bellies hung over matching linen shorts belted in red, white, and blue sharks. Each wore a pair of navy blue Docksiders.

"That's him!" one of the men yelled. "The mad fucking cowboy! He's the one should be arrested. He threatened us with that goddamn machete. We have rights, you know!" The men struggled against their binds.

The policeman tipped his hat to Fish and then shoved the prisoners into his patrol car.

Fish turned to Winston. "Yachties on a bender. Motored in a few hours ago and mistreated my barkeeper. Thought they'd bully her for stronger drinks. Then they demanded their change in dollars instead of pesos, and when Isabela told them we didn't have enough in the register, they became unpleasant."

Fish reached the entrance just as two college-aged girls in tight shorts, bikini tops, and lace-up sandals stumbled out. "Give me back my boyfriend!" the lead girl whined. "He's my boat ride home."

"Mine too," the second girl slurred, and she dropped her sunglasses to the sand. "Shit, those are expensive." She bent forward, lost a sandal, tripped, and toppled over her friend. Both girls collapsed.

"Hot, hot, hot!" they stammered and scuttled crablike back inside the bar.

"Interesting establishment," Winston said.

"Comes with the booze. But it's mostly friendly. Locals and vagabonds. Our town cop, Xavier, takes care of the occasional riffraff. He'll hold them awhile, charge a hefty fine for disturbing the peace, and send them along with a stern warning not to return. They usually get the message." Fish stepped inside.

"A week ago you and the *Rhapsody* are motoring by my rancho promising a boatload of fish stories. Next thing I know you show up in a wrecked pickup with a limp and a hell of a shiner." He eyed his friend's attire more closely. "Hospital gown?"

Winston's face paled. "A drug dealer named La Cucaracha thought Weevil stole his drugs."

Fish glanced down at the unconscious boatman in his arms.

Winston continued, "I didn't know anything about it until yesterday."

Fish nodded absently and walked through the door toward the doctor who sat at the bar. "I was planning to fly down and surprise you for your fortieth birthday. I got distracted, so I called you on the radio instead. It was late in the afternoon yesterday. I even tried your cell but got nothing. I got worried and flew down this morning. The *Rhapsody* had already left—in the middle of the night."

Winston sighed. "I'm sorry for all the trouble."

"Trouble? Hell, you saved my life. Flying down to Cabo was the least I could do."

"Doesn't make it right."

"Doesn't matter." He readjusted Weevil in his arms and asked, "Is Big Joe still working for you?"

"He was in Cabo looking for Weevil when the drug dealer attacked me."

"You think he might be driving the *Rhapsody*?"

"And leave us stranded? Never."

"So the boat's collateral?"

"I think so."

Fish thought of the millions hidden in the hull and said, "You didn't have any work done recently on the hull, did you?"

"No, why?"

"Just curious." He hurried to the curved bar and added, "As soon as the doctor cleans Weevil up, we'll fly over to my island and rest up for a bit. It's close by. Ten, fifteen minutes tops."

Fish arrived at the circular pier-plank bartop and whispered into the ear of an elderly woman squeezing limes over a plateful of shrimp. She wore a vibrant serape and sat beside a large black satchel. She wagged a finger at the empty space between her plate of food and a pair of comatose iguanas. Then she reached into her satchel and removed a small glass container. She unscrewed the lid and scraped out a fingerful of salve. The smell of tidal mud and dried kelp wafted over the fried shrimp and beer.

Fish laid Weevil gently on the bar and removed the bloody gauze tied around his shoulder. Weevil stirred at the familiar undercurrent of alcohol and gazed lovingly at the bottles lining the back of the bar. He propped himself up with his good arm and licked his lips. The old woman reached out her hand and applied the salve.

Weevil let out a bloodcurdling howl. He fish-flopped across the bar, nearly knocking the drunken iguanas to the floor, his cries for mercy drowned by the beat of a Carlos Santana riff emanating from the jukebox.

Winston cringed.

Pike grinned.

Fish headed for the phone to call Toozie with the news: Winston and the first mate were safe, but Big Joe and the boat were still missing.

Through the pain Weevil felt his mind whirlpool. As he lost consciousness, he swore he saw the silhouette of an old Indian woman, the head of a shrimp dangling from her mouth, her finger buried knuckle-deep in his shoulder muscle.

PART II

CHAPTER 30

TUCSON, ARIZONA

Private detective Toozie McGill spent the morning returning telephone calls and tending her horses. Lunch was homemade fish tacos and a Negra Modelo, and by early afternoon she was sitting in her seventeen-foot Ranger bass boat flipping a willowleaf spinner bait into the cattails along the shores of Arivaca Lake. Located sixty miles west of her rancho and eleven miles north of the Mexican border, Arivaca Lake was her escape. Even in the late afternoon heat. A place to ponder in solitude, to plan investigative strategies, to solve cases.

She held the Arivaca Lake record for largemouth bass and had recently hooked and lost a fish nearly twice its size. She christened the bass Big Julie and spent her fishing hours hunting for a second try at the big bucketmouth.

On this late summer afternoon, she was work-free as she made an underhand cast to the edge of a weedline when her cell phone rang. She ignored it, waited for the spinner bait to sink a few feet, and cranked the reel. Moments later the water erupted with the strike of a hungry bass. The small fish swung its head against the pull of the line. It flipped into the air, belly-flopped, and surged for the safety of lake weed. Toozie calmly turned its head and eased it to the surface. She brought it alongside the boat, pinched its lower lip with thumb and forefinger, and hefted it into the air. She kissed it on the head and released the two-pounder back to the water. Her phone vibrated with a message.

The sun dropped low to the hills, and Toozie stowed the rod and reel and motored back to shore. She backed the trailer down the dirt ramp and slid the Ranger over the carpeted bunk boards. After hitching it tightly, she pulled it from the lake and unscrewed the drain plug. Then she sat in her truck, opened a fresh Negra Modelo, and retrieved the phone message. The sound of Atticus Fish's voice brought a smile to her face. He said the captain and two of his deckhands were safe. Her smile faded as she heard him explain that the third seaman, Big Joe O'Ferrill, was missing. So was the eighty-two-foot *Wahoo Rhapsody*. But it was the next sentence that caused her to set down her beer:

I need you to look into a drug dealer who goes by the name La Cucaracha. The captain thinks he's behind all of this. I've got a local cop helping down here. I'll call you as soon as I know anything more.

Toozie felt the familiar corkscrew of discomfort when drug dealers became involved in a case. The discomfort was magnified by the fact that she'd seen the name La Cucaracha mentioned in the morning paper along with tabloid quotes from federal prosecutor Rent Barnhouse. Barnhouse was Tucson's most celebrated and sleaziest barrister, and Toozie distrusted anything the man said publicly. Barnhouse was more politician than prosecutor, a wannabe officeholder with a win-at-all-cost mentality.

Toozie tossed her baseball cap to the dashboard, shook loose her ponytail of strawberry blonde hair, and took a long pull of beer before dialing her assistant, Foley Hayworth. He answered on the first ring.

"Rent Barnhouse is on the front page again," she said.

"Rent's a news whore. What else is new?"

"Have you heard of La Cucaracha?"

"The song?"

"The drug dealer. Paper says he's a spin-off of the Escarabajo cartel. They're the ones who killed those journalists in Tijuana a few years ago. Apparently Barnhouse has the kingpin in jail. A guy named Ernesto Camacho."

"*The* kingpin? Sounds fishy coming from Barnhouse."

"My thoughts exactly."

Foley chuckled and said, "Barnhouse really believes some Mexican drug boss is calling himself the cockroach? Hilarious. That song's all about smoking pot."

"It isn't," she exclaimed.

Foley began to sing, "*Porque no tiene, porque le falta, marijuana que fumar. La cucaracha—*"

Toozie cut him off. "Okay, I believe you. But what's really crazy is it's the second time I've come across it in the last hour."

"The lyrics to the song?"

"The name La Cucaracha. My ex-brother-in-law called me from Mexico less than an hour ago. His friend had a run-in yesterday with the supposed La Cucaracha. Lost a fishing boat and a deckhand."

"I thought Barnhouse has the guy in jail."

"Exactly."

Foley was silent.

Toozie said, "Call your friend Larson at the DA's office and see if you can get your hands on that indictment."

"I'd rather get my hands on Lars," Foley said dreamily.

"First the indictment."

"Your brother-in-law, is he the rich guy who sued the pope?"

"Something like that."

"He's in Mexico?"

"Hiding from the fanatics."

"I read somewhere that he has more money than God. Is he single?"

"Foley!"

"I'll call Larson."

Toozie ended the call. She closed her eyes and thought about her brother-in-law living in Baja. How much she suddenly missed him. Missed the romance of Mexico. It had been nearly four years since she'd visited Baja California. It had been a quick trip to La Paz with a new boyfriend. An even quicker breakup after she'd chosen marlin fishing over lounging by the pool. The note on the hotel bed said something about her needing to relax. She'd smiled at that one. Fishing was the one thing that *did* relax her.

That and abruptly finding herself unhitched in Baja. She vowed to only date fishermen in the future. Then she celebrated the breakup with a bottle of tequila and a walk through old town La Paz. Which is where she spotted the two life-size, hand-painted wooden skeletons that stood together in her tackle room back at the rancho. They were dressed as vaqueros, embracing in a macabre pose.

The two skeletons had been standing at the open doorway of an indigenous art store, away from the bustle of trinket stores and tourist shops. Inside were hundreds of hand-painted masks hung from the walls. Animal faces and devils, and combinations of both. But the skeletons drew her attention back to the doorway.

They were fashioned after the work of Mexican folk artist Posada, whose skeletal portfolio mocked the ruling class during the last revolution.

Toozie had to have the colorfully painted couple. Had to be near their hollow faces so full of mirth. Their fleshless bodies so full of life.

As if the dead were more alive than the living.

CHAPTER 31

TUCSON, ARIZONA

Federal prosecutor Rent Barnhouse was craving a Tom Collins. He was also craving Octavia Ortiz, his star witness against Ernesto Camacho, aka, La Cucaracha. Octavia had been flirting with him for weeks. Ever since last month at the Samaniego House, a lawyer-friendly cocktail lounge in downtown Tucson. Ever since she overheard him bragging about his political future and the drug dealer who smuggled cockroaches in his pot. An hour later, over margaritas, she told him she knew a drug dealer in Cabo San Lucas who had a thing for cockroaches. She said her cousin worked for the man. Said the man's name was Camacho. That they sold skunkweed to the tourists. Rent asked her out. Then he asked her to testify.

"I think you've finally got it," Rent said, strolling to his wet bar and pouring gin into a glass of sparkling lemonade. He checked his profile in the mirror and said, "Just remember to say Camacho approached you a year ago at a bar in Cabo San Lucas and asked if you were afraid of cockroaches."

"Sounds corny."

"It'll soften the jury for your next statement."

She grimaced. "You really want me to say that Camacho offered me ten grand to recruit elderly illegal women to smuggle pot across the border in their wigs?"

"Exactly."

"Grandmas?"

"Camacho needs to look like a pig."

"I'm not even a citizen."

"But you're beautiful, and that's all the jury will see. Plus the media will love you." He scanned her body with viper eyes.

Octavia ignored the leer. "How soon can you deposit the money?"

"As soon as you testify."

Octavia walked to the bar and made a margarita. "Half now, half after I testify. And I want double our original deal."

"What!" Rent coughed out a mouthful of Tom Collins.

"For the ogling."

"I can have you deported."

"Not if we're having drinks later."

"Really?"

Octavia leaned forward, allowing a full view of her terracotta cleavage. "I have a surprise for you tonight. Meet me at the Green Dolphin at nine o'clock."

"Nine o'clock."

"My cousin is joining us."

"The pot dealer?"

"A different cousin."

"Oh," Rent said dejectedly.

"I think you'll like her. She's into rodeo."

"I like rodeos."

"She's a clown."

"I love clowns."

"I'm not surprised."

"Should I wear cowboy boots?"

"Wouldn't hurt." Octavia downed her drink and walked to the door. "Bring cash. It could be quite a night."

CHAPTER 32

PACIFIC OCEAN, BAJA CALIFORNIA, MEXICO

By the time Big Joe and the *pangero* arrived at the small dock outside Cantina del Cielo, the sky was a blur of stars and the two fishermen were out of tequila. They secured the *panga* to a cleat and hauled the dead hammerhead to shore. Two hours of backward towing had kept oxygen from entering the shark's gills, asphyxiating it underwater.

The two men stumbled up the clamshell path to the open-air bar. Dozens of tourists and a handful of locals populated the stools lining the open walls. A parrot cawed high in the palapa, and an iguana walked with an unsteady gait among the random puddles of beer. It stopped to lap up a particularly inviting wet spot and then ambled onward. Johnny Cash belted out a live version of "Folsom Prison Blues" from the jukebox. Big Joe and the *pangero* entered the bar.

"*Tequila con sangrita,*" Big Joe ordered from the female bartender. "*Dos, por favor.*"

"*Y dos Carta Blancas,*" the *pangero* added.

Isabela nodded.

Someone tapped Big Joe on the shoulder. "*Con san*-whata?" she asked drunkenly.

Big Joe turned. A twenty-something woman in a bikini top and a wraparound skirt smiled. A pair of broken sunglasses sat perched on a tangle of salon-streaked hair.

"I'm Roxy," she said and extended a well-manicured hand.

Big Joe shook it.

"Pepe," the *pangero* blurted and reached for her hand.

A second similarly clad woman stumbled to the bar and took Pepe's hand. "*Me llamo* Rose," she hiccupped in barely recognizable Spanish.

"Rosalinda," Pepe repeated dreamily.

"Sounds so beautiful when he says it like that," Rose crooned.

Big Joe added two more tequilas *con sangrita* to his order.

"You didn't tell me," Roxy complained, wrapping her arm around Big Joe's neck. "The Santa Rita stuff."

"*Con sangrita*. Little bit of blood."

She untangled herself from his neck and frowned. "Disgusting!"

"It's a metaphor," Big Joe explained.

"A whatafor?"

"It's not real blood."

"Oh good." She rewrapped her arm around his neck. "Do you own a boat?"

Big Joe glanced at Pepe.

Roxy leaned in close to Big Joe's ear and whispered, "Is it a big boat?"

"Sort of."

She dropped her arm from his neck. "It isn't a trick question."

"We have a small boat. The bigger boat's tied up at the moment."

She turned and winked at her friend. "How tied up?"

"Well—"

The drinks arrived, and Pepe passed everyone a shot glass. "*Salud*," he said and dumped the tequila into his mouth. He quickly passed around the chaser of *sangrita*.

"*Otra vez.*"

They downed the *sangrita*.

"Hot! Hot! Hot!" Roxy complained and chugged a third of Big Joe's Carta Blanca.

Pepe laughed.

"Ever seen a hammerhead shark up close?" Big Joe asked.

"Don't fall for that one, Roxy," Rose chimed in. "Not until we're safe and secure on the *big* boat."

"You two are stranded?" Big Joe asked.

"Sort of," Roxy mumbled.

"It wasn't a trick question."

She punched him playfully on the shoulder.

"We really did catch a big hammerhead shark today. It's on the beach right outside."

"And we really are stranded. Our ride's in the local jail."

"Maybe we can help."

"*Ayúdeme*," Pepe said and winked a glassy eye.

"Is he your boat captain?"

"Something like that," Big Joe said and led the trio out toward the dock and the shore-bound hammerhead.

CHAPTER 33

SAN DIEGO, CALIFORNIA

Edwin had waited for the last of the employees to leave before overloading his Celica with cases of canned tuna. Then he locked his car and hurried back up the stairs to his office to light his final Swisher Sweets of the day—hopefully the last of his tuna-canning career. He opened the office window and looked longingly across the swath of honking asphalt toward the setting sun. The tide was low, and Mission Bay smelled of gangrenous shellfish and Sea-World offal. Edwin welcomed it. The smell would help encourage his departure from the fish business. And his pyromania.

As Edwin watched the sun fade into the low-lying marine layer, he pulled the half-smoked cigar from his mouth and set it on the tin ashtray. He adjusted the seesaw of tobacco with his fingers and scooted the newspaper into place. The newsprint fluttered. A sudden gust levitated the ashtray and toppled its contents to the front page. The headlines smoldered and burst into flames. Edwin raised his chubby arms in celebration.

A second gust spread the flaming ink across the desk, and Edwin watched in awe as the San Diego Padres baseball team went up in smoke. A sudden pang of guilt sent him scrambling beneath the desk for the metal trash can. Above him, the smoke began to swirl about the room. He emerged with the canister, kicked off a shoe, and swept the burning sports section toward it. As the newspaper edged over the desk, a third blast of bay breeze scattered the new sections across the floor. Edwin gaped in horror as the stock market turned red hot. The lifestyles section sizzled and popped. The personal ads burned scarlet. The editorials erupted in heated debate, and the funny pages burst in a comical flare. Topwater Tuna had become a media firestorm.

Edwin slipped his shoe back on and charged from the office. He wondered briefly where he kept the fire extinguisher and then bounded down the stairs and bolted from the building. He barreled into his car and gunned the engine. But the overloaded Celica whined in protest. Edwin stopped to empty the hatchback of its pallets of canned fish. One glance in the rearview mirror changed his mind. Topwater Tuna was belching black smoke.

Edwin approached the freeway, and for the first time he was able to merge into traffic without braking. It seemed a few hundred extra pounds of canned tuna made for optimum rush hour speed. He arrived at his condo an hour later in darkness. He changed into black jeans and a black long-sleeved shirt. He paused briefly to boost his confidence with a beer and a painkiller and then rummaged through his closet for a can of black shoe polish. Like a cowboy sleeving snuff, he shoved the can of polish into his back pocket. Then he returned to his driveway, stowed the cases of tuna in his garage, and minutes later was back on the freeway.

As he passed Topwater Tuna, he saw the fleet of fire trucks in the parking lot. He jammed on the gas pedal just as his cell phone began to ring. He picked it up and read the name on the caller ID:

Doris Dockweiler. She'd know of the fire by now. Probably be in a panic on her way to the cannery.

Edwin set the unanswered phone on the passenger seat and rolled down the window. He inhaled the polluted bay air and felt suddenly sentimental. Something about the aroma brought a Swisher Sweets to his mouth. He lit the cigar.

Through the toothsome smoke and the Mission Bay muck, Edwin could just make out the familiar scent. Slightly different than boiled tuna. Stronger, yet not wholly unpleasant. Then it dawned on him. The freezer at the cannery had been compromised. The frozen fish were thawing.

And flame-broiling.

CHAPTER 34

MAGDALENA BAY, BAJA CALIFORNIA, MEXICO

After leaving Cantina del Cielo, Fish loaded the *Rhapsody* crew into the seaplane for the short thirty-mile hop to his island home. It was dusk, and the outlaw sky was drunk with color. Weevil, who had passed out from the pain of the *curandera's* magic paste, stirred during takeoff. He wore a baggy Cantina del Cielo cotton shirt above his board shorts, and his wounded arm was curiously numb from shoulder to elbow. His eye patch and nose bandage had been replaced with fresh dressings, and the smell of damp hay hung in the air.

Weevil rubbed at his unbandaged eye and saw a large animal with a muzzle and erect ears. The animal stared through a porthole window, and for a moment Weevil wondered if he was back aboard the *Wahoo Rhapsody* sharing quarters with a barn animal. Then the seaplane banked sharply, and Weevil's stomach knuckleballed his thorax.

"Ughhh," he moaned, uncomfortably familiar with the rising motion sickness. The gentle leveling of the seaplane briefly quelled the uprising.

Pike, who wore red plastic earmuffs over his freshly bandaged scalp, sat strapped to a parachute seat near the front of the aircraft; he flashed Weevil a thumbs-up. Weevil ignored him. He craned his neck and saw a tall man at the controls wearing a cap that seemed to be made of fish skin. Winston sat in the copilot seat, his hospital smock replaced by a Cantina del Cielo sweat-shirt.

Weevil sat upright on the seam of two straw bales that had served as his makeshift bed. He scanned the wide-bellied plane. Plastic crates lined the concave walls, each bungeed to a stainless steel ring. The crates held an array of spectacular shells and drift-wood, barnacled buoys, glass floats, whale vertebrae, bleached bird skulls, and a stack of turtle shells in varying stages of decay. At the back of the plane near the hay bales was a makeshift stall with a wooden whisky keg sheared in half, its matching ends set side by side. A hitching ring had been welded to the frame just below the window with a rope that led from the ring to the ani-mal's neck. Above the window was a hand-painted sign.

It read "Mephistopheles."

Pike flagged an arm toward the empty parachute seat beside him where a second set of red earmuffs lay coiled. Weevil saun-tered forward and sat. He placed the earmuffs over his head and heard Fish say, "Bought her from a retired air traffic controller who had a thing for Howard Hughes. Damn near perfect replica of the *Spruce Goose*. Smaller, of course, and she flies better. Ret-rofitted both diesel engines to run on fish oil. Right over there's one of the largest fish factories in Baja." He motioned through the windshield at a smokestack. "They've got planeloads of it. Cheaper than Pemex if you can haul it away. Burns clean. Good use of byproduct."

"Fish oil?" Weevil stammered, his stomach trampolining.

"Welcome back," Fish said into the speaker. "How's the arm? The *curandera* said you'd be up soon."

"I can't feel it. What's a *curandera*? And what's with the horse?" He looked around frantically. "I think I'm going to puke."

Pike glared at Weevil. "That witch doctor may have fixed your arm and stopped the nose whistle, but your brain damage seems permanent."

"You're one to talk."

Pike elbowed the first mate in the gut.

Weevil folded forward and dry-heaved into his hands.

"*Curandera's* a shaman," Fish continued. "Shawoman, actually. A folk healer. She's the one who fixed you up. And Mephistopheles isn't a horse. She's a mule. Loves to fly. Pegasus reincarnated. I think she's disappointed each time we touch down."

Fish dipped a wing of the plane.

Weevil fell to his knees.

"If you're going to be sick," Fish said, "use the hay in the back, but watch yourself. Our four-legged friend's territorial about her paddock." He motioned out Winston's window. "Down there are the largest mangrove forests in Baja."

Winston glanced at miles of twisting river glinting in the setting sun. The tangle of water created a jumbled geometric pattern in the distance as if a basket of gargantuan snakes had been spilled across the bay.

"Shangri-la," Fish offered. "One of the few remaining stretches of unmolested coastline. No docks. No marinas. No homes or resorts. Nothing for miles. Only the small fish camp over there, and even then you rarely see the *pangeros*."

A ruffle of headwater signaled a school of rising minnows, and seconds later a flock of seabirds crashed headfirst into the riotous water.

"Hang on," Fish said. "We'll circle back and buzz the fish camp. I see Xavier's patrol car down there. Probably buying fresh lobster." He banked hard and turned for a tiny spit of sand where a scattering of canoe-like boats canted sideways on the shore.

Fish flew over the fish camp and dipped the wings from side to side. He dropped low and then pulled back on the yoke for altitude. Weevil, still on his knees, began to cough.

"Hairball?" Pike asked and clapped Weevil hard on the back.

Weevil toppled forward and rolled armadillo-like toward the makeshift paddock, the cord of the headset wrapping tightly around his neck. He came to a stop behind Mephistopheles and heard Fish say, "Would you look at that! The longest green flash I've ever seen."

Fireflies sparked in Weevil's vision. His eye bulged. His face bloomed a horticulturist's dream. He clawed at the choking headset cord and flailed at the air. His hand found Mephistopheles's tail, and he yanked himself from the floor, loosening the garrote. He sucked in a lungful of air. Then he hunched forward and patted Mephistopheles appreciatively on the flank. Pike waved frantically. Weevil glared back angrily.

Pike shrugged.

Mephistopheles kicked.

Weevil's face went sunrise-red. His legs buckled, and like a catcher covering home plate, he dropped to his knees, slowly rolled to his side, and passed out.

"There she is!" Winston yelled into the headset and pointed through the windshield. "The *Rhapsody* coming into the bay!"

"I see her, partner," Fish said and banked hard to the right.

CHAPTER 35

PACIFIC OCEAN, BAJA CALIFORNIA, MEXICO

The capitán's death was an accidente, Memo typed on the keys to his cell phone. He stood at the helm of the *Wahoo Rhapsody* and finished his text. *I have gabacho's boat AND our fish.*

A few minutes later came the reply: *And what will you do now? Take the boat to San Diego? Pretend you are the new capitán? Estúpido! Look in the mirror! Even in Mexico you look out of place on the water.*

Memo had never known La Cucaracha to be so enraged. *We are heading to Mag Bay. The fish plant there. Socorro knows someone. We will offload tonight.*

And the boat? They will be looking for it.

Sink it outside the bay. Before dawn. No one will know. We have panga to return to shore.

Think, Memo! The boat is worth more than the fish. Unload then repaint boat. Call it the Espíritu Santo. Take to Ensenada and hide among the tuna fleet. I will meet you there.

And the fish?

Call cannery man. Tell him to meet Socorro in Mag Bay. Bring his canning labels. He and Socorro will can everything there.

They can drive it by truck to San Diego. No one will suspect a gringo to use his own labels to smuggle mota across border.

Memo considered telling his boss about Edwin's attempted double-cross. Instead he typed, *What if he refuses?*

Kill him.

CHAPTER 36

TUCSON, ARIZONA

Rent Barnhouse could not believe his luck. After meeting his star witness, Octavia, and her cousin at the Green Dolphin Bar, both women agreed to accompany him to his mountaintop getaway at nearby Mount Lemmon. Rent drove alone in his volcanic black Corvette. The women followed in Octavia's equally black Mercedes Benz.

Once inside the cabin, the cousin changed into her clown outfit as Octavia lounged on the couch smoking a joint and sending text messages. Rent uncorked a bottle of cheap wine. He wore a white cowboy hat tilted back and a plastic gunslinger holster over a snakeskin belt. The belt matched a pair of shiny snakeskin boots. He brought the wine to Octavia, who flamed the end of the joint just as the bathroom door hinged open. Octavia choked back a laugh.

"I know the shoes are a kinda weird," the clown-faced woman said, adjusting the bulbous red nose. "But the suspenders are perfect." She pulled back the stretchy fabric and snapped them across her bare breasts.

"Yeehaw," Rent said, and he hurried to the liquor cabinet for a bottle of Cuervo. He poured a quick shot.

"To clowning around," he toasted.

Octavia puffed on the joint and watched Rent spill out a second shot and hand it to the clown, who was busy adjusting her rainbow-colored wig. Octavia held out the joint. The clown downed the tequila and clopped across the living room floor.

"Thanks," she said and sucked in a lungful of smoke.

"Why don't we take our private rodeo into the bedroom," Rent suggested and hurried to the kitchen. "I'll grab the wine and be right in. Leave the light on, okay?"

The clown took another puff on the joint and whispered, "My fee just went up." She waddled into the bedroom and set her small handbag on the television. She adjusted her baggy pants and slid onto the bed.

Octavia sank into the couch and yawned. "I'm taking a nap," she said as Rent hurried by and closed the bedroom door.

Rent stripped from his clothes. He re-cinched the holster, snugged his cowboy hat tightly to his head, and began hula-hooping his hips in harmonious bliss. He reached around and pinched the clown's rubber nose.

"Giddy-up, cowgirl!"

The clown neighed halfheartedly and said, "Ride 'em cowboy."

Rent redoubled his efforts and then fell back unsatisfied against the pillows. "Seems the stallion needs a little pick-me-up."

He logrolled to the edge of the bed, badly bending one of the phony holsters, slid open the bedside drawer, and uncapped a bottle of blue pills.

"Horsepower," he announced, chomping the pill to powder. He stood and shook out his legs, seized the bottle of burgundy from the nightstand, and chugged half straight from the top.

"Only takes a minute."

The clown reset her wig and lit a cigarette.

"Back in the game!" Rent announced proudly as the clown finished the last of her cigarette. He climbed into position, removed his hat, and slapped it against the clown's backside.

"Hi-ho, Silver!" he squealed and pounded his chest like an aging ape, unaware of the tiny red light glowing from the handbag above the television.

CHAPTER 37

MAGDALENA BAY, BAJA CALIFORNIA, MEXICO

After splash-landing on the shallow inlet on the eastern side of his sand dune island, Fish tied the seaplane to its buoy, loaded the three passengers into his awaiting *panga*, and sped the short distance to shore. A seasoned dune buggy, its keys permanently rusted to the ignition, carried them over the hard-packed sand for the two-minute drive to a sparse canopy of elephant trees. The sky was the color of busted beets, and the air smelled of salt marsh and seaweed.

"You got a plan?" Winston asked Fish as they exited the dune buggy.

"Yep. I'll tell you all about it over dinner."

Two Labrador retrievers, wet with ocean water, galloped down the sand to greet them.

"The black one's Sting," Fish said. "She's a few years younger and a whole lot smarter than Ray." He waited for the yellow Lab to catch up and bent to scratch it behind the ears.

"Cool to name them after a fish," Weevil commented. "I always liked the name Mullet for a cat."

"There's a surprise," Pike scoffed.

"Not a stingray," Fish said. "Musicians. I saw Ray Charles in concert back in the nineties. The next day I went out and bought every album I could find. And who doesn't like Sting?"

Pike raised his hand.

Fish ignored him and handed Winston his crutch. They walked a cobblestone-like path of chocolate clamshells up and over a small rise and stopped. Wedged into a chasm of sand was an octagon-shaped edifice four stories high made from wood and adobe. It had a turret-style balcony at the top and a towering *palapa* roof. Dozens of salvaged nautical windows green with patina were set into the walls. Every window was hinged open, each bracketed by old glass fishing floats, some the size of basketballs. The floats hung in nets fashioned from heavy buoy lines that draped the windows like makeshift shutters.

Winston crutched down the walkway to an entryway fashioned from an antique red phone booth, the glass panes of its accordion door cracked and clouded with age.

"Phone booth?" Winston asked.

"Coastline north of here catches half the Pacific as it goes by," Fish explained as they entered the house.

The floor was made from intricately placed driftwood packed with sand in a herringbone pattern that drew the eye to the center of the room where a branchless redwood soared sixty feet high. Coiled from trunk to top was a spiraled iron staircase that resembled an enormous rusted spring.

"Currents from as far away as Japan and Alaska bring in flotsam by the ton," Fish continued. "Everything you see except the staircase came from the beach. Those beams running from the redwood to the walls came from an old hickory pier that floated ashore in pieces. It had Canadian maple leaves burned into the grain. The heaviest planks are now the circular bartop at del Cielo."

Pike walked to the center of the room and slapped the varnished bark. "This thing's real?"

"Washed up at Malarrimo. Completely waterlogged. Just what I needed to anchor this sand castle."

Weevil, who had explored much of Baja's coast, chimed in. "You dragged that thing all the way from Malarrimo?"

"Towed it by barge and beached it out front for a summer. Had to roll it every few days to dry it out. After three months we dragged it here. Took us a month and hundreds of wooden skids. We felt like Egyptians building a pyramid. Counterbalance pulleys, fulcrums, even an old farm tractor with sand chains on the tires. Hired half the town to help out. Paid the *pangeros* to ferry the workers out here in their *pangas*. Had to sink the rootball twenty feet deep and then added a five-foot ring of concrete." He patted the redwood admiringly. "Old girl probably fell from a cliff along the Northern California coast. Lucky for the both of us. If the loggers had gotten her, she'd have been ripsawed into a thousand picket fences by now."

Pike gazed up the redwood trunk into a wagon wheel pattern of roughhewn beams each attached to a corresponding wall like spokes to a wheel. The beams were off-centered so that the walls were supported concentrically from top to bottom. Near the top was a series of eight rope bridges that led to arched passageways extending into eight small rooms, and above that a balcony and the towering *palapa*.

"No elevator?" Winston lamented, leaning heavily onto his crutch.

"We're strictly solar out here, but there's a pulley for the heavy stuff." He stole a glance at his friend. "Or I could carry you up."

"Like hell."

"Some kind of a turret up there?" Pike asked, pointing to the double doors winged open to allow in sunlight and sea breezes.

"Porch," Fish said. "Living quarters. Kitchen. Workshop. All the rest of this is basement, really."

"We're below ground?"

"Below the base of a moving mountain range of sand."

"Moving?"

"Sand dunes are like giant sea urchins. Always moving in slow motion. Which accounts for the octagon shape of the house. The eight walls work like sand repellent. They transfer the weight evenly on all sides. All I do is keep the entrance clear."

"With what, a bulldozer?"

"Could use one at times. The windy season's like a tropical version of a snowstorm."

A loud creak echoed across the room.

"Uh-oh!" Weevil blurted, the nose whistle suddenly returning.

"Sands of time," Fish explained. "Just moving around the house."

Weevil swallowed dryly. "What if a wall caves in?"

"Impossible. But a crack is possible. If that happened, all six thousand square feet of her would fill up like an hourglass."

The dogs started to bark.

"Sounds like Xavier's here. Wings are marinating topside. Cold sodas in the fridge." Fish started up the spiral staircase. "One step at a time, Captain."

Pike turned to Weevil. "Guy's a bigger nutcase than you."

Weevil ignored him. His face was pale, and he was backing toward the phone booth entryway.

"You coming, Cyclops?" Pike asked, placing a hand on the iron staircase.

Weevil didn't answer. He crashed through the accordion door and straight into the outstretched arms of a policeman.

CHAPTER 38

SAN DIEGO, CALIFORNIA

Edwin parked his Celica in the underground parking lot near La Jolla's shopping district, three blocks from Mrs. Dockweiler's seaside mansion. The night was cool and heavy with sea mist. Throngs of well-dressed tourists crowded the sidewalks, clogging the foyers of high-end bars and five-star restaurants. Edwin felt out of place in his sneakers. He also felt light-footed with opiates. He veered away from the crowds and ducked into an alleyway one block from the beach.

The alley was quiet and uncomfortably clean. Fenced alcoves hid trash cans from sight. Cars were ensconced behind baroque garage doors. No weeds sprouted, no litter congregated, no discarded furniture or toys, not even a cigarette butt marred the blacktop. Dogs didn't bark at his progress. Cats didn't lurk in the shadows. It was as if such high-priced square footage lured life indoors.

Edwin tucked his chin to his chest and ambled to the end of the alleyway, where Mrs. Dockweiler's mansion rose like nacre glowing beneath the night sky. The Mediterranean-style architecture was enclosed by a thick wall, its turn-of-the-century bricks coursed in thick ivy. An olivewood gate barred the entrance beneath an archway of Torrey pines. The detached garage, larger than the average middle-class home, stood in the darkness, its tiled roof glistening with mist. Edwin hurried to the fenced alcove shielding her trash cans from sight.

He unlatched the gate and ducked into the shadows. He applied the black shoe polish to his face, upended a large trash can, and hauled his girth over the wall. On the way down, he grabbed a handful of ivy, slipped, and landed with an ankle-twisting thud. Sufficiently anesthetized, he glanced around the darkness and nearly whooped with excitement. No motion detectors had been triggered, and no alarm had sounded. He saw no movement through the windows, and as he drew in a celebratory breath, his stomach knotted and he gagged. Something foul engulfed him. He wheezed and spat and tried to hold his breath. He failed, and the odor barged into his nostrils like barnyard sludge. It was worse than boiled fish guts. It was rank and rancid.

And it was everywhere.

Edwin pushed himself from the ground when he heard a rustle from across the yard. The sound was followed by a ballyhoo of snorts. Edwin froze. The rustle became a gallop, and from across the yard came a swarm of hoofed feet. Edwin yelped. He fell back against the wall and kicked out with his feet. Ivy jabbed at his back.

"Shoo!" Edwin shouted in a panicked whisper. "Shoo pigs!"

He was morbidly afraid of pigs—dead or alive. The phobia began with *Charlotte's Web* and its blathering porker, Wilber. Then it was *Animal Farm* and its creepy revolutionary pigs. But it was Babe, the wannabe sheepherding piglet, that turned Edwin into a certified swinophobe. He'd been eating pork rinds in the theatre when Babe learned of his eventual slaughter. Edwin choked back tears, shoveled in another handful of fried pigskin, and gagged. He gripped his throat and tried to free the wayward snack, but his airway was blocked. Edwin collapsed to the floor. Paramedics were rushed to the theatre. A successful Heimlich maneuver and a night in intensive care permanently cured Edwin of his taste for all things piggy.

Now he was confronted by dozens of the creatures. He willed himself forward and booted the lead sow in the nose. The pig clamped down on the tip of Edwin's shoe and shook her head. Edwin lost his balance and fell into the muck. The sow tugged like a mastiff mouthing a chew toy, and Edwin yelped again. He felt the shoe slip free and watched the pig saunter away triumphantly. He scrambled to his feet and stared in terror as the remaining herd charged.

Edwin backed against the ivy-strewn wall, incensed at the idiosyncrasies of the rich. He'd read about potbellied pigs. How the dwarfish farm animals could grow to immense size. How owners expecting years of fun with their piggies were soon caring for hundred-pound rooting ungulates. Veterinarians and humane societies were inundated with the abandoned novelties. Saving such swine from certain euthanasia was just the sort of eccentric hobby a tuna-millionairess would enjoy.

Edwin cursed. To hell with the heist and the sudden scourge of pigs. He pulled at the thick vines and inched up the wall. The pigs crowded in. Half a dozen rooted into his pant legs. One managed to worm its nose up his calf, tearing the seam to the knee. Edwin gave a muffled scream. He grasped at the tendrils of ivy and yanked when a pig nicked his calf with a tooth. Edwin bleated in pain. The pigs squealed in response.

More meddlesome than malicious, the pigs closed tightly around Edwin's legs. Another snout invaded his untorn pant cuff. The seam split like Velcro. Edwin kicked out like a chorus line dancer. Snouts raised and lowered in response. Tails wagged. Snorts filled the night air.

Edwin turned and clambered up the ivy with both hands. He dug the toe of his sock and his remaining sneaker into every available crevice. Pig heads butted his every move. Bristly noses nudged him higher. Desperately he pulled. He found purchase, but then suddenly the foothold crumbled and he slipped. But instead of crashing into an orgy of hooves, Edwin landed feet first onto something solid.

And undulating.

The pigs in their wild rush had crammed themselves into the base of the wall, creating a solid bench of living ham. Edwin sprang from the rioting backs like a crazed zookeeper. He fingered the ledge of the wall, scraped himself over, and landed on the upturned trash can with a loud crash. He scarecrowed to his feet and hobbled away, pig slop dropping from his clothes like mud from a wrestler.

He drove the side streets home and coasted up his driveway after midnight. As he stood fully clothed beneath the hot shower, disheartened by his prospects for early retirement, he thought of Derek Moneymaker and the ambulance-chaser's slam-dunk lawsuit.

Class-action lawsuits aren't about greed, Moneymaker had told him. *They're about keeping the consumer from risk. And you*, he had warned Edwin, *are a very substantial consumer at risk.*

Come to think of it, Edwin thought as he stepped gingerly from the shower, toothpicks did seem sharper these days.

CHAPTER 39

MAGDALENA BAY, BAJA CALIFORNIA, MEXICO

After colliding into Xavier, Weevil collapsed in the phone booth, paralyzed by the thought of drowning in sand. Ironically, it was Pike who came to Weevil's rescue, recognizing the paranoia caused by the *curandera*'s mangrove elixir. Pike called up to Fish, who calmed Weevil with another glop of the mystery goop. Within minutes, Weevil was two-stepping up the circular staircase commenting on the ingenuity and workmanship of the towering sandcastle.

Soon Weevil was on the porch at the top of the sand dune settled into a canvas-backed chair between Pike and Winston, chattering about the summer he'd spent surf fishing Baja. Xavier stood a few feet from Fish and whispered something into his ear.

Fish nodded. He glanced out at the mirror of stars masking the Pacific Ocean and said, "*Sí.*"

"You own this whole island?" Pike blurted suddenly.

Fish stepped to the mesquite-fire barbecue and flipped medallions of sizzling wings into the air. "I prefer caretaker. Ownership's a fleeting concept. But technically I own the island. Buried millions into it, actually. Makes for the perfect savings account."

Weevil frowned. "You don't use banks?"

"Don't trust bankers," Fish said. He dribbled a spoonful of homemade barbecue sauce over the wings and removed them from the fire. "Bastards smile in percentages and sleep with their spreadsheets. Haven't met one who could look me in the eye without seeing dollar signs. I guess you could say I prefer more creative means of securing my retirement."

"Like burying it in the sand?" Weevil chirped.

"From the mean tide up."

"But somebody could come along and steal it."

"They better have a big shovel."

Weevil shuffled to the solar-powered icebox and rooted around for a beer. "I thought you owned a bar?"

"The only one in town."

"And you're out of beer?"

"Used to have a drinking problem."

"So you bought a bar?" Pike sputtered.

"Keeps the demons close." Fish handed out the dinner plates. "Just not too close." He sat in a driftwood chair and said, "Besides, hanging around drunks all day's a good reminder to stay sober."

Pike forked food into his mouth. "Hey, these chicken wings are great. How'd you get the bones out?"

"Baja secret," Fish said and winked at Xavier, who knew the wings were medallions of washed-up stingray.

"You don't worry about drug dealers way out here alone?" Pike asked.

Weevil choked on a bite. "Sorry," he said and plucked an opaque shard from his mouth. "Kind of thin for a chicken bone."

Fish swallowed a laugh and said to Pike, "Drug dealers aren't a problem out here. They prefer the calmer Sea of Cortez to run their dope. It's the developers that keep me up at night. Those jerk-offs are worse than bankers. Of course I've got the advantage when it comes to buying beachfront."

"You do?" Pike asked, shoveling in another forkful of fish.

"They're in it to make money. I'm not."

"You're in it to lose money?"

"Can't take it with me to the underworld. So when the time comes, I've left instructions with Xavier to donate it to the Nature Conservancy. Along with instructions to bury me with my assets. Six feet down in all this precious sand."

"Why leave all that money in the sand?" Weevil groused. "That's crazy."

Winston said, "No crazier than suing God. *That* was sheer madness."

"You sued the Almighty?" Pike asked and quickly crossed himself.

Fish squeezed a wedge of lime over his food. "Organized religion, actually. But it wasn't madness. Madness is the system that allows insurance companies to blame deities for trillions of dollars in losses. They write it into the policies. Call it the 'acts of God' exclusion and use it to deny payment to millions of people. Victims of earthquakes, lightning strikes, floods, forest fires. Almost any natural disasters you can think of the insurance companies try to blame on God."

As everyone finished their meal, Fish explained his lawsuit. How his high school friend turned bishop, Douglas McFetters, had been struck and killed by lightning while conducting an outdoor funeral in Flagstaff, Arizona. How the life insurance company had denied the claim by the bishop's sister. How the insurance company claimed that the lightning bolt was an act of God.

How Fish got angry.

"And so," Fish continued, "I filed a lawsuit on behalf of the bishop's sister. Wrongful death. Against the Catholic Church, which employed McFetters. I argued that because the church represented God, and God caused the lightning strike, Bishop McFetters was killed in the course of his employment. He worked for God, after all, and if God was this all-powerful and all-knowing being, and the lightning was under His control, and He throws one of His zillion-volt bolts at one of His bishops instead of, say, a palo verde tree, then it's a clear case of workplace negligence."

Weevil bobbed his head up and down while Pike crossed himself again.

"I couldn't exactly get God to appear in court," Fish continued, "so I went after God's representatives. The entire American diocese, for a start. And guess what? They quickly settled the case. Apparently they didn't want to admit that God was not all-knowing and all-powerful—and if He was, they didn't want to admit that He lost control of His temper and zapped the good bishop. Next thing I knew, more and more people were coming to me with insurance company denials based on the acts of God exclusion. So I filed a class-action lawsuit.

"Then I went after all of them. The Vatican with its deep pockets, all the Christian spin-offs including the Mormons, the Baptists, the Presbyterians. Then I went after the Jews, Muslims, Hindus, every major religion I could think of, including all those creepy televangelists. Every organization that sold their version of God as a product, through donations, fundraisers, charity events, and so on. And here's the best part: none of them wanted to admit that their version of God lacked the foreknowledge that His acts would cause injury. Or if they did, that He either couldn't or wouldn't stop it. What it all meant was that any legal defense of God required a sacrifice of one of the big three godly qualities: omniscience, omnipotence, or omni-benevolence. And that scared the hell out of them."

"Omni-what?" Weevil yawned.

"All knowing, all powerful, all good," Pike said gruffly.

They all stared at him.

Pike dropped his fork to his plate. "I'm really not comfortable with this conversation."

Fish smiled. "It's okay to be a believer, Willie. This isn't a church, and I'm not a preacher. My personal opinion is that God, if He exists, is a real SOB. But you can relax. Lightning hasn't struck me yet."

"It's blasphemous. You can't blame God for stuff like that. He's got His reasons. It's not for us to judge."

"Except that the law doesn't work like that. Under the law, you slay, you pay."

"Amen," Weevil said and raised his soda.

"Like hell," Pike snapped.

Fish chuckled. "More like a single day of worldwide donations. That was the final settlement. Just one-three-hundred-and-sixty-fifth of each religious institution's annual donations. Not much of a sacrifice, really."

"Sounds more than fair to me," Weevil offered sleepily as the magic mangrove paste wore off. "So you settled your case against God and retired down here?"

"Pretty much. I had quite a few death threats, as you can imagine. Remember Salman Rushdie? He only pissed off one religion. I had them all gunning for me."

Winston cleared his throat. "About the *Rhapsody*."

"We go at midnight," Fish said. "Xavier spotted the boat on his way out here. He says two people are aboard unloading dead tunas into a *panga*. A man and a woman. They're ferrying about ten fish at a time through the mangroves to the fish cannery."

"Those two are psychopaths," Weevil said with a shudder.

Fish motioned toward the boatman's wounded eye and nose.

Weevil nodded. "Guy's name is Memo. The woman calls herself Socorro."

"Why unload the fish?"

"It's where I hid the drugs."

"Inside the fish?"

"Double-wrapped the pot and shoved it down their frozen throats."

"Dumbass," Pike commented.

Fish let out a boisterous laugh. "How many did you stuff?"

"Fifty."

"Will they know which fifty?"

"Doubt it. I clipped the tails, but if you're not looking for it you wouldn't notice."

"Okay, then they'll have to unload them all." He looked at Winston. "How many fish total?"

"Hundred and fifty-five," Winston said.

"Ten fish per load, that makes about fifteen trips to the cannery and back. Figure about thirty minutes per trip. They'll be at it all night."

"They could be armed," Pike interjected.

"I'm counting on it."

Pike frowned. "But we don't know anything about these guys."

"I've got a private investigator working for us stateside. She's trying to identify La Cucaracha. I'm also calling in a friend. A local Indian who's good with knives."

Winston stood. "I'm really sorry about all of this."

"Me too," Weevil said sleepily and crawled into the nearby hammock.

Fish shrugged. "I would have drowned if it wasn't for you two and Big Joe. This is nothing compared to that." He motioned inside the house. "We've got three hours to showtime. Beds are down the hallway. I'll get a blanket for Weevil. He can stay out here tonight."

Winston couldn't help but smile. He turned and limped inside, his favorite Guy Clark song suddenly ringing in his head.

Old friends, they really did shine like diamonds.

CHAPTER 40

TUCSON, ARIZONA

Toozie opened a fresh Negra Modelo and watched the sky blossom through the window of her kitchen. Skeins of fire streaked across clouds as large as mountaintops. She sat at a denim couch in the den of her rancho. Above her spun the thick wooden blades of a ceiling fan.

She flattened the creases of the La Cucaracha indictment surreptitiously copied by Larson the courthouse clerk and smuggled out in his bikini briefs. How he managed to fold eighteen pages of legalese into the size and shape of an athletic cup was a mystery to Toozie. Foley said it was something about the practical applications of origami. Impressed, Toozie gave him a bottle of organic Mexican wine for him and Larson to enjoy at their leisure.

With Foley now gone, Toozie read Rent Barnhouse's accusations. The drug dealer known as La Cucaracha was allegedly Ernesto Camacho, a two-bit coyote who border patrol officers had apprehended leading a troupe of elderly women with pot hidden in their wigs. The women claimed to be seeking work cleaning University of Arizona dormitory rooms when Camacho offered them guaranteed passage across the border. All they had to do was carry the marijuana. Apparently the women's wigs were also infested with dead cockroaches.

Barnhouse made no mention of the college administrators' willingness to hire the illegal workers and instead focused on the danger of such an influx of south-of-the-border septuagenarians. The fact that no legal resident would scrub dormitory toilets at less than minimum wage went without mention. Barnhouse supported his rant against illegal immigration by citing recent calls by a concerned group for electric fencing along the border. "A vital step in keeping out the scourge of illegal laborers." No matter that the "concerned group" was a posse of middle-aged white men who liked to carry guns and who covertly paid their Spanish-speaking nannies and fern-cutting landscapers pennies on the dollar.

Barnhouse also cited the powerful Washington lobbyist group known as JuHSTICE (Jesse Helms Strom Thurmond Institute of Constitutional Ethos), whose members erected border town banners that read "Grannies Without Green Cards Go Home." He even included copies of anti-immigrant recruitment advertisements placed by Tea Partiers in *AARP Magazine* as an example of the seriousness of the issue.

"Camacho the Coyote is the worst kind of criminal," Barnhouse wrote. "One who must not be gently booted across the border where he can regroup and resmuggle to the detriment of not only Arizona, but of the whole of the United States of America."

Apparently the judge agreed, and Camacho was given full room and board at the local Pima County Jail. Toozie assumed that the man was more than a little bewildered by all the attention, especially since only a nitwit would hide cockroach-littered pot in the wigs of grandmothers. But Barnhouse wasn't finished.

He claimed that the real reason the old women were smuggling pot was because they were terrorists supporting unemployed sons who were intent on retaking Arizona for the homeland of Mexico. Such a crime triggered the Patriot Act, and as such the court could confine their ringleader, Camacho, indefinitely.

And while Camacho may have been as corporately-minded as any hard-working patriotic American—offering low wage, union-less, benefit-deprived workers employment without benefits—Barnhouse claimed that the partially melted stick of sealing wax along with a metal stamp embossed with the initials LC found in his pockets was proof of his guilt. The plastic film canister stuffed with dead cockroaches was only added proof. Barnhouse argued that Camacho was far more sinister than some shabbily clad coyote. He was the infamous La Cucaracha, responsible for importing much of the confiscated contraband coming through the southwestern border with Mexico.

And in case there was any doubt remaining, Barnhouse claimed that an unnamed female witness would prove beyond a reasonable doubt that Ernesto Camacho was the man behind the buggy smuggling operation. Then, in tabloid flourish, Barnhouse wrote, "As surely as the common cockroach is squashed beneath the treads of our citizenry, so too must Mexico's most notorious drug dealer be stomped asunder by the steel boots of the American justice system."

Toozie tossed the indictment to the floor and dialed Foley Hayworth at home.

"Hey, Tooz," he answered in a slightly slurred voice.

"The indictment's rubbish," she said.

"What else is new?"

"Remember the recent arrest of the granny smuggler?"

"Sort of."

"A young coyote named Ernesto Camacho. Barnhouse claims Camacho's our notorious drug lord."

"No way. Drug lords don't accompany the illegals. They pay coyotes to do it."

"Exactly. And get this, Barnhouse claims Camacho was caught with a stick of wax and the branding seal of La Cucaracha in his pocket when they nabbed him."

Foley chuckled. "One of those old-fashioned letter things?"

"There's more. Camacho was apparently also carrying a small container of dead cockroaches."

"He wasn't!"

Toozie couldn't contain her laughter. Then she liberated a fresh Negra Modelo from the fridge and said, "Can you say setup?"

Foley said, "Obviously we need to talk with Camacho."

"Unfortunately, Rent figured out a way to trigger the Patriot Act."

"Camacho's also a terrorist?"

"Threat to national security."

"Of course."

"I'm working a way around it." She swallowed a mouthful of beer. "Meeting with an old professor. Constitutional law guy. He'll know what to do."

"Let me know if I can help. Oh, and Lars loved the wine. He and I are planning to hike Mount Lemmon tomorrow. Breakfast in Summerhaven. Want to join us?"

"Can't. But keep your phone. I may need you."

"Will do."

She hung up and finished her beer. Rain from a lingering monsoon pelted the tile roof of her rancho, and as she breathed in the rising aroma of wet sage, she uncapped another Negra Modelo and dialed Fish's number in Mexico.

CHAPTER 41

SAN DIEGO, CALIFORNIA

After showering away the pig slop, Edwin nodded off on his couch wearing only his towel. He was dreaming of buxom Alaskan women in salmon-choked streams when an incessant knocking woke him.

"Mr. Sparks!" came a rough voice from beyond the front door. More knocking followed. "San Diego Police Department. We'd like to talk with you about the recent fire at Topwater Tuna."

Edwin rolled from the couch and crawled to the sliding back door. He stepped quietly to the wooden balcony and glanced out at the darkness. The piercing lights of a plane barreled down the runway. The knocking grew louder.

"It'll only take a minute, Mr. Sparks!"

Edwin scaled the railing and crouched at the edge. Ten feet below was hillside, its dead brush coursed with debris triggered by the unrelenting takeoffs.

"Mr. Sparks, we advise you to cooperate!"

Edwin heard a plane taxi down the runway. He crouched low and felt the railing begin to vibrate. He dropped to his belly and slid over the edge, both hands gripped tightly around the corner post. He knew Mrs. Dockweiler had called the police, and he expected them to bust down the door at any moment. He was inching himself lower when the bath towel loosened at his waist. He instinctively grabbed for it and slipped. He sailed backward like a leaden blimp, the towel in his grip resembling a pennant in the wind.

He landed on his back and slid headfirst down a channel of loose rock, coming to rest at the base of the chain-link fence surrounding the airfield. The airplane noise dissipated, and Edwin waited for the detectives to shine their flashlights on him, supine and naked as a sumo wrestler. Instead he heard car tires squealing in the distance.

Edwin slowly sat up. He stared into the bleakness. The lights of the airport cast a hazy glow across the hillside. He looked up and saw the difficult climb back to his balcony. He heard a cricket's harried chirp, the insect desperate to serenade a mate before the next takeoff. Edwin reset the towel and began his ascent of the hillside. His back burned and his head throbbed. He made it a few feet and slid back down the rubble.

Another plane taxied down the runway, and Edwin waddled to the dirt path paralleling the outer boundaries of the chain-link fence. The path was frequented by transients and drug dealers who camped in a ravine a quarter mile away. The ravine cut through Edwin's subdivision and had a hiking trail that led to his street. Edwin ducked as the plane roared overhead. As the noise subsided, he began to trot down the rocky path. His feet were soft as caramel.

He paused, looking for a discarded shoe or an old pair of socks, but then the sound of a police siren propelled him forward. Fifteen minutes later he turned into the ravine and froze. In a nearby clearing was a bonfire and a group of youths huddled over a boom box. Loud music exploded into the night. The huddle broke, and the teenagers danced around the fire. Edwin reached up to cover his ears.

"Hey, check out the naked freak!" a young man cried out.

"Sick!"

"Pervert!"

Edwin waved hesitantly. He peeked up the path that led to the street less than a hundred feet away. The scent of marijuana was heavy in the air. He saw the large collection of beer cans piled near the fire and the glitter of broken bottles. A few of the teenagers wore wireless headsets clipped to their ears. Others typed furiously at their cell phones. When Edwin stepped toward the street, a beer can erupted at his feet.

"What the hell, man!" hollered a powerful boy in a hooded sweatshirt. He took a step toward Edwin.

"It's not what you think," Edwin stuttered. "I fell from my balcony." He pointed back the way he'd come. "After my shower." He turned to show the boy his back.

A cluster of smoking girls yelled, "Gross!"

"Rad," came a baritone chorus.

The powerful boy stopped and said, "Fuck, man, your back is toast. Want a beer?"

Edwin nodded.

"Give him your sweatshirt, asshole," one of the girls hollered. "He's fucking shivering."

"Give me head," the boy fired back.

"In your dreams, jerk-off!"

Someone lit a joint, and the crowd hived. Edwin waited for the beer. When no beverage appeared, he shuffled up the path and merged into the darkness.

"Hey, where'd the fat guy go?" Edwin heard someone wheeze seconds later. The question was followed by a fit of coughing.

"Hallucination," came another voice.

"Cool," someone answered to the sound of a jet lifting off.

CHAPTER 42

TUCSON, ARIZONA

After their tryst at the mountaintop cabin, Rent Barnhouse and his clown awoke late and drove to the town of Summerhaven for a morning-after breakfast. Edgy with hangover, Rent wondered why Octavia had departed during the night, taking most of his cash without leaving a note. He also wondered why she'd left her cousin behind. He was about to ask when the Corvette hit a pothole, exacerbating his pain. He gently rubbed his temples and pulled into the crowded parking lot.

He muttered for the clown to wait in line for a table while he remained in the car with the air conditioner cranked to arctic. Ten minutes later, the waitress led them to their booth near the front door. Rent slumped in, his face shaded by an old Tucson Toros baseball cap. He growled an order for pigs in a blanket, two sides of crispy bacon, an extra large soda, and an icy glass of milk. Then he hid behind his Saturday morning paper and chomped breath mints like a salesman at a strip club.

"Last night was one of a kind," the clown said from across the table. She reached out a pantyhosed toe and tickled Rent's leg.

Rent grunted.

"I need to buy a new wig."

Rent gave another grunt.

"I do clown parties."

Rent popped another breath mint and pushed his wallet across the table. "There's not much left."

The cafe's front door jangled open.

"Shit," Rent mumbled and pulled the brim of his cap low.

"Rent Barnhouse!" Foley Hayworth called out. He held a varnished hiking stick in one hand and a water bottle in the other. A younger man walked beside him wearing cotton shorts and a fitted T-shirt emblazoned with an oversized photo of Boy George dressed as Jesus Christ with a banner reading "Do You Really Want to Hurt Me."

Foley touched his companion on the shoulder. "Rent, this is Lars. From the courthouse."

Rent forced a finger waggle and returned to his paper.

"Congratulations on the La Cucaracha indictment," Foley continued. "They're calling you the Exterminator. Sounds provocative, don't you think? Like the Terminator."

Rent ignored him

Foley waited for Rent to introduce his friend, and when he didn't, said, "Hi, I'm Foley Hayworth. This is my friend Lars. He's a clerk at the appellate court."

Lars held out his hand.

Rent rustled his paper.

"Bunny," she said. "A pleasure to meet you both."

Foley glanced back at Rent, whose face had reddened considerably. "Well, you two enjoy your breakfast. Nice to meet you, Bunny."

Lars waggled his fingers energetically. "See you around."

Rent flinched.

Bunny watched them stroll to the takeout counter. Then she rifled through Rent's wallet and yanked loose the remaining cash. "You could be more sociable."

"You could get a real job."

"You didn't seem to mind last night."

"Guys like that make me sick."

"They were being nice."

"Like nuclear waste is nice."

"You need to eat."

"Sometime today would be helpful."

Bunny shrugged. She snapped a piece of chewing gum between her teeth. "Tell me more about this La Cucaracha."

CHAPTER 43

SAN DIEGO, CALIFORNIA

Minutes after escaping the crowd of pot-smoking teenagers, Edwin made it to his street. He stood for a moment to catch his breath and then re-cinched the towel around his waist. A light fog had rolled in from the bay, and as he turned the corner on his block, he heard a car engine come to life. He crouched behind a low hedge and spotted taillights backing from his driveway. The car braked under the glare of a lone streetlight, and Edwin saw the black-and-white markings of a police car.

He dropped to the neighbor's lawn and wormed his way to the edge of a planter, careful not to lose his towel. The police car was moving slowly, and Edwin could hear conversation through the open windows.

"Next shift comes in at six," came a gravelly voice. "That gives us an hour to hit up Denny's for a free breakfast."

"Isn't that against the law?" a younger man responded. "I mean, can't we get into trouble for doing that?"

"For fuck's sake, kid. We're cops. Eating at Denny's is a public service. You know how many robberies are averted by our presence?"

"But they shouldn't have to pay us extra for it. We're not private security. We're already being paid."

"So you're telling me you'd turn down cookies from an old lady whose cat you just saved?"

The car had stopped, and through the bushes Edwin could see the silhouette of the younger cop shake his head.

"Damn right you wouldn't. But technically it's payment for the work you've already been paid for. Same as a free Denny's." The cop lit a cigarette. "Half the gooseneck politicians in this city eat for free. And I guaran-fucking-tee it ain't at Denny's."

Edwin felt a tickling sensation on his feet. He kicked his legs against the grass. The tickling increased and moved up his thighs.

"I didn't mean anything by it," the young man said. "I just don't want to screw up my career before it gets started."

A distant rumbling signaled the start of another takeoff. Edwin glanced down at his legs and saw a swarm of red ants. He logrolled across the lawn.

"Yeah, well it sounded accusatory," the senior cop said. "But don't sweat it, kid. That's why they put you with me. Teach you the ropes. As for our arsonist, he can't hide forever. Mrs. Dockweiler's done a lot for the department. The chief wants him brought in for questioning. We'll come back after breakfast and rough him up a bit."

"Mrs. Dockweiler?" The young cop raised his voice as the airplane soared overhead.

"The widowed millionaire," he said loudly.

"But isn't that favoritism?"

Edwin scissored his legs. He grabbed his knees and rocked on his back in a perfect imitation of an upended sea turtle. A series of sharp pains stung his belly. Edwin shrieked. The ants burrowed beneath his towel, and Edwin shrieked louder. He lunged to his feet, hopping and swatting and not caring if he was arrested. Then the roar of the jet faded, and Edwin stared into the street. The police car was gone. The takeoff had muffled his screams.

He wrapped himself in the towel and moments later entered his condominium. His back was stiff with dried blood, and his feet were swollen. He drew a bath and submerged his wounds. Ant welts pocked his belly and thighs. He closed his eyes when the showerhead began to vibrate. A roar filled the bathroom, and a ceiling tile dropped to the floor.

Edwin thought of the cop car and smiled.

"Thank you, Wright brothers," he said. "Thank you. Thank you. Thank you."

CHAPTER 44

TUCSON, ARIZONA

Rent Barnhouse felt rejuvenated. Breakfast was better than antici-
pated, especially after popping another blue pill and spending ten
minutes reclined in his Corvette with Bunny. She'd agreed to wear
the clown wig again if Rent wore the red nose. She'd also agreed,
over a plate of runny eggs, to testify against La Cucaracha. And
for a lot less money than Octavia, who Rent planned to indict for
witness tampering—just as soon as he could find her.

Now, three hours later as he stood at his den's wet bar and
poured a tumbler of premixed Tom Collins, Rent felt celebratory.
He doused the drink with imitation limejuice, swirled it thought-
fully, and lit an authentic Cuban cigar—a gift from an ex-prosecu-
tor turned appellate judge. Rent puffed at the cigar and replayed
the slideshow of the previous night's rodeo through his head.

He downed his drink, stubbed the cigar, and pocketed his
wallet and car keys. Happy hour lingered on the horizon and
lightened his gait as he skipped out the front door. He skidded to
a stop seconds later beside his Corvette. A small brown package
sat snuggly against the windshield.

Rent glanced around uncertainly. Mail bombs were back in vogue, and prosecutors were a favorite target. This bomb, however, was too conspicuous. It was also nowhere near his mailbox. Reassured by the large red letters, Rent approached the package. The note was printed in lipstick and signed with a heart.

Rent tore off the brown paper wrapping and stared at a DVD case. The label read:

GIDDYUP!

CAMACHO IS INNOCENT

AVOID PRIMETIME DISASTER AND DROP ALL CHARGES

LA CUCARACHA

Rent felt his heart begin to race. He rushed back into his house and placed the disc into the DVD player. The flat screen whirred to life, and Rent Barnhouse, Tucson's most recognizable federal prosecutor, cringed.

He'd forgotten all about that plastic gunslinger belt.

CHAPTER 45

MAGDALENA BAY, BAJA CALIFORNIA

After cleaning up the barbecue and feeding Sting and Ray, Fish climbed to his rooftop radio tower and dialed Skegs's cell from the satellite phone.

"Authentic Indian Artifacts," Skegs answered against the audible backdrop of tourists singing "La Bamba."

"How soon can you be here?"

"Sandman?"

"Hey, Skegs."

"You run out of ironwood already?" The noise in the background was reaching full pitch.

"Can you go outside?"

"I am outside."

"I can barely hear you."

"Hang on a minute."

Fish heard the music die, and then a chorus of boos was followed by bottles shattering. Next went up a loud cheer, and Skegs said, "How's that?"

"You okay over there?"

"Pulled their power cord and had to dodge a few beer bottles. Nothing a case of free mescal couldn't solve."

"I need your help, amigo."

"I thought we were painting the community center next week?"

"Drug dealers stole my business partner's boat. They're anchored in the bay ferrying our fish to the cannery."

"You have a business partner?"

"Long story."

"And they stole your boat for a load of fish?"

"These are some rare fish."

"No fish are *that* rare."

"They're stuffed with pot."

Skegs laughed. "*Mota* hidden inside dead fish? Man, you white guys think up some crazy shit."

"I'm planning to retake the boat tonight."

"What about the crew?"

"They aren't exactly the raiding type."

"What you need is a warrior."

"Exactly."

"Man, I'm touched."

"Can you be at the ranch by midnight?"

"It'll be close. I'm out at Tecolote. Place is turning into a mini-Cabo. But if I leave now and don't hit a cow or a drunk trucker, I'll be there."

"I owe you one."

"Naw, man. I just want to meet the cat who shoves dope up a dead fish's ass."

"Down their throats."

"*Lo mismo.*"

"Thanks, Skegs."

"Give me 'til twelve thirty. I'm on the way."

CHAPTER 46

TUCSON, ARIZONA

Toozie drove from her foothills ranch toward Rent Barnhouse's ninth-hole estate. The desert air poured through the driver's side window like lava. Her old diesel pickup had no air-conditioning, but Toozie didn't mind. She'd grown up in the Tucson heat.

Born Harriet Collingsworth McGill, Toozie was a tomboy, unlike her older sister, Elizabeth, whom her father had lovingly called Onezie. And unlike her sister, Toozie had embraced the ranching life. She learned to ride as soon as she could walk and was soon spending summers on horseback with her Irish father, Ian McGill, working cattle with the Mexican cowhands.

Toozie thrived in the sweltering Arizona climate, walking the desert barefoot and climbing every tree with reachable limbs. She was also a natural acrobat with a penchant for trick riding that rivaled riders twice her age. Her mother was thrilled and horrified by Toozie's fearlessness. Determined to make a lady out of her daughter, she insisted Toozie balance her rodeo with ballet. And so three nights a week, the trick-riding, tree-climbing tomboy was shuttled into town wearing tutus and toe shoes to attend classes with Tucson's top ballet instructor. To everyone's surprise,

Toozie merged her outdoor skills into soaring *grand jetés* and dizzying pirouettes.

By seventeen, she had become a rising ballerina sought after by some of the country's best ballet companies. Unfortunately, she soon learned that to study professional ballet was to move to a sprawling metropolis without horses or heat. The only opportunity that appealed to her was an offer from Mexico City. But her mother was afraid of a country where drug dealers killed indiscriminately and massacres were front-page news. Plus, the government was corrupt, and the female population far from liberated.

Toozie appealed to her father, whose stories of riding bareback as a teenager across Ireland's green hills had mesmerized her. Her father understood her passion for adventure, but not at the expense of her safety. Toozie was inconsolable. She was also determined. Late one night she scribbled a letter to her parents and left for Mexico—on horseback.

She was an unusual sight, riding alone through machismo country, her red hair braided tightly beneath a turquoise studded cowboy hat. Years of working with Mexican ranch hands had given her confidence and a background of fluent Spanish. It had also given her reliable contacts at ranchos throughout Northern Mexico.

Toozie made it as far as Zacatecas near the center of mainland Mexico, a state known for its vast plateaus and deep veins of silver. She had stopped for a few days of rest, finding work at a large rancho, when word of the traveling Ballet Folklórico reached her. She hung up her spurs and danced into town. The troupe was impressed by her striking beauty and rapid footwork, and they soon added the first gringa to ever dance in the traditional show. For three years she traveled Mexico before the news of a family tragedy reached her. Her father had been gunned down by a disgruntled cattle rustler.

Toozie returned home to comfort her mother. But when the local sheriff's investigation failed to apprehend her father's killer, Toozie started a search of her own. Within months she'd tracked the murderer to Monterrey, Mexico, and arranged for his arrest by local *federales*. Extradition was swift, due in large part to Toozie's insistence that the killer not be given a death sentence. Soon, the tomboy ballerina was primetime news.

The media focused on her doggedness and fairness and christened her the "Prancing PI." Toozie hated the moniker, but the public loved it, and soon she was inundated with investigative requests. That was fifteen years ago. Since then, the soaring *grand jetés* may have been replaced by flipping jigs for bass, but her doggedness remained feisty as ever.

Now as Toozie pulled into the guest lot of Rent Barnhouse's gated community, she checked the breast pocket of her cowgirl shirt for the folded copy of the incendiary photograph. It was taken by Foley and Lars a few hours earlier while they were blazing a trail near their favorite mountaintop restaurant. They'd stumbled across the sleek black Corvette parked on a dirt road near a copse of ancient pines. The car's convertible top had been disengaged, and Rent was sitting naked and fully reclined, his thin white legs wrapped around the head of a woman wearing a rainbow-colored wig. In the photo Rent's arms were raised above his head, his mouth agape, his nose covered by a red ball of foam.

Toozie parked, removed the photo, and slipped into a pair of coveralls with an innocuous landscaping logo. She snatched a wide-brimmed straw hat from the passenger seat, grabbed a rake from the bed of the truck, and headed for the air-conditioned guardhouse. The man waved her through without opening the sliding glass door. It seemed refrigerated air trumped security during a triple-digit heat wave.

Toozie made her way up the lane to a two-story house landscaped with pansies and geraniums. She stepped to the oversized double doors, ignored the brass lion-headed knocker, and rapped with bare knuckles. Cowboy calls and coital sounds emanated from behind the doors. She rapped again and heard a crashing sound. Toozie stepped to the side and extended her hand over the peephole.

"I don't want any!" came the sound of Rent's voice. "Reveal yourself or I'll shoot."

Toozie stepped in front of the door. "Don't be a horse's ass, Rent. Open the door."

"I have company."

"Not a chance. We all know bad porn when we hear it. Open the door."

"You know I don't talk to private investigators. Especially defensive ones." He paused, and she wondered if he was confused by his own conjugation. "Go back to the ghetto and bother one of your criminal clients."

She slid the copy of the photo under the door and waited.

"Son of a bitch!" The lock clicked, and the double doors winged open.

Toozie stepped back, surprised to see middle age in such crisis. The prosecutor wore a crisp pink polo shirt with the collar turned up, perfectly creased khaki pants, and shiny tasseled animal-skin loafers. Not a dyed hair on his head was out of place. And yet everything about the presentation seemed to sag at the edges. His eyes were watery, and his jowls drooped. The pigment-colored foundation did little to hide the veins at his nose or the brown splotches on his manicured hands.

"You can't come here and blackmail me. I'm a member of the bar, goddamn it!"

Toozie smiled. "Who mentioned blackmail?"

"Give me the camera before I arrest that little prick who works for you. How much did you pay him?"

"Less than you paid that clown. By the way, it's a crime to engage in a sex act in public. Regardless of its comedic quality."

"The camera!"

"Aren't you going to ask me in?"

"Goddammit, Toozie!"

"Invite me in, and we'll discuss your political future, your sordid past, or your distasteful present if you prefer. But we're not doing anything while I'm standing on the front doorstep."

Rent stepped to the side, and Toozie walked through the foyer

"Don't touch anything," Rent snarled. "I've got security cameras."

"Oh goody," Toozie said and snatched a large brown wrapper covered in lipstick from the floor.

CHAPTER 47

MAGDALENA BAY, BAJA CALIFORNIA

Big Joe and Pepe carried a bucket of Dos Equis down the pathway of broken shells to the small dock in front of Cantina del Cielo. It was midnight, and the Milky Way illuminated their way like a specter. Roxy and Rose tottered behind, their lace-up sandals scuffing as they tried to catch up.

"I have to pee," Roxy complained and veered into a cluster of mesquite trees. She squatted.

"Yuck, it smells like a barn."

She stood too quickly, lost her balance, and toppled into a pile of mule manure.

"Oh my God!" she screamed and raced toward the bay.

Big Joe and Pepe doubled over with laughter.

"Hey, that's not funny," Rose said. "She smells really bad."

In the distance they heard a splash and then a scream.

"Shark!"

Roxy raced past them, an ashen look on her face. Big Joe found her minutes later cowering behind the back wall of the bar.

"You're shivering," he said. "Here, take my shirt."

"I almost got killed," she cried.

"The shark's dead."

She pulled the shirt over her head and tied the loose end into a knot above her waist. "It was swimming in the water."

"We should have pulled it farther up the beach."

"It tried to bite me."

"Spring tide's coming up."

"But it's summer."

"It's the name of the highest monthly tide."

"You're cute."

"You're still shaking." He held out his arms, and she fell into him. "I'll walk you back, and we can check out the hammerhead together."

"I think we should stay right here," she said and pulled him to the ground.

CHAPTER 48

TUCSON, ARIZONA

Toozie followed Rent through the foyer, reading the lipstick on the brown paper wrapping. "Fan mail?"

"I said don't touch anything."

She crumpled the paper and tossed it to the floor. They followed a vanilla-scented hallway past vases of silk magnolias, Rent's steps clicking loudly on the polished marble floors.

"Nice shoes. Gecko?"

"Gator," he said as they entered the den, where he grabbed a half-empty Tom Collins from the wet bar. "Want one?"

"And leave you with only one shoe?"

"Huh?"

"Here's the thing, Rent. Everyone knows you've indicted someone named La Cucaracha. But we both know your suspect Camacho is nothing but a low-level coyote. He's incapable of running a major cartel."

"The indictment's sealed. How the hell—"

"Doesn't matter."

Rent's mannequin eyes blinked vacantly.

"The real La Cucaracha, Rent—who is he?"

Rent finished his Tom Collins and made another.

Toozie tried again. "I want the real drug lord. You want those photos. Sounds like a win-win."

"How should I—" He stopped and narrowed his eyes. "The photos are a separate matter. The real La Cucaracha is sitting in jail. I've indicted him because he's guilty."

Toozie peered past him through the room's plate-glass window. The ninth hole of the golf course spilled across the desert like a toxic algae bloom. The scene reminded Toozie of the frequent press conferences Rent held at golf courses. He used tee boxes like grandstands to spew his propaganda. Most recently it was the overblown dangers of the neophyte drug dealer named La Cucaracha. Before that it was the unwarranted scare over a hallucinogenic mushroom found on a Hopi Indian reservation that turned out to be nothing more than moldy button mushrooms growing in the rafters of an elderly man's hogan. And then there was the ordeal involving a snakehead fish found in the luggage of an exchange student from Vietnam.

The juvenile freshwater fish was wrapped in a wet towel and stuffed inside the woman's toiletry kit. A voracious predator able to walk on its fins and breathe air, the fish was still alive when customs agents confiscated it. Unsure of how to dispose of the foot-long predator, the fish was brought into the animal importation room and left on a table, where it wriggled into a load of live Japanese breeder carp destined for a Scottsdale koi farm. Upon arrival two days later at the pond in the upscale suburb, half the carp were gone and the snakehead had doubled in size.

Barnhouse claimed it was the second snakehead confiscated in as many days and proof of a new and powerful illegal fish trade. He alerted the citizens of Arizona to be on the lookout for the killer fish as well as female Asian exchange students. Then he arrested the young woman responsible for importing the fish and charged her with multiple causes of animal poaching and smuggling.

In front of a collection of bored cameramen while standing on the eighteenth tee box at the Raven Golf Course overlooking an enormous blue-green lake, he promised to have the snakehead-importing student expelled from her high school exchange program, deported, and fined thousands of dollars to pay for a special snakehead customs agent as well as compensation for the Scottsdale koi farm's loss of Japanese carp. The woman's host family hired Toozie, who quickly disproved Barnhouse's allegations. She also exposed the negligence of the customs agents who initially confiscated the exotic fish and allowed it to escape into the carp tanks. Barnhouse was forced to drop all charges against the student and issue an apology to all visiting Asians.

Toozie turned her attention back to Rent. "A client called yesterday and told me someone named La Cucaracha stole his boat. In Baja California. If La Cucaracha is sitting in jail, how the hell can he be in Baja? "

Rent slammed his tumbler of Tom Collins to the bar. "Maybe your client's full of shit, Toozie. Camacho's the guy. Got caught with all that La Cucaracha stuff. Even the little bugs in his pocket. Whatever you're thinking, forget about it. This case is as open-and-shut as it gets."

"I'm offering you a hell of a deal here, Rent. I'll even help you find the real La Cucaracha. You'll get all the glory. My client gets his boat back, and Camacho can quietly be deported. It's not too late to amend the indictment. No one will ever know."

"I sure as hell will know."

Toozie walked to the front door. "Twenty-four hours, Rent. I want copies of your investigation file. Everything that has anything to do with Camacho and La Cucaracha. *Comprende?*"

She opened the double doors and pulled a second photograph from her breast pocket. "Camera phones are incredible these days. Did you know a person can download a photo to the Internet in seconds? The whole world can have access to a person's most intimate moments with the click of a button. Fascinating, isn't it?"

She tossed the photo to the floor. "Twenty-four hours, Rent. And not a second longer."

CHAPTER 49

TUCSON, ARIZONA

Octavia Ortiz sat across the thick glass and watched her real cousin enter the visitor's room of the Pima County Jail. She smiled as he sat at the plastic chair and lifted the phone from its cradle.

"I can't believe they let you in to see me," Camacho said.

"It is not so different in this country," Octavia said. "*Mordida* offered to the right person at the right time."

"Especially when it's offered by a beautiful señorita to a fat guard on a slow Sunday morning."

"It helps to be dating the federal prosecutor in charge of your case."

Camacho's eyes widened.

"Dating might be too strong a word. Flirting is a better characterization of our relationship."

"How—"

She held up a hand. "With all due respect, *primo*, men are interested in only one thing. Dangle it in front of them and they lose all sense of reason."

Camacho nodded. "An unfortunate truth, I suppose."

"I know you are not La Cucaracha. And the prosecutor knows it too. He needs a big bust to get elected governor. I pretended to know a drug dealer with a thing for cockroaches. The prosecutor offered me thousands of dollars to testify in court that the drug dealer is you."

"The *coño!*"

"Instead, I have suggested rather strongly that he drop all charges against you. I believe he will. In fact, I'd be surprised if you weren't released within a couple weeks. And when you return to Mexico, I have a job for you."

"I'm finished as a coyote."

"You'll never have to cross the border again."

Camacho raised his eyebrows in interest.

"Meet me in Ensenada. At the old port where the shrimp boats dock."

"Then what?"

"A surprise."

CHAPTER 50

SAN DIEGO, CALIFORNIA

The barrage of turbines overhead hardly stirred Edwin. After his shower, he disinfected the ant bites and downed what remained of his painkillers with a bottle of yard sale wine. But he hadn't meant to pass out. Not with detectives threatening to return at dawn.

He lay naked on the couch continuing his dream of feasting on moose steaks with his busty fishwife—*what was that incessant knocking?*—her gentle hands unraveling his furs—*more knocking*—the furs falling away—*louder knocking*. The door to Edwin's mind swung open, and he blinked. He was aroused, half-sliding from his living room couch. The knocking was so loud it reverberated through the room. He was pulling last night's towel from the floor when a woman's shrill voice startled him.

"Edwin! You open up this goddamn door this minute! How dare you try and hurt my pigs. Topwater's been burned to the ground. Probably one of your goddamn cigars!"

Edwin quickly got to his feet and regretted it. Fireflies popped in and out of his vision. He wobbled on his swollen ankle and toppled to the coffee table. The sound of splintering wood was mercifully blotted out by a 747 soaring over the condominium's roof. The powerful afterburners also muffled Mrs. Dockweiler's ranting. Edwin lay trancelike on the shattered table. The plane passed, and the loud rapping resumed.

"Edwin, goddamn you! You're fired! Open this door right now! You do not want me to call the police again. The chief's a friend of mine. I can have you arrested *and* jailed with a single phone call!"

Edwin looked down at his leg. Thunderclouds of skin welled around his ankle. His back ached, and the pig bite on his calf waved the red flag of infection. He wormed to his knees and crawled to the kitchen under the camouflage of another takeoff.

He pulled himself up by the handle on the refrigerator door, found a bottle of aspirin, swallowed what remained, and limped slowly to the front door. Mrs. Dockweiler was kicking the door with her high heels when Edwin freed the lock. The door was flung open, knocking him backward. He lost his footing and his towel and crashed to the floor. Mrs. Dockweiler's heaved a manure-saturated tennis shoe over his head.

"For the love of God! Cover yourself up, Edwin."

She stomped inside and slammed the door. "And air this goddamn place out. It smells worse than my backyard."

Edwin sat up and re-cinched the towel. "I'm sorry about the factory. I—"

"Who gives a goddamn about that pile of fish bones. My accountant says it's the best thing that could have happened. Insurance is going to pay me a bundle. And to be honest, Edwin, with all this hot air about overfishing, polluted oceans, and sea-rising environmental whacko bullshit, it was just a matter of time before I sold out. Last night I was going to give you a bonus for your cigar-smoking sloppiness. Until this morning when my nosy neighbor told me about a fat man falling off my wall last night."

Edwin reddened.

She held out her cell phone. "Want to see?"

"No ma'am."

"Can you believe two old ladies were trading pictures on their mobile phones like a couple of teenagers?"

Edwin was speechless.

"Jesus Christ, Edwin," she said, staring at the phone. "You look like an idiot in that black makeup. What the hell were you thinking?"

"I wanted to call you about the fire," Edwin croaked out the lie. "But I couldn't find my cell phone. I drove to your house, but you weren't there. I was scared. I didn't know what to do. I jumped the wall to see if you were in your backyard, and then—"

"And then you thought you'd rub black shoe polish on your face and play with my pigs for a while?"

"I didn't know about the pigs."

"Funny little animals. Friendly as poodles, except they shit every goddamn place."

"They attacked me."

"Attacked? Are you out of your mind, Edwin? They're docile as oversized gerbils."

"I can prove it," Edwin protested, pointing at his inflamed calf.

"You must have provoked the old gal. She's just as cuddly as a teddy bear. But I will say, you look rather worse for wear. Maybe I should take you to the doctor."

Edwin shook his head. "No medical insurance, remember?"

"Just because I won't pay a king's ransom for bad healthcare doesn't mean you can't take some of that savings I've allowed by way of free tuna and go see a doctor directly. I know a good one in La Jolla. Pricey, but you get what you pay for."

"I'll be okay."

"Suit yourself," she said cheerily. "And now that I've heard your explanation for damaging my vines and scaring my pigs, I'm pleased as peaches. Your trespassing and attempted burglary have saved me money once again." She reached into her pocketbook and removed the bonus check. "Ta-ta, Edwin." She tore the check into dozens of pieces and flung them into the air. "And stay away from my pigs!" She strode through the door and into her idling Rolls Royce.

Edwin dropped to his knees and watched the bits of paper flutter across the floor. The deep rumble of another takeoff caused the pieces to dance. Edwin slumped to his side and closed his eyes.

As the condo quaked, he wondered about toothpicks and how hard it would be to swallow one.

CHAPTER 51

TUCSON, ARIZONA

Toozie sat in the far corner of Bob Dobbs Bar and Grill sipping a draft beer and discussing the Patriot Act and its implications for Camacho the Coyote with Professor Danesh Tandon, University of Arizona's professor emeritus of law and expert in all things constitutional. Professor Tandon wasn't thinking about anything scholarly at the moment. The aroma of the bar's famous garlic burger was wafting from the kitchen.

"If I could just get inside and see him," Toozie said, snapping Professor Tandon out of his reverie. "But this damn Patriot Act bars most visitation rights."

"You know what I miss most about teaching?" he asked, seemingly unsympathetic.

"The grading?"

The professor's gray mustache caterpillared into a grin. "Optimism. The classroom's full of it. Young people think the future will always be better than the past. Maybe they're right."

"Hard to see how the Patriot Act makes us better."

"The pendulum swings both ways, Toozie, but eventually it does moves forward. I think sometimes it's easy to lose hope."

"Especially in those burgers." She looked around for the waitress.

"Do you remember the Carlin case?"

Toozie gave him a look of puzzlement.

"In 1978 George Carlin went on Pacifica Radio to spoof profanity. He focused on the seven dirtiest words. And he said them repeatedly. A father was driving his young son home from school when it aired. He was incensed by the comedian's use of language, and he got the FCC to sue Pacifica Radio, claiming that Carlin was breaking the law by using unprotected speech—obscene speech. The lawsuit made it all the way to the Supreme Court. Do you know what the justices said?"

"Cursing is fucking funny?"

Professor Tandon spotted the waitress and waved her down. He ordered two garlic burgers and turned to Toozie. "The justices ruled that Carlin's seven dirty words lacked value. That the words weren't worth protecting."

Toozie scowled. "I hear foul language on the radio all the time. Not to mention cable TV."

"Exactly. The pendulum has swung back. Obscenity has made its way into primetime. And now the pendulum is swinging back from the Patriot Act."

"And that gets me in to see Camacho how?"

"People assume the Patriot Act is insurmountable, but it's not. Judges are chipping away at it. Even the Supreme Court has joined in. The government's backpedaling like crazy, and prosecutors are getting desperate."

"Barnhouse seemed far from desperate."

"Oh, he's desperate. The government needs good PR at the moment. Waterboarding, Gitmo, the John Yoo memos—all very bad for public relations."

Toozie's face dropped. "I need to hire a PR firm?"

Five minutes later, the burgers arrived, and Professor Tandon took a bite. He closed his eyes and swallowed. "Outstanding." He took another bite and said, "Camacho's a Mexican national. Immigration is a big issue here in Arizona, and because of all the government abuses, humanitarian groups are gaining ground. And respect."

"You want me to join an immigration rights group?"

"I thought you'd never ask." He pulled a business card from his shirt pocket and handed it to her.

"Border Crossing International?" Toozie asked, confused.

"I'm a founding member."

Toozie's mouth hinged open.

"My parents were immigrants."

"But—"

"Dad was from India. My mother was pure Azteca. Both illegal when they first arrived."

"I had no idea."

"Join our legal team, Toozie. We could use help with the investigative work. Camacho is just the kind of person we like to help. The feds would be crazy to bar you access—a well-known female investigator working for free on behalf of Border Crossing International? You're all but guaranteed a cell-side seat."

Toozie leaned back, her eyes bright as opals.

"Talk to him, Toozie. Then build your case against Barnhouse. As we both know, the man's a menace to the legal profession. I'll write an amicus brief. If we can't get him to release Camacho, maybe we can get him disbarred."

"Or jailed."

Professor Tandon's gray mustache curled upward again. "I like the way you think."

CHAPTER 52

SAN DIEGO, CALIFORNIA

After pulling himself from the floor of his disheveled condo, Edwin collected Mrs. Dockweiler's shredded bonus check from the carpet and taped it back together. He wondered why he bothered. The amount was ninety-nine dollars and ninety-nine cents. The pig-loving miser couldn't even bring herself to write out a full hundred.

As he wondered whether to insult himself further by trying to cash it, he noticed a message on his cell phone. It had come in during the night from the brute Memo telling him to fly down to La Paz and drive to Magdalena Bay where he and Socorro were unloading the stuffed fish. La Cucaracha wanted Edwin to process the pot personally. Can it right there in Baja with Topwater Tuna labels and have it shipped by truck to the San Diego cannery. Memo finished by assuring Edwin that border inspectors would never suspect a well-known California fish factory of smuggling canned pot to its own headquarters.

Edwin felt a rush of excitement. Memo wouldn't know about the fire or the permanent shutdown of Topwater Tuna. If Edwin moved fast, he could be in sole possession of a fat retirement.

Drive it across the border and never stop. Not until he made it to Alaska. Warehouse the dope and piecemeal it to customers. One can at a time. Avoid arousing suspicion. Or the web of La Cucaracha.

Edwin called Alaska Airlines, bought a next-day ticket to La Paz, and rented the cheapest car available: a cherry-red Volkswagen bug. Then he crumpled Mrs. Dockweiler's check, rummaged through his cupboards for a can of free tuna, and downed it without utensils, straight from the can.

Planes roared overhead.

Edwin hardly noticed.

He clomped to the bedroom, where he dressed hastily, and by nightfall he was sitting at the Fish Market's aquarium bar. He ordered a double martini with extra olives.

"On toothpicks, please," he told the barman while staring forlornly at the imprisoned fish.

An hour and four double martinis later, Edwin was staring at the toothpick design he'd made on the bar. The crowd of drunks was thinning. The imprisoned fish were sleeping. And Edwin's courage was waning. He wanted in on Moneymaker's class-action lawsuit. As a backup in case something went wrong with the Alaska plan. All he had to do was clamp the toothpick between his front teeth, and when the bartender wasn't looking, yank his upper lip down and over the end. But an earlier practice run had hurt worse than he imagined and only hastened another stiff drink.

Now, as he squared the toothpicks into a frame over the top of a drifting neon goby, Edwin fidgeted. The fish appeared to be headed for a whirlpool much like Edwin's resolve. He fingered one of the toothpick corners and wondered, as he had since scraping his inner lip, how he could match a pierced septum. A wrecked larynx. A pincushioned palate.

"Another?" the bartender asked, slapping his hand over the circling goby. The toothpicks scattered, and the startled fish caught a current down the bar. "Blind as bats. I told the owner to soften the lights, but he said it'd ruin the ambiance. Ambiance? What ambiance? It's a fucking fish bar. Guy's a douche bag."

"You got any of those plastic spears?" Edwin asked. "Maybe with some of those little red cherries?"

"Cherry bombs? Those babies got enough toxins to kill a sewer rat. I got a whole jar of them. How many you want?"

"Three would be good," Edwin slurred. "Just make sure the toothpick is plastic not wood. Save a tree, right?"

"Tell that to the prick who owns this place. The other day he brought in a case of old-growth toothpicks. Said they'd bring a premium. Made me add two bucks to the drinks. Fucking thousand-year-old trees! Christ, man, I don't know who's worse, the idiot owner or the idiots who pay extra for the toothpicks."

The bartender shook the martini tumbler. "You want plastic, I'll give you plastic. But don't think you're doing Mother Nature any favors. Those little spears last a million years. You want do something for the environment, jump off a fucking bridge. Overpopulation's our doom."

"I don't like heights."

The bartender shrugged and shoved a trio of cherries over a miniature yellow spear. "On the house," he said and whisked down the bar taking last call orders.

Edwin chugged the martini and gummed the first maraschino into his mouth. The taste reminded him of a Swisher Sweets cigar. He pinched off the cherry's stem, swallowed the marble of preservatives, and quickly slipped the entire spear with its two remaining cherries into his mouth. Edwin's adrenaline surged. He locked his front teeth around the spear and prepared to suck it and the cherries into his throat when someone grabbed his shoulder.

"Edwin!" Derek Moneymaker bellowed. "Twice in one week! Can you believe your luck?" He clapped Edwin hard between the shoulder blades.

Edwin involuntarily clamped down on the plastic spear. The cherries slingshotted down his airway, anchoring into a fleshy crease of trachea. Edwin couldn't breathe. He opened his mouth to cough, but nothing emerged from his trapped airway. He tried to swallow, but that too failed. His red face reddened. His mouth carped open and closed, and the crushed remnants of the plastic spear tumbled to the bar.

"Hey, buddy," Moneymaker called out. "Cat got your tongue?"

Edwin goggle-eyed the class-action attorney. He gagged and convulsed. He leaned forward and slapped his palms hard to the aquarium glass, cherry saliva dripping from his lips.

"One hand, pal!" the bartender hollered over a trifecta of foaming beer mugs. "You'll scare the little guys to death."

Moneymaker suddenly noticed the red saliva pooling next to a collection of wooden toothpicks. "I think you're bleeding there, bud." He leaned in close to Edwin's ear and whispered, "Quick, put your face down on the bar next to the toothpicks. I'll snap a picture with my cell phone. Guaranteed payday, Edwin. Guaranteed."

Edwin flapped his arms. He grabbed his neck and squeezed. A strand of maraschino spittle pole-danced to the bar. Edwin's head lolled forward.

"Good idea," Moneymaker said. "Keep your mouth open just like that. Drama equals money, old buddy. Make it real." He took a picture and then angled the cell phone and took another. "Way to hold your breath like that, man. Makes your face extra red. Looks real, too. Oscar performance, baby. I'm telling you, this is a slam dunk. Especially with that swollen eyeball trick."

As Moneymaker clicked away, the bartender leaped over the bartop, shattering Edwin's empty martini glass and sending a pair of damselfish into a frenzy. He landed on the floor behind Edwin's stool, wrapped his arms around Edwin's substantial chest, and knuckled the tunaman's sternum, squeezing all three hundred pounds of him off the stool. Both men crashed to the hardwood floor.

"Hey, that's a tort!" Moneymaker yelled. He aimed his phone and clicked. "Assault *and* battery."

Edwin stirred and released a series of soggy, red-stained coughs.

The bartender stood and helped Edwin to his feet. "I told you those cherries are deadly, man." He jumped back across the bar.

"That's intentional infliction of emotional distress!" Moneymaker continued. "Maybe even attempted murder! You're finished, I'm telling you!"

The bartender leaned across the bar. "I just saved his life, asshole. Go sue your mother for defective birth."

Someone in the crowd started to clap.

Moneymaker turned to Edwin. "You mean that was for real?"

Edwin nodded sluggishly.

"Even better," Moneymaker said. "You just upped the payoff. Forget assaults. They're peanuts compared to defective products. Choking on a cherry, man. That was brilliant! All these witnesses." He tapped his phone loudly. "And these photos. Priceless, man."

Edwin sucked in another deep breath and watched Money-maker pluck a squished cherry from the floor.

"Edwin, my man! The pit's still in this one!" He draped an arm across Edwin's shoulder. "Like I said. Lucky you ran into the Moneymaker today. Lucky, lucky, lucky."

CHAPTER 53

MAGDALENA BAY, BAJA CALIFORNIA, MEXICO

Just after midnight, Fish stood at the stern of his *panga* motoring through the mangrove channels toward the main body of Magdalena Bay. Winston sat on the center thwart. Pike and Skegs knelt at the bow. Weevil had been left behind at the rancho, high on the *curandera*'s homeopathic poultice, promising not to take any more of the medicine until daybreak.

Fish kept the throttle open. He knew every channel of the mangrove swamp. Knew every dead-end branch and circuitous offshoot. He knew where to find the snook holes, the fattest of the mangrove groupers, and the thick schools of mud shrimp hidden beneath the tangled roots. Knew where the egrets and the herons nested, and where, on just the right neap tide, a local pod of killer whales was known to corral manta rays and feast on their livers, leaving the rest to the sand sharks. But most importantly, Fish knew the fastest and most direct route to the *Wahoo Rhapsody*. Twenty minutes at full speed, thirty if he wanted to enjoy the ride. Tonight was a bit of both.

Minutes earlier Skegs had arrived at the rancho, and Fish explained his plan to retake the boat. He'd sent Xavier into town to watch the *Wahoo Rhapsody* from shore. The policeman had called at midnight to confirm that the boat was still anchored in the bay, and that the man and woman continued to unload the fish and transport them by *panga* through the mangrove swamp to the cannery. Fish left Weevil sleeping in the hammock with a supply of magic mud and a cautionary note reminding the first mate of the poultice's power.

Now, as Fish pulled into a dark cluster of mangroves near the opening to the main bay, he went over their plan. He and Skegs would board the *Rhapsody* first with the speargun and machete in case a guard was on board. Pike would remain with Winston as lookout until the boat was secured.

Fish shut down the engine and whispered, "Xavier says they make a run every thirty minutes or so. We'll wait for them to pass by before moving on. Once they're gone, I can have us at the stern of the *Rhapsody* in minutes."

When Pike began to protest, Fish raised a finger to his lips. The low rumble of an outboard engine filled the night sky. Seconds later the tuna-laden *panga* lumbered through the darkness. Fish waited until the sound faded around a bend of water before pulling the starter cord and racing into the big bay. The wide expanse of water stretched nearly half a mile, slick and shadowless and flat as a headstone. The marine layer had drifted offshore, and the sky hung thick with stars. In the distance the *Wahoo Rhapsody* lay at anchor, its outline barely visible on the bituminous bay.

Fish shut down the engine for the second time and handed Skegs one of the two paddles. "The quieter the better."

Skegs took the paddle and together they directed the *panga* across the bay, the slow rhythm of their strokes flaring bioluminescence in their wake. Pike and Winston crouched catlike at the bow, and within minutes they were sidled against the *Rhapsody*'s stern. Fish reached out and gripped the edge of the dive step.

"On five," he whispered to Skegs and held up a closed fist. When he raised his index finger indicating one, Pike grabbed the machete and sprang to the dive step. He ascended the stern ladder in two lunging steps, pommel-horsed over the transom, and disappeared into the darkness.

"What the hell?" Winston muttered.

"Marine boy's gone ninja on us," Skegs said, hefting the speargun. "Hope he knows how to use that thing."

Skegs scaled the ladder. He peered over the transom and then dropped to the deck and sprinted into the galley. Fish followed, angling portside, and froze. A tiny red glow was moving along the upper deck. As it emerged from the shadows, Fish saw the outline of a man—a man with a shaved head and a neck crowded with tattoos. Fish recognized him immediately.

The Chula Vista Chicano exhaled a stream of smoke and stared across the bay toward the mangrove thickets. A sudden clatter inside the boat brought a long-barreled pistol from his waistband. He flicked the cigarette into the water and hurried back toward the helm. He raised the weapon and charged up the gunwale and disappeared into the shadows.

Fish moved fast along the lower gangway, pausing to tug a long-handled gaff from its fixture. He tucked the weapon against his side and climbed onto the splash rail. The beveled wood was wet with mist. Fish gripped the rail with bare feet and raised the gaff above his head, the tip of stainless steel sharp as an adder's fang. Halfway to the bow he paused again.

Overhead near the upper bow he could hear the low hum of electronics emanating from the wheelhouse. He took another step and heard a flurry of footfalls followed by a grunt and the thud of a body landing hard on the upper deck. Fish waited for Skegs or Pike to speak. Instead he saw a match flame high above. Fish slowly crept forward, his eyes locked onto the shoulders of the Chula Vista Chicano. The gangbanger leaned back against the upper railing, craned his neck upward, and blew smoke rings into the sky. Fish saw the red tip of the cigarette motioning toward the wheelhouse.

The gangbanger said, "Step outside, *buey*, before I start pumping holes through you."

Fish was wondering which *buey* he was speaking to when he heard Skegs call out from the helm, "How do I know you won't put holes through me anyway?"

"'Cause I got integrity. And because you're going to toss out that speargun. I ain't about to shoot an unarmed Mexican."

"Indian."

"Same fucking thing, *ese*."

"How about I get back in my boat and pretend we never met?"

"And leave your friend lying here all by himself?"

"He's not my friend."

"The two of you board my boat in the middle of the night and I'm supposed to think it's a coincidence?"

"It's not your boat."

"Three seconds and I start shooting."

Fish heard the speargun clatter across the upper deck and saw the back of the gangbanger's head give an abbreviated nod.

"That's good, Geronimo. Now tell me who your *jefe* is."

"I work for the owner of the boat. He offered me a thousand bucks to get it back."

The Chula Vista Chicano whistled his approval. "This generous owner, where is he now?"

"At his bar probably."

"The *chinga* who rides around on a burro like Clint Eastwood?"

"That's the one."

"I should have killed him the other day."

"Maybe he'll give you another chance."

"He'd be dead if the fucking gun hadn't jammed."

Fish saw the cigarette cartwheel into the air and heard the hammer click back on the pistol.

"Whoa, man," Skegs's voice rose. "You said you wouldn't shoot."

"Changed my mind."

Fish leaped from the gunwale, swinging the gaff high overhead. It buried into the gunman's Adam's apple and exited through his spine. Blood erupted from the tattoos, and Fish heard the gun clatter across the deck, firing a round into the steel hull. Fish heaved back, and the Chula Vista Chicano flopped over the railing and crashed into the bay, the handle of the six-foot shaft following him stiffly into the darkness.

"About time," Skegs said, leaning over the railing.

Fish hopped back to the gunwale. "You're welcome."

"He was about to kill me."

"I'm glad you're okay."

"That's more than I can say about our ninja."

Fish stretched out his hand, and Skegs helped him over the railing and onto the upper deck. Pike was sitting near the bow, his temple swollen, a rivulet of blood trailing down the side of his face. His head bandage had come unwrapped.

"Guy pistol-whipped me," he said groggily. He balled up the bandage and tossed it toward the scupper.

"Hey, Saviorman," Skegs called out. He was kneeling near the bullet hole in the hull. "You're not going to believe this, but I think there's more than air in your hull." He held up part of a hundred-dollar bill.

"Drug money?" Pike asked.

"Bank account," Fish corrected him.

Skegs shook his head in disbelief. He picked up the gangbanger's gun and heaved it into the bay.

Pike scrambled to his feet. "Hey, that was evidence!"

"Not without a body," Skegs said. "The tide's about to peak and carry our dead guy far out to sea."

"But—"

Winston limped out from the helm. "Heard a gunshot and a splash and came as fast as I could." He spotted the blood on Pike's temple. "You all right, Willie?"

"Better than the guy who pistol-whipped me," Pike said.

Winston turned to Fish and held out a cellular telephone. "You may want to see this. It was vibrating in the helm beneath the charts. There's a text message in Spanish."

Fish translated: *I hired a capitán for the gringo boat. He's meeting us in Ensenada. Be there as soon as you can. Is everything set with our cannery man?*

Fish typed in Spanish: *I've decided to keep my boat.*

Minutes later the phone vibrated. Fish read: *Who the fuck is this?*

Owner of the boat.

Where are Socorro and Memo?

In handcuffs.

You are the policía?

Hardly.

What do you want?

Out.

Not until I get back the stolen marijuana.

Don't have it.

Then you better come up with half a million dollars.

Meet me at Catalina Island at midnight. Avalon pier.

I deal only in cash.

We should get along fine.

Half a million and not a peso less.

Not a problem.

How do I know this is not a trap?

You don't.

I could have you killed.

I understand.

Half a million. Midnight.

Roger.

What do you look like?

Tall guy. Fishskin cap. Long goatee.

Double-cross me and you die.

Ditto.

Fish pocketed the phone. "Change of plan. Skegs, you and I are heading to the bar. I need to call Toozie from a landline. Have her focus on finding Big Joe." He turned to Winston. "You and Willie take the boat out to sea and dump any remaining fish. Then head to San Diego. I should be fueled up and overhead by early afternoon. Need to make Avalon in time to make a little withdrawal."

"I'm coming to Avalon with you," Pike said, touching his swollen temple.

"I don't think so. The captain needs a deckhand."

Winston shrugged. "Actually, I'd rather go it alone."

Pike smiled and turned to Fish. "You said a withdrawal. I thought you didn't trust banks?"

"Who said anything about a bank?"

CHAPTER 54

MAGDALENA BAY, BAJA CALIFORNIA, MEXICO

Weevil peered over the sandy lip of the nearly six-foot-deep hole. Ten feet away he could see the foamy tide line and beyond that the arena of stars reflecting off the dark waves. He was bare-chested and wore badly scuffed flip-flops beneath his board shorts. His skin was sweaty and covered in beach grit, and his bad arm hung heavy as ironwood by his side. His nose and eye patch were grimy and beginning to loosen. He wore a headlamp low on his brow.

It was the third hole Weevil had dug in the last two hours, after disregarding the note from Atticus Fish reminding him not to apply too much of the *curadera's* magic salve. Too much could cause hyperactivity and hallucinations, the note said. Weevil had grinned eagerly, crumpled the note, and slopped the remaining salve over his wound, anesthetizing more than his shoulder. His neurons popped and buzzed. His heart thumped.

Now, as he peered above the hole, his mind whirred to the thoughts of buried treasure. The millions Fish had buried in the sand. Weevil knew he could find it. He *had* to find it. It was the only way to pay off La Cucaracha, the gambling debt, and reclaim the *Rhapsody*.

Above him the Milky Way burned through the fabric of clouds like sparklers through fogged glass. Weevil took a fast breath and one-armed himself from the hole. He upturned the empty five-gallon bucket requisitioned from Fish's tool shed and buried the borrowed pickaxe into the sand. He clicked off the headlamp and sat on the overturned bucket feeling like a spelunker with a bum arm and a world-class buzz.

The *curandera's* magic mud didn't allow him to sit for long. He reengaged the headlight and skipped toward the shovel lying in the sand beside the flagpoled Hawaiian sling, its three prongs buried deep, his Cantina del Cielo shirt hanging from its handle. Weevil had shot the sling from the porch hours earlier, willing it to find Fish's money, following its flight down the sand dune like a dowser seeking liquid gold.

Weevil was staring at the Hawaiian sling, wondering whether to shoot it skyward again, when the sound of an outboard engine startled him. The drone approached from the south, paralleling the shoreline. Weevil felt a fishtail of panic. Why would his friends return from the ocean side of the island? And more importantly, the beach was a mess. How would he explain his handiwork to the eccentric ex-lawyer?

His medicated mind settled on the obvious. He had to fill the holes. And fast.

Weevil dropped to his knees, one-arming sand like a defective bulldozer. He peddled his legs around the first hole, scooping piles over the edge. Sweat rained down his face. His bad arm flopped beside him like a dead eel. The pitch of the outboard engine increased. It grew closer. Too close. Weevil collapsed into the half-filled hole and tried to catch his breath.

He heard voices and periscoped his head above the sand. The headlamp had angled upward, and as he pulled it down the tri-bulbed lamp cast a sharp light over the shorebreak. The *panga* was just outside the combers, its occupants blurred by the misty air. Weevil climbed from the hole and stepped sheepishly toward shore. He would have to tell Fish the truth.

As Weevil stepped to the tide line, the engine unexpectedly surged. He aimed the spotlight and watched the *panga* turn sharply. Its two occupants were crouched low among a forest of fish tails. Weevil could just make out the driver manning the throttle. He recognized the man's wide shoulders, his thick, squat neck. The passenger was at the bow, her unmistakable hair fluttering like a pirate flag among the yellowfin tuna.

Socorro was grinning madly.

"*Oye!*" came Memo's angry call.

Weevil's thinning hair nearly stood on end. He spun and charged up the wet sand, stopping just beyond the three holes. He glanced up the mountainous dune, eyeing the porch and its outdoor kitchen. A kitchen with its array of knives more than a football field away. Weevil swallowed. The *panga*'s hull scraped loudly over the sand, its engine sputtering to a stop.

"*Maricón!*" yelled Socorro.

Weevil willed himself forward. He kicked off his worn flip-flops, made a single stride, and tripped over the upside-down five-gallon bucket. The plastic pail cartwheeled into the air, clattering loudly over the back of the buried pick like a disc in a game of quoits. Weevil lost his balance and landed facedown among his holes, his mouth agape, his unbandaged orb clogged with sand.

"*Mira!*" Memo cried and leapt from the *panga*. Socorro hurdled the boat's gunwale and plunged through the spill of semi-frozen fish.

Weevil scrambled to his feet and thumbed sand from his eye. The fall had knocked the headlamp up his forehead, sending a beacon of light skyward. He coughed out a sand ball and peered over his shoulder. Memo was lumbering up the beach like a beer keg on legs. The man still wore cowboy boots, wet and covered in sand.

Socorro kicked off her sandals and sprinted past Memo. Weevil scooped the shovel from the sand. He turned to face his tormentors, his mind wallowing in a witch's serum of psychedelics.

Memo saw the threatening shovel and grinned.

Socorro cackled.

Weevil raised the shovel, waggling it in a one-armed batter's grip. He focused a blurred eye on Memo and immediately lost sight of Socorro. He jerked around, but quickly lost sight of Memo. A guttural howl spun Weevil back again. Socorro gave a shrilling wail, and Weevil swiveled once more. Then he dizzily dropped the shovel and ran toward the Hawaiian sling. The sand was spongy, and as he neared the spear his left foot burrowed and his right ankle keeled. Weevil toppled forward and belly-flopped inches from the Hawaiian sling. Air fled his lungs like smoke from a fire.

As Weevil struggled for breath, he heard Memo's huffing growing louder. He heard Socorro caterwauling and closing fast. He knew they would kill him this time, maybe mash him to the sand like a fist into clay. Weevil inched his hand forward and touched the shaft of the six-foot sling. He felt the weapon slip into his grip, the loop of tubing stretching across his palm. He rolled to his back and raised the cocked weapon.

In the glare of the headlamp, he saw Memo lunge through the air, his face a portrait of hate. He saw the big arms stretched wide, the fists opening into claws. He watched the killer's flat teeth grinding, his cruel lips curling into a sneer. Weevil released the Hawaiian sling.

The three-pronged weapon rocketed through the air, each of its razor-sharpened points glinting in the headlamp. Weevil watched in wonder as the top prong pierced the socket just above Memo's left eye. He watched the lower two prongs form a deadly triangle, one threading the hit man's nostril and the other punching through his sinus cavity. All three spikes plunged into brainy softness.

Memo's teeth stopped gnashing. His eyes glazed over, and his sneer slackened. The force of the sling spun him off course, and he landed on his back, sliding past Weevil and dropping headfirst into one of the freshly dug holes. Weevil scooted away, unsure if the man would rise zombie-like and finish him off. Instead, the wet cowboy boots dropped from sight.

Weevil crawled catlike to the hole where the yellow handle of the sling jutted above the sand. Weevil plucked it with a finger and quickly backed away. Nothing. He crept back and peered inside. Coiled into a misshapen heap six feet below was his hole-punching nemesis. Weevil angled the headlamp, mesmerized by the brightness of the crimson sand. Then he remembered the woman.

"Socorro?" he offered, his voice unsteady. He stood and scanned the pockmarked beach.

"I'm stuck, baby," he heard her gasp. "In some kind of hole. I think I broke my leg."

Weevil stepped cautiously and peered into the nearest crater. Socorro leaned awkwardly against the wall of sand, her foot winged out like a broken flipper. She looked up, her eyes seductive in the spotlight.

"I'm so happy you are safe, *mi amor*. I told Memo not to hurt your eye, but the *cabrón* didn't listen. I hope you killed him." She held up her arms. "Help me out so we can be together."

Weevil felt his face flush. He scanned her body with a gimlet eye, breathing in her perfume.

"Take me in your arms," she purred. "Like a lover."

Weevil's head began to swim. In the spotlight he saw the woman at the base of the Squid Roe tree. He saw her fling the hole punch to Memo. Felt the cold jaws of steel clamp over his nostril, then his eyelid. The memory crashed into him like a closed fist.

"No thanks," he said.

He dropped to his knees and one-armed a pile of sand into the hole. Socorro sputtered. Weevil treadmilled his feet, circling the hole like a shark stalking prey. Socorro screamed profanities. Weevil ignored her. She tried to pogo one-legged over the rising sleeve of sand, but tired quickly. Within minutes, she was buried neck-deep in the hole, her eyes level with the incoming tide.

Weevil retrieved the pickaxe and touched it to her nose. "How did you find me?"

Socorro laughed nervously. "Memo has the eye of a killer. Not you, baby. He killed your captain. He stole your boat."

"*Had* the eye of a killer," Weevil said. "Memo is dead. But the captain is very much alive. Aboard our boat you left anchored in the bay."

"I am glad. All of this was Memo's idea. I had no choice."

"You chose to Mickey my drink, Socorro. You chose to take me to Squid Roe so Memo could torture me. And you would have let me die tonight. Maybe even killed me yourself."

"Because he would kill me if I didn't," she protested. "But he is dead now, so put away the pickaxe, baby, and dig me out."

Weevil let the handle drop to the sand. Socorro was right. He wasn't a killer.

"That's better," she said softly. "Free me, and I will tell you where we hid the other fish. We can disappear. I have many friends. La Cucaracha will never find us."

"I quit the drug business," Weevil said. He turned and walked to the waterline, the air cool against his bare chest.

"Wait!" Socorro screamed.

Weevil scooped an armful of rotting seaweed from the wet sand and carried it back to his prisoner.

"What are you—"

He shoved a handful of dripping kelp into her mouth and then wrapped a leafy cord around her neck and coiled it up and over her nose. Sand fleas scurried up both nostrils and into her ears. Socorro released a muffled scream. The fleas swarmed over her tongue and down her windpipe. She shook her head violently and sent a platoon of winged insects airborne. She bucked her head and spluttered, and when she finally fell silent the cloud of insects kamikazied en masse.

Thousands of flying poppy seeds zoomed in and out of her vision. They swarmed her tear ducts and skated across her corneas. She shrieked and snorted and blinked vigorously. Her flapping eyelids trapped dozens of bugs, clouding her view of the boatman. A large sea beetle tunneled into her eardrum. Socorro begged and blubbered for salvation.

"How did you find me?" Weevil asked again, unwinding the cord.

She spit out a mouthful of seaweed. "I knew you would help me."

"How!" Weevil demanded.

She tongued sand from her teeth and explained: "A tattooed Chicano guy at the gringo bar said a rich American lived out here. Said there were visitors with him who were hurt. The captain of a fishing boat and a deckhand with bandages on his nose and eye. We knew it had to be you."

"So you came here to kill us."

"No, we were going to leave you alone and take the *Wahoo Rhapsody* to Ensenada, but then someone stole it from the bay. We followed it out to sea, but with all the fish we were too heavy to catch up. That's when we saw your light on the beach."

"And that's when you decided to kill me."

"I was going to make sure Memo *didn't* kill you. La Cucaracha wants you alive. To finish the job. I've had enough, baby. Let's take the drugs and sail off together—"

Weevil shoved the plug of seaweed back into her mouth. "The only place you'll be sailing off to is a jail cell. Here's a little something to chew on while we wait for my friends."

He re-slung the thick cord of seaweed across Socorro's mouth. She clamped her jaw, freeing a tiny crab from its hiding place. The crab scrabbled into her hairline and disappeared. Socorro let out a throaty squawk.

"Focus on the nutrients," Weevil offered. "People pay big money for this stuff."

He candy-caned the kelp around her face and eyes. Then he hefted a second load of seaweed and spun it down from the top of her head. A third handful completed the wrapping, and as Weevil stepped back to survey his handiwork, a swarm of castaway sea lice the size of potato bugs scampered into the moaning kelp.

Weevil turned away. His shoulder throbbed from the waning effects of the medicine, and his head felt hollow. His legs felt weak, and he shivered at the loss of adrenaline and the nearness of his own death at the hands of Memo. His working eyelid began to droop, and as he trudged up the dry sand to retrieve his shirt, he was hardly aware of the quickly rising sea. The past few days had distracted him from the rhythm of the moon and its affect on the ocean. Had he been aboard the *Rhapsody*, he'd have checked the charts. He would have known that the planets were aligned this month—that the tug of the tide was especially strong on this night.

Instead, Weevil knelt to the sand. He grabbed his shirt and felt exhaustion spread across his body. The sound of the incoming waves lulled him to lie down. He tucked the shirt beneath his head and closed his eye.

Less than a fathom away, the tide rushed over Memo's body, filling the hole with sand. With each passing minute the water inched higher, and soon Socorro felt the sea lap against her neck. She welcomed its coolness and its loosening effect on the seaweed—but mostly she hoped it would scare away the bugs.

CHAPTER 55

TUCSON, ARIZONA

"It's Sunday fucking morning," Rent Barnhouse growled at the phone ringing beside his calfskin loveseat. His voice was nasally with hangover.

Rent hadn't slept much the night before. He was worried about the blackmailer who placed the DVD on his car windshield. At first he was sure it was Octavia, his original witness against La Cucaracha. Now he wasn't so sure. Especially after that two-bit detective showed up with the photograph of him and Bunny in his sports car. Maybe Camacho the Coyote had bought himself a dream team of tampering sleuths. It would be just like Toozie and her flamboyant assistant to pay a tramp like Bunny to set him up. At least that was his conclusion after downing an ocean of Tom Collins and watching his performance on the DVD loop until he passed out.

The phone jangled again, and Rent grudgingly picked it up. "Whoever you are, you must have a goddamn death wish!"

"I saw Camacho yesterday," Toozie said, her voice cutting like razor wire into Rent's brain.

"The fuck you did."

"Oh, and I heard from my client in Mexico. La Cucaracha is on his way to California. To pick up a half million bucks. In exchange for the boat he stole. You've indicted the wrong guy, Rent. Sweet dreams." She hung up the phone.

Rent rolled angrily out of the loveseat, made a sloppy Bloody Mary, and saw the red light blinking on his digital-switch recording device. It had been installed by a friendly FBI agent who owed Rent a favor. Rent pressed play and listened to the conversation between Toozie and a man named Fish. Then he pressed redial on his home telephone and waited for Toozie to answer.

"Top-notch Detective Agency, Toozie speaking."

"You're an asshole," Rent said.

"I see you've cheered up."

"La Cucaracha's in jail. End of story."

"Apparently not."

"I know all about your friend, Fish-fucker or whatever. And I know all about his little flight to Avalon tonight. Doesn't mean shit."

"You're wiretapping my phone?"

"I didn't say that."

"That's illegal."

"Not when the wiretapee is aiding and abetting a known terrorist."

"You think I'm aiding and abetting?"

"A known terrorist."

"Camacho's no terrorist."

"Call him what you want. He's been identified as La Cucaracha."

"Give me a break."

"I didn't arrest you."

Toozie laughed. "You'll never get away with it, Rent."

"Is that supposed to scare me?"

"You're not at all curious about the meeting at Avalon?"

Rent snorted. "Toozie, you're in way over your head. Camacho's going away for a very long time. Your rich client can hand out his half million bucks to whoever he wants. I don't give a rat's ass. He's being had. Some copycat read about my bust in the papers, and he's about to make a bundle off some schmuck at the Avalon pier. I'm going back to bed."

"You're making a mistake, Rent."

"Not a chance, honey."

There was a long pause, and Toozie said, "The file, Rent. Today."

"How about we meet tomorrow after work? Have a cocktail. Maybe a few cocktails. Get to know each other a little better. You haven't even seen my fun side yet."

"I've seen it, Rent. And I wasn't impressed. Noon today. Or the deal's off."

Rent heard the dial tone, and he felt his hangover ease. He wandered back to the wet bar and made another Bloody Mary. He thought of the upcoming La Cucaracha trial, the media interest, and his rocketing fame. The accolades would fly. The governorship would land in his lap. And women would beg for his attention.

He returned to his DVD player, a spry bounce in his step.

"To La Cucaracha," he toasted gleefully, and pushed play.

CHAPTER 56

LA PAZ, BAJA CALIFORNIA

Edwin Sparks arrived in La Paz, plunked down his credit card for the cherry-red Volkswagen bug, and made it four blocks before the front left tire shredded. Edwin pulled to the side of the road. He rummaged through the front trunk, found no tire jack, and trudged back to the rental agency. The door was locked, and the lights were off. He was cursing under his breath when he heard footsteps and turned to see a middle-aged woman weaving up the sidewalk, her extra-large sundress billowing in the breeze.

"Siesta time," she slurred, stopping beside Edwin.

"It's not even noon," Edwin complained.

"Don't be rude. It's five o'clock somewhere. Come have a drink with me."

"My car has a flat."

"A drink will make it better."

"Do you think the rental car agency will reopen soon?"

"Who cares?" She wobbled on her pair of new huarache sandals. "Time to enjoy your vacation and come have a drink."

"I'm not on vacation," Edwin said.

"You live here?"

"No, I—"

She leaned close and whispered, "Are you on the lam?"

"What? No, I—"

"Come on, I won't tell. Is it the IRS? An ex-wife? Murder?"

"I think you're drunk."

"I think you're cute."

"I need to get to Magdalena Bay. Someplace called Puerto San Carlos. My boss'll kill me if I don't show up."

"I have a car."

Edwin raised his brow. "You do?"

"Uh-huh."

"Magdalena Bay is a three-hour drive."

"I've got all week."

"You're alone?"

"Not for long."

"But what if I really am a murderer?"

"Then we should have that drink before you kill me." She winked. "What's your name, killer?"

"Edwin," he said and reached out his hand.

She grabbed it and yanked him into a bear hug. "Peggy from Juneau."

Edwin's eyes widened. "Alaska?"

"Cute *and* smart," she said and nibbled on his ear.

CHAPTER 57

LOS ANGELES, CALIFORNIA

Rent Barnhouse exited the airplane and hurried through the gate into the crowded Los Angeles airport. He was still fuming about the photographs of him and Bunny in his Corvette that Toozie had released to the local media just after noon. Rent had called her bluff. Had ignored her demand to meet him for lunch. Now he was regretting it. A law clerk at the prosecutor's office had called at 12:01 with the unfortunate update. Fox News reporters were heading to his townhouse. Rent raced out the door and headed for the airport. He needed to hide out for a few days and let the brouhaha blow over.

On the way to the airport Rent had one of his prosecutorial epiphanies—the perfect revenge for Toozie's juvenile attempt to embarrass him. Apparently some La Cucaracha copycat was heading to Catalina Island to extort half a million dollars from Toozie's rich client. Hell, Rent thought, why not cash in himself? The whole cockroach cartel was his fabrication anyway: the bribery of the border patrol agent that led to the arrest of the recidivist immigrant smuggler, the planting of the buggy evidence, and of course the coup de grace—Rent's new star witness, Bunny.

238

Rent was suddenly eager to visit Catalina Island. While he hated any kind of forced exile, he was happy with the idea of profiting from his mini-vacation. Afterward he'd deny the validity of the sex photographs as some weak-minded attempt by Camacho's defense team to discredit Bunny. Then he'd file a lawsuit against Toozie for harassment, swiftly convict Camacho the Coyote, and waltz into the governor's mansion a hero. A rich hero with half a million in cash tucked into his wall safe.

First, though, he had four hours to kill until the ferry would take him to Avalon. Rent ducked into an airport bar and ordered a Tom Collins. Beside him sat a middle-aged woman with a watery stare and an overly lipsticked smile. Rent quickly downed his drink and was ordering another when a Fox News bulletin interrupted a preseason football game. The patrons booed.

A rail-thin commentator in a low-cut blouse said, "This just in: Arizona federal prosecutor Rent Barnhouse has been caught having sex in public. As troubling as this sounds, an even more surprising wrinkle is the attire that was worn at the time of the incident. Mr. Barnhouse is clad not only in a white cowboy hat, but a red rubber nose as well. The woman in his convertible Corvette is attired solely in a rainbow-colored clown wig."

The bar erupted in laughter as the headshot of a red-nosed man in a white cowboy hat filled the screen. A second close-up showed the out-of-breath prosecutor with a blue pill in his teeth. A quote at the bottom of the screen read, "Viagra anywhere anytime!"

The drinkers roared appreciatively and then toasted the return of their football game, unaware of the red-faced man at the bar. Rent felt nauseated. He set his drink down and fished a credit card from his wallet. The bartender returned moments later with the bill.

"Thank you, Mr. Barnhouse," the man said with a wink.

The lipsticked woman turned her head at the mention of his name. "You look sexy in a big red nose."

Rent pushed back from his stool.

"Don't go," she slurred. "I have a few of those blue babies in my purse. Just in case." She tried to wink, but both eyes closed simultaneously.

Rent charged from the bar and raced through the terminal. He hurried past baggage claim and onto the crowded sidewalk. The line for taxis was long, so he tucked his chin to his chest and waited.

He needed a disguise.

And soon.

CHAPTER 58

FIFTY FEET ABOVE THE PACIFIC OCEAN

As morning turned to afternoon, Fish reviewed the last few hours from the cockpit of his seaplane. After killing the Chula Vista Chicano, he, Skegs, and Pike stopped at Cantina del Cielo where, while calling Toozie with news of the recapture of the *Wahoo Rhapsody*, a muscle-bound American and his girlfriend came stumbling in from outside. It was after midnight, and the man was shirtless, covered in hickeys, and had fresh scratches down his back. He also seemed distraught about a missing boat. The girl, on the other hand, beamed with happiness. Fish approached the couple and immediately recognized Captain Winston's chief engineer, Big Joe.

The search was off.

The crew was safe.

Fish was pouring fresh celebratory beers when Xavier walked in with a grim look on his face. The drug dealers never made it to shore, but a heavily laden *panga* was seen leaving the bay and heading into open ocean. The boat thieves, it seemed, were in pursuit of the *Rhapsody*. Fish radioed Winston to be on alert and then ferried everyone back to the rancho, where they found

Weevil half-submerged in the tidal wash and mumbling something about a *panga* flipping in the surf. The *Rhapsody's* first mate seemed perplexed by the power of the high tide and the clean state of the beach. He was sure the bodies of the two drug dealers had washed ashore. All that remained, however, was a pile of rotting fish and an overturned *panga*.

Now, as Fish and his passengers neared Catalina Island, the radio crackled with the sound of Big Joe's voice. He and Roxy had been picked up by the *Rhapsody* and were backtracking to a nearby fish camp to retrieve Rose, who'd accompanied Pepe and his shark to a beachside celebration. They'd be headed for San Diego within the hour.

"Excellent," Fish radioed back. "See you after midnight. By then you should be somewhere near Cedros Island."

Weevil stretched in the copilot seat and asked, "You think it'll be that easy to do this?"

"Why not?" Pike interjected from the parachute seat in the back of the seaplane. A fresh butterfly bandage covered the stitches at his hairline. "We're entering the country illegally and flying under the radar so Captain Fantastic here can pay off a drug dealer for dope *you* stole and left floating somewhere in the middle of the fucking ocean."

"Buckle up," Fish said. "Splashdown in thirty seconds."

Fish landed and taxied across the water toward a sheer cliff of broken granite half a mile from downtown Avalon. He knew the anchorage well, having flown to Catalina Island every few years to handle occasional stateside business. Catalina Island was almost a straight shot from Magdalena Bay, and the local population was as secretive about their island life as Fish was about his expatriate status.

He set the anchor, deployed the dinghy with a four-horse-power four-stroke Yamaha outboard, and at sunset nosed ashore near the lights of Armstrong's Seafood Restaurant.

"I need to meet La Cucaracha alone," he said and handed Pike a roll of cash. "There's a doctor I know just up the hill. Retired, but moonlights out of her house. Use my name and pay her what she wants to look at Weevil. Take what's left for the ferry back to LA." He turned to Weevil. "After the doc checks you out, meet me here. Not long after midnight. I plan to have you back aboard the *Rhapsody* by first light."

Pike started to object, but Fish stopped him. "I can't risk you running off the rails like you did back on the *Rhapsody*. That was reckless. Although, I have to admit, I was impressed with your ambition."

Fish tipped his fishskin cap and climbed the concrete stairs to the boardwalk, where he merged into the burgeoning crowd of tourists.

"I don't need a doctor, I need a drink," Weevil said, following Pike up the stairs.

Pike peeled a few twenties from the rubber band, his attention on Fish's shiny cap visible in the distance.

Weevil reached out and snatched the sixty dollars. "Care to join me?"

"Not a chance."

"Don't you ever relax?"

"Not in a bottle of booze."

"Listen, land worm," Weevil snipped. "You might want to butter up your old boss. Especially since the captain's not around to save you this time."

"Save *me*?"

"That's right."

"I never really thought of you as my boss."

"Good, because you're fired!" Weevil turned to go, but Pike caught him by the arm with surprising speed and placed two powerful fingers over Weevil's bull-horned shoulder.

"Ouch!"

Pike moved his lips close to Weevil's ear and spoke quickly. Weevil listened, his working eye widening. "No way," he uttered.

"Way, deckboy. Now, go have your drink and hope to God you never see me again."

"I can't believe you're—ahhh!"

Pike rammed a knuckle into Weevil's shoulder bandage. "For once, just do what you're told."

Weevil nodded quickly. Pike released him.

"I'm really sorry about putting those hooks in your bed. It was a stupid thing to do."

"You're still talking."

"Right." Weevil made a zippering motion across his mouth.

Pike lobbed the money into the air. "Take it. And try to save a little for the captain. He deserves something for his loyalty to a louse like you."

Weevil caught the roll of bills. "Yes sir."

"Smartest thing you've said since we met."

Pike sprinted across the cobblestones and up the paved side street, following the path Fish had taken only minutes earlier.

CHAPTER 59

LA PAZ, BAJA CALIFORNIA, MEXICO

Edwin tried to stop at one drink, but Peggy was insistent. She said tequila was God's natural air conditioner. Why else would a country as hot as Mexico have invented it? Six mango margaritas later they were on the road to Magdalena Bay, a cooler of icy Pacificos in the back of her cherry-red Jeep.

"The agent at the counter said the color was a proven accident deterrent," Peggy explained, handing Edwin a fresh beer. "More visible to other drivers."

"And car thieves."

"You're getting burned, baby. Should we stop and put up the top?"

"Too hot to stop."

"Hand me your arm."

Instead he unfolded a map of southern Baja. They'd bought it from the Pemex station on the way out of La Paz. "It says the next mile marker is a shortcut to Magdalena Bay."

Edwin turned onto the dirt road. Peggy squeezed sunscreen into her hands and rubbed it across Edwin's reddening arms. Then she rubbed it across his cheeks and face. She reached into her purse, found a Shawn Mullins CD, and slid it into the slot on the dashboard. "This guy's dope. I saw him in Juneau last summer."

"Please don't say dope."

"We should try to buy some," she said excitedly. "I bet every rancho out here grows it."

Edwin flinched.

"Have another beer, baby."

"I haven't finished this one yet."

"The road looks like a minefield. Drink up."

Edwin slowed the car to a crawl and weaved between the cavernous potholes.

Peggy traced her finger down his arm. "Want to make out?"

"I need to watch the road."

Peggy shrugged. She chugged her beer and opened another. "Mind if I sunbathe? These babies need some color before I go home." She slipped her sundress down to her waist and reclined her seat. The car jarred over a deep dirt hole.

Peggy sat up. "I thought you were watching the road?"

"Sorry."

Thirty minutes later Edwin was shirtless and hitting potholes with abandon. The song "Goin' to Alaska" was cranked to high volume, and he and Peggy were belting out the chorus.

"I need some more sunscreen, baby," Peggy said, interrupting their crooning. She leaned across the center console. "See where the tops are getting red?"

Edwin emptied the tube into his palm and was turning toward Peggy's chest when she bolted upright.

"Stop the Jeep!" she screamed.

Edwin jammed on the brakes and followed her stare to the center of the road. A large farm animal stared at them, pawing angrily at the dirt.

"I think that bull has udders," Peggy said.

"That makes it a cow."

"With horns?"

"Is that a car door around its neck?"

"Oh my God. The poor thing."

"Maybe we should stop drinking."

"I just thought of something," she said and reached out and poked her finger against the flimsy material. "These doors are fabric."

"And red," Edwin added.

"Should we turn around?"

"Uh-oh."

"What?"

"She's snorting at us."

"Drive!"

"Please tell me you rented a four-wheel drive."

"I'm from Alaska, baby."

"I love you!"

Edwin punched the accelerator and cranked the steering wheel. The Jeep rocketed over a barrel cactus and plowed into the desert. Peggy wrapped a protective arm around her chest and another around Edwin.

"I love you too!" she hollered and reached in the backseat and plucked two fresh beers from the cooler.

CHAPTER 60

CATALINA ISLAND, CALIFORNIA

Islands are loners. Separated by time and water, many offer the allure of comfort with their welcoming marinas and seaside resorts. Others offer only icy stares and hardscrabble beaches. But a few, like Catalina Island, are hybrids.

Rising from the Pacific Ocean, this 168-square-mile island has only one square mile of human habitation. The town of Avalon. A borough where golf carts outnumber cars. An island unsullied by development where Garibaldis thrive and buffalos wander freely.

A place where at seven o'clock in the evening, the daily ferry from downtown Long Beach arrived to unload its usual band of weekend couples, returning locals, vagabonds, and a middle-aged man in a really bad disguise.

Rent Barnhouse carried no luggage other than a small backpack emblazoned with a superhero cartoon—to carry the money back home. He'd purchased the backpack a few blocks from the Los Angeles airport, at a drugstore where he'd also bought a canary yellow tennis visor and a pair of Harry Caray oversized sunglasses. The taxi driver then took him to a nearby strip mall

populated by porn shops and prostitutes, where he found a wig
store with peroxide mullets, mohawks, and the perfect replica of
a black Afro rock star wig.

Now, as Rent made his way down the short road to downtown Avalon, tourists did a double take, hoping to identify a
famous actor in disguise. Their excitement quickly turned to disgust when they realized the middle-aged man in the Afro was
nothing more than another island oddity. Rent ignored the stares.
For the first time in his life he was pleased to be incognito.

By ten thirty that evening, Rent had settled into a dark corner
of a boardwalk restaurant overlooking the Avalon pier. His disguise seemed to be working, and other than the occasional rubber-
necker, Rent had eaten his double buffalo burger with chili-cheese
fries in blissful anonymity. Less joyful, however, was his mood.

Rent was particularly perturbed at the attempt by his enemies
to derail his political ambitions—even if it allowed him the chance
to possess half a million tax-free dollars. Releasing those bawdy
photographs to the media may have been embarrassing, but it
was hardly career-ending. He wondered why Toozie had done it.
But mostly he was bored. Hiding out on the island may have been
politically prudent, but it was also downright drab. What he really
wanted was to wander into a tourist bar and charm some tourist
back to a hotel room. Entice her to join him for a nightcap or two.
Instead, he dutifully kept watch over the pier and went over the
events that led to his stakeout of the man with a long goatee and
fishskin cap.

Camacho the Coyote was in jail set up on drug charges as
the notorious drug lord La Cucaracha. The star witness, Bunny,
was relaxing at a spa paid for by him on the promise of her prac-
ticing the scripted testimony and memorizing her new name,

Jessica Coneja. Meanwhile, Tucson's most annoying private investigator had wormed her way into the case and was working for the world's dumbest client—an expatriated weirdo willing to pay some phony drug dealer half a million dollars for nothing. And then there was Octavia, Rent's original fake witness who had mysteriously disappeared after setting him up for the night with Bunny. Rent was certain she was in cahoots with Toozie. He just didn't know exactly why or how. Not that it mattered. Rent was about to impersonate his own fictitious drug lord, make off with a bundle of loot, and return home a slightly sex-tarnished hero of the criminal justice system. Of that the Afro-wigged prosecutor was certain.

Rent gave a silent toast to his new moneymaking scheme when the Tom Collins caught in his throat like a carbonated fishhook. He'd been watching for a goateed man carrying a half-million-dollar satchel when he spotted a familiar figure pausing by the pier before hurrying off in an overcoat and high heels.

Rent coughed into his napkin, dropped four twenties to the table, and hurried out the door. The cobblestone waterfront was restricted to pedestrian traffic, and the earlier crowd of partiers had thinned to tipsy couples and random drunks huffing down cigarette smoke. Rent tracked his quarry across the rocky avenue, stepping briskly to keep pace.

The cobblestones turned to asphalt at Armstrong's Restaurant and then plunged into semidarkness along the old seawall. Rent was pushing his sunglasses over his yellow tennis visor when a crack in the pavement caught the toe of his loafer. He tumbled to the ground, rolled awkwardly to his knees, and found himself staring into a pair of fishnet stockings.

"Is this some kind of joke?" came the woman's voice. "Who the hell wears a wig like that?"

Rent kept his head down and lunged for the woman's waist. He felt a knee drive into his stomach, and then the two were rolling down a set of concrete steps. They landed on a rocky beach, where Rent locked an arm around his opponent's neck.

"Enough, Octavia."

"Rent?"

He tightened his grip. "What the hell are you doing here?"

"I can't breathe."

Rent released some pressure.

"I'm meeting a friend."

"Don't bullshit me. I knew you set me up with that video. You're working for that private eye, aren't you? The one who released the photos to the media!"

"What are you talking about?" Octavia asked.

"How did you know I was here?"

"I didn't." She narrowed her gaze. "What are *you* doing here?"

"Some idiot's pretending to be La Cucaracha. Thought I'd see who it was."

"You bugged my phone?"

"What? No, I bugged Toozie's phone."

"Who?"

"Never mind," he said and hefted a large rock above her head. "No more lying, Octavia."

She spoke fast. "Okay. Camacho's my cousin. You and I both know he has nothing to do with La Cucaracha. He finds people jobs in America."

Rent lowered the rock. "I thought Bunny was your cousin."

"I lied about that."

Rent cleared his throat. "Camacho traffics in pot-carrying aliens."

"I may be illegal, but I'm not stupid."

"You flirted with me, for Christ's sake! Told me your cousin worked for a drug dealer in Cabo."

"That's actually my sister, Socorro. Along with her boyfriend, Guillermo."

"I can have you arrested right now."

"Not if you want to keep your private rodeo with the clown out of the papers and off the Internet."

"My sex life with Bunny's already gone public. You and your friend Toozie are wasting your time. And mine." He raised the rock again.

"I came for the half a million," Octavia blurted. "We can split it. Go into business together. Socorro and Memo seem to have disappeared. I could use a business partner. A silent one with border patrol connections. We can take La Cucaracha to the next level."

Rent narrowed his eyes. "*You're* the idiot impersonating La Cucaracha?"

"Surprise, surprise."

"But you're a woman."

"Last time I checked."

"Nobody will believe it."

"Exactly."

"Camacho has a drug dealer for a sister?"

"Camacho's not my brother, he's my cousin."

"He's my prime suspect. You're just trying to ruin my plans for the governor's office."

"I'm a businesswoman," Octavia said coldly.

Rent swung his arm downward and watched the rock strike the crown of Octavia's head. She grunted, and he watched her eyes roll up into her head. She slumped to the side, breathing softly.

Rent didn't have the nerve for another blow. He also knew she was no threat to him anymore. He knew her scheme now. Knew she tried to turn his fictitious drug dealer into a full-blown cartel. She was also an illegal immigrant who had tried to blackmail a federal prosecutor. He was certain she would return to Mexico and disappear from his life forever.

He quickly unlaced his gator skin loafers and tied her hands and feet. He removed his belt, gagged her, and wrapped it twice before buckling it against her cheek. Then he slid her unconscious body into the shadows at the base of the concrete landing, scrambled up the steps, and clopped lacelessly toward the pier.

As he approached Armstrong's Restaurant, he checked his watch: eleven o'clock.

One hour to showtime.

CHAPTER 61

DOWNTOWN AVALON, CATALINA ISLAND, CALIFORNIA

Fish keyed in the combination and unlocked the all-night storage unit. He'd only visited twice in the last five years, both times at night and both times to withdraw cash from the "safe."

He entered the dark room, rummaged for the battery-powered Coleman lantern, and illuminated the relics of an expatriate. Old couches, moldy rugs, rusted bicycles, and even a cracked full-length mirror lay strewn across the concrete floor. Fish bought all of it the week before he permanently flew south. Visited every yard sale on the island. He made a show of loading it all into the unit, leaving the door open for hours at a time while he scoured the island for more rubbish. Gossip runs rampant in communities like Avalon, and he wanted the locals to think he was just another eccentric hoarder of junk. Then, the night before he expatriated, he returned and stuffed every moldered couch cushion with brick-size bundles of hundred-dollar bills.

Fish closed the door behind him and pulled a tattered rucksack from a pile of old blue jeans. He unzipped a cushion and removed ten bundles. Each bundle held five hundred Benjamin Franklins worth fifty thousand dollars. He filled the rucksack, re-zipped the cushion, and headed back into town.

Ten minutes later he entered the Seahorse Saloon, a local dive bar with a view of the pier. He was immediately accosted with uplifting music and bright lights. The freshly painted walls were stenciled in smiling pastel seahorses, and the floors gleamed in a skin of polished linoleum. Even the hardwood bar had been laminated in aluminum, reflecting the bright lights like a welder's torch.

"Coke please," Fish grunted. He was squinting into the bartender's eyes.

"Pepsi okay, cowboy?" The man was not much older than twenty-one and wore a white blazer covered in seahorses.

"Huh?"

"We don't sell Coke."

Fish looked around with a scowl. "What the hell happened to this place?"

"Please," the bartender said with a tight smile. "The language."

"You've got to have a Coke in there somewhere."

"We only carry Pepsi. They give us more free stuff." He reached beneath the bar and raised a cardboard drink coaster. He spun it on the aluminum top and slid a napkin beside it. Both bore colorful Pepsi logos. He turned to grab the Pepsi bottle from a glass shelf, and Fish noticed the geometric pattern on his belt. It was landscaped in Pepsi products. Fish felt sick.

"Never mind," he said.

"How about a mixed drink? Maybe a Jack and *Pepsi*?"

"Doesn't quite sound right."

"I wouldn't know."

"How about water."

"Aquafina okay?"

Fish frowned. "What?"

"Aquafina. Bottled water made by Pepsi."

"You're kidding."

"Dead serious."

"Tap water's fine."

"No can do."

"Why the hell not?"

"Tsk-tsk." He made a slashing motion through the air with his index finger. Then he smiled and said, "Tap water's strictly for cleaning. Aquafina's made for drinking. Company policy. Cost you two extra bucks, but it's well worth it." He held up a plastic bottle of Aquafina. "Did you know the engineers at Pepsi filter all the bad stuff out of the city aquifers to make this water purified? It promises to give you less of a hangover."

Fish adjusted the rucksack and said, "The hangover's half the fun. No truer gauge of the previous night's exploits."

"Sounds like you should come to one of our meetings."

"Meetings?"

"Sponsored by Pepsi and AMADD—Alcohol Manufacturers Against Drunk Drinking. See, it's printed right here under the napkin and coaster." He proudly displayed the acronym. "We only sell half shots here, and we limit our patrons to one drink an hour. Cuts way back on liability insurance."

"And customers," Fish said, glancing around the empty bar.

"It's a slow-growth movement."

"I'll say."

"All of our Saloons of Salvation are. See the halo over the heads of the seahorses?" He pointed at his white blazer.

Fish shaded his eyes against the glare and saw the rings of silvery As over every horse head. "You've got to be kidding. It's like an undercover Alcoholics Anonymous."

"Better, actually. A wholly owned subsidiary called Altruistic Alcoholics. A market-driven concept. If you can't beat 'em, join 'em. And what better way to tend to our flock of addicts than on their own turf? We buy old bars across the country and refurbish them to save customers from themselves. Next meeting's at midnight." He peeked at his watch. "Less than thirty minutes."

Fish removed his hat and ran his fingers through haulms of sun-bleached hair. "Let me get this straight. A company designed to aid alcoholics is now selling alcohol to them."

"Brilliant, don't you think?"

"Diabolical."

The man was about to respond when the front door swung open. "I'll bet he's here for the meeting."

Fish turned with a look of surprise. "Bet he's not."

CHAPTER 62

MAGDALENA BAY, BAJA CALIFORNIA, MEXICO

By the time Edwin and Peggy pulled into Magdalena Bay, it was nearing midnight. Their escape from the door-wearing longhorn cow led them across the desert and into a spider web of back roads. By the time they found the rusty sign to Puerto San Carlos, it was well past dark. Now, as they coasted into town, the emptiness was eerie and the one hotel was closed.

"We're out of beer, sugarplum," Peggy said, rooting through the slushy ice.

"And gas." The Jeep shuddered to a stop, and Edwin shut off the headlights. "I forgot to take it out of four-wheel drive."

"What's that light down there?" Peggy pointed toward the bay. "Looks like cars are parked out front. Maybe it's a restaurant."

"Or a trap."

"Don't be a grumpy bear. We made it. Your boss will be happy."

Edwin glowered and followed Peggy on foot. Five minutes later they stepped onto the sandy floor of Cantina del Cielo.

"Look, Edwin!" Peggy exclaimed, pointing at the chalkboard menu hanging over the circular bar. "Sanddab tostadas are on special."

"I work at a tuna cannery."

"I work at a salmon factory!"

"You do?"

"Senior filet machine supervisor. You'll never guess how many dogs we process a day for Costco."

"Dogs?"

"Dog salmon, also known as chum. Locals won't eat them."

"But their dogs will?"

"Exactly. And once we stamp wild salmon on the package, so will most of the lower forty-eight."

Edwin puffed out his chest. "I invented Salisbury Tuna."

"The stuff that actress peddles on TV?"

"Yep."

"Edwin, how exciting! It's like we were destined for each other."

"I'm famished."

He held out his hand and led her to the bar, where they ordered the sanddab special and two Pacificos. Thirty minutes later Edwin inquired about a large fishing boat named the *Wahoo Rhapsody*.

"Sorry, amigo," Isabela said. "It left early this morning. Before dawn."

"What about its captain and crew?" Edwin asked, alarmed.

"Gone as well."

Edwin was speechless.

"You need a room?"

"Um..." Edwin glanced at Peggy.

Isabela said, "It is not safe to drive at night. Longhorns and *barrachos* on the roads."

Peggy nodded. "Ditto to both." Then she frowned. "But the hotel is closed."

"*No problema.* My cousin, Xavier, can take you to a rancho out on the island. Xavier is the caretaker for the owner. Fifty bucks a night." She paused. "And very romantic."

"We'll take it," Peggy said.

"Is it far?" Edwin asked.

"Twenty minutes by *panga*. My cousin's right there at the end of the bar." She pointed to the man in the *federales* cap sitting on a stool scratching the belly of a passed-out iguana.

"A cop?"

"Oh, yes, señor. You and your fiancé will be very safe tonight."

CHAPTER 63

AVALON, CATALINA ISLAND, CALIFORNIA

When the man in the yellow tennis visor, oversized Afro, and rumpled superhero backpack entered the bar at Armstrong's Seafood Restaurant, Weevil hardly noticed. Weevil had entered the bar thirty minutes earlier to wait for Fish to return. He was also intent on drinking up most of Fish's money—the money Pike had thrown at him before trotting off into the Avalon night.

But as the goofy man in the bad disguise ordered a Tom Collins, Weevil stared sullenly down at the bar, his one eye fixated on his half-empty beer. He was trying not to scratch at the skin itching beneath the nose cone while thinking about all the trouble he'd caused. Days ago when he'd re-marked La Cucaracha's bale of floating cannabis, he was high as a frigate bird. When he'd fallen under Socorro's spell at the Giggling Marlin, he was drunk as a frat boy. He'd been so hard up for a drink that he swallowed the mescal worm after the longhorn attack, and when he couldn't find any booze at the rich lawyer's house, he'd abused the *curandera*'s magic mud. And what had resulted?

The captain nearly lost his boat *and* his life. Three people were dead, and the man who saved them was about to hand over a half million bucks for a stupid deckhand's greed. Weevil felt contemptible. The one person trying to save them, and Weevil had been so stoned on mangrove paste that he'd even tried to steal the man's buried millions.

A sudden news bulletin brought Weevil from his ruminations. He raised his eye from the bar to the wall-mounted television screen. A buxom waif on Fox News was introducing the show's most requested photographs.

"Startling new images of Arizona's Rent Barnhouse," she was saying through a perpetual smile. "Our team of experts has successfully micro-edited into today's most riveting news item: *Clowning Around with the Cowboy Prosecutor.*" She paused to ratchet her eyebrows in practiced anticipation. "Hold onto your snakeskin boots, viewers, because that's about all the federal prosecutor is wearing. That and his hat and a fake rubber nose."

As the close-up of Rent's raised boots filled the screen, Weevil saw the man in the Afro two seats away spill his Tom Collins and rush out the door.

"What's that guy's problem?" Weevil asked no one in particular.

The bartender mopped up the icy spill and said, "Bad hair day."

Weevil glanced down at his lukewarm beer.

"Freshen your beer?" the bartender asked.

"I need some fresh air."

"Six bucks then."

Weevil dropped a ten on the bar and walked outside. He wandered toward the dark seawall and stared longingly at the rows of mastheads bobbing on the bay. The sound of their riggings made him homesick for the *Rhapsody*. He climbed to the top of the seawall and breathed in the briny air. The tide had hit its nadir, and the exposed marl was crackling with thousands of mud shrimp calling for a mate.

Weevil climbed atop the seawall and unbuttoned his board shorts. He quickly checked the street behind him for late-night revelers, relaxed, and began to relieve himself onto the rocks eight feet below. A muffled scream stopped him midstream. He saw a movement near the rocks and started to re-button with his working arm.

"Sorry," he blurted out, fumbling with the fly of the board shorts. He lost his balance and toppled from the wall, landing on a patch of wet sand with a grunt. He rolled over and bounded to his feet. In the rocks sat a woman with a belt buckled across her mouth. Weevil reached out and released the belt.

"You peed on me!" Octavia shouted.

"I didn't know you were here."

"Jesus, what happened to your face?"

Weevil knelt down and inspected her bloody hairline. "I was about to ask you the same thing."

"It's nothing." She glanced around nervously. "The asshole said he was coming back to kill me. He hit me with a rock and tied me up. I don't know who he is, but you should untie me. He's dangerous. We need to get out of here."

"He tied you up with all of your clothes on, hit you in the head, and said he was coming *back* to kill you? Did he have a meeting to get to or something?"

"How the hell should I know? At least he didn't pee on me!"

"I said I was sorry." Weevil untied her ankles. "These are shoelaces."

"Guess he was out of handcuffs."

Weevil freed her hands. "You sure you're okay?"

Octavia jumped to her feet and charged up the concrete steps.

"Hey, don't you think we should go to the cops!" Weevil called after her.

Octavia didn't reply. She turned up the street away from Avalon and sprinted into the darkness.

Weevil shrugged and tossed the laces into the rocks. Then he trudged up the steps and back to the bar, brushing sand from his jeans.

"Same as before?" the bartender asked.

Weevil shook his head. "Just a coffee, if you don't mind."

At two minutes to midnight, Fish slung the rucksack across his shoulder and ambled to the pier. Built in 1920, the poorly lit stretch of planks extended little more than a football field into Avalon Bay. Short by California standards, the pier housed some tourist shops, a bait shop, and a fish and chips restaurant. All had been shuttered for the night.

Iron benches were spaced along the railings, and Fish paused halfway to the end, where a homeless woman snored beneath a section of newspaper. He made a note to give her some money before he left and continued toward the far end of the pier, eyeing the seagulls and night herons perched on the covered trash cans.

At the end of the pier a young couple stood arm-in-arm watching the mast lights sway with the tide. They leaned together and kissed passionately. Fish took a few more steps and stopped. He bear-hugged the half a million dollars against his chest, leaned back against the wooden railing, and waited.

Five minutes passed, and then a shadow emerged from the boardwalk and sauntered past the shuttered shops. As it moved into the frosted lamplight, Fish saw a man in an ill-fitting Afro clopping along the thick wooden planks. The man wore a yellow sun visor and a pair of oversized sunglasses. Fish straightened. He slid the rucksack to his side and let it fall down his arm, catching the strap in his left hand. The heavy weight of half a million dollars swayed from his grasp.

The Afro approached with an awkward gait, and Fish saw that the man carried a child's backpack festooned with cartoon characters.

"Nice cap," Rent Barnhouse commented, stepping to the railing. "Fish skin?"

"You a fisherman?"

Rent ignored the question. "Those aren't cops making out at the end of the pier down there?"

"That would be a first."

"Who's the old lady on the bench?"

"Beats me. Go ask her. I've got time."

Rent shrugged. He pointed at the rucksack. "That the money?"

"You ask a lot of questions."

"I need a lot of answers."

"See you around." Fish took a step.

Rent yanked the glasses from his face. "I'm *La* fucking *Cucaracha*, you idiot."

"And?"

"And I'm here to collect my half million bucks." He pointed at the rucksack with raised eyebrows.

Fish said, "Why would I give you half a million dollars?"

"In exchange for not slitting everyone's fucking throats." He took a step toward Fish. "Hand over the money so I can get off this shitty island."

"I heard a rumor recently," Fish said, "that La Cucaracha is sitting in an Arizona jail. That's peculiar since you seem to be a free man. You also don't look Mexican. At all."

Rent gave a hearty laugh. "I made all that shit up. Television loves a good pseudonym. And everyone knows about Mexico's drug problem."

"Funny, I thought the Americans had the drug problem."

"The money!"

"You haven't explained who's sitting in jail impersonating you."

"Every good setup needs a fall guy. Camacho's mine. Now hand over the money before I change my mind about our deal."

Fish held out the knapsack. "All obligations and debts are hereby satisfied."

"Whatever." Rent snatched the bag of money and nearly fell from his lace-less shoes. "Heavier than it looks," he panted and backed away from the railing.

"Don't you want to count it?"

"You'd be a fool to cheat La Cucaracha." He shouldered the rucksack and began backing away. "Don't try anything stupid. I've got a gun in this backpack, and I'm not afraid to use it."

"Deal's a deal," Fish said coolly. "Wouldn't hurt to use some of that money to buy some new laces."

"Nice doing business with you."

When Rent turned to run, the snoring bag lady sprang up. "Rent Barnhouse, you son of a bitch!"

"Toozie?" Rent tucked the money against his chest and sprinted, his shoes flinging behind him like mud from a tractor.

"Toozie?" Fish echoed, wondering why she didn't tell him she was flying in from Arizona as backup.

Toozie didn't respond to either man. She was already running. Fish took a lunging stride and saw a shadow move from behind the seashell store. A leg with a shiny black shoe extended into Rent's path.

Rent, preoccupied with the money and his pursuer, tripped over the shoe and crashed to the pier. His wig flew off, and his yellow visor crumpled. The rucksack rolled a few feet, spilling bundles of money from its loosened flap.

Willie Pike stepped from the shadows and placed a shiny shoe over Rent's chest. Above the shoe were belted black pants, a dark blue windbreaker, and a badge pinned to the front.

"DEA!" Pike yelled. He pulled a gun from the back of his waist. "You're under arrest."

The young couple at the end of the pier materialized with guns drawn. "Freeze!" they shouted at Toozie, who quickly raised her hands.

Fish turned to Pike. "She's with me, Willie. PI from Arizona. I didn't know she'd be here."

Pike motioned for the agents to lower their guns. Then he turned to Fish. "It's Dilts, remember? Special Agent Tyler Dilts. Willie Pike's history, thank God."

Fish nodded. The undercover agent had found him earlier, inside the Seahorse Saloon, and offered him immunity to help nab La Cucaracha. Dilts had explained how the arrest of a San Diego drug dealer named the Angler led local authorities to a canning operation called Topwater Tuna. Surveillance of the cannery led to a long-range fishing boat named the *Wahoo Rhapsody* whose crew was planning to bring in a haul of pot-stuffed tunas from Mexico. The manager of Topwater Tuna was planning to transfer the marijuana into lead-lined tuna cans and truck them across the country. It was the intention to smuggle drugs across the international border as well as transport them across state lines that triggered jurisdiction by the DEA, which brought in Special Agent Dilts.

Dilts explained how he was chosen by his superiors to masquerade as a USC graduate student studying marine biology and approach the captain of the *Wahoo Rhapsody* about a summer internship. How everything began to unravel when Weevil stole from the drug lord: first the booby-trapped bunk, and then the stolen boat and the loss of the drugs on board. Add the disappearance of boat thieves and the gaffing death of the Chula Vista Chicano, and Dilts's evidence was quickly disappearing. Even the San Diego tuna cannery had mysteriously burned to the ground. Not to mention its manager was missing. Capturing La Cucaracha was the only hope of saving the operation.

Fish initially refused to cooperate—until Dilts agreed not to press charges against the captain or crew of the *Rhapsody.*

"I kind of liked Willie Pike," Fish said wryly.

"He had his moments," Special Agent Dilts responded. He bent down and handcuffed the shoeless prosecutor. "Let's get him on the chopper," he told the assisting agents.

The two agents pulled Rent Barnhouse to his feet.

"But I didn't do anything!" Rent shouted. "I'm working a case. Impersonating a drug dealer to help identify the real La Cucaracha. I know who she is. That money's evidence. You can't arrest me. I'm innocent!"

"*She?*" Toozie chimed in. "I thought the real La Cucaracha was Ernesto Camacho?"

"There," Rent spluttered. "She knows all about it. She can vouch for me. Toozie, tell them. Tell them I'm the one—"

"Who knowingly indicted an innocent man," Toozie finished his sentence.

Rent shook his head vigorously. "It was all part of the sting," he lied. "Camacho's working undercover for us too." Rent's face was reddening, his speech growing louder. He jabbed a finger toward Fish. "Arrest this man. He's the one paying blood money for the drugs. He tried to blackmail me. His fingerprints are all over this thing."

Special Agent Dilts motioned toward Fish's guayabera shirt. Fish grinned and revealed the wires that Dilts had taped to his chest inside the Seahorse Saloon.

"So what?" Rent implored. "I was acting out the part. I can prove it. La Cucaracha is here. On the island! I caught her. Tied her up on the beach. Next to Armstrong's. Go look. She's near the landing on the bayside of the seawall."

Dilts nodded to the two agents, who hurried toward the restaurant.

"Her real name's Octavia!" Rent called after them. "Don't let her fool you!"

Toozie began to laugh. "Octavia, as in your star witness?"

"Former star witness," Rent spat. "She's a Mexican national. Her family runs the Baja corridor. She played us all along."

"Sounds like she figured out your setup of Camacho. And your play for half a million bucks."

Rent shrugged. "See for yourself. It won't be long."

Fish untaped the wires and removed the small recorder from his back pocket. He handed the device to Dilts. "All of it caught on tape, per your request. And, as agreed, any and all charges against the *Wahoo Rhapsody* and/or its captain and crew are hereby dropped."

"Indeed." Dilts pocketed the evidence. "An interesting few weeks, to say the least."

"Now with your permission, I'd like to head south for the rest of my foreseeable winters."

"Be my guest."

Fish took a step, and then Dilts said, "I gave your man Weevil all the money. He didn't want a doctor. He wanted a drink. He's probably comatose over at Armstrong's."

Just then the two agents returned, panting and shaking their heads. "No one there, sir," they said in unison.

"She has to be there!" Rent whined. "I hit her with a rock, tied her hands *and* her feet! She couldn't get away! She couldn't…!"

Dilts gestured, and the agents escorted their prisoner down the pier and into a waiting patrol car.

Toozie watched them drive away, then scooped the fallen bundles of cash back into the rucksack, and handed it to Fish. "I believe this belongs to you."

"Keep it," Fish said, buttoning his shirt. "Think of it as a life-time retainer." Then he added, "Didn't think I could handle it alone, huh?"

"Just looking out for a favorite client," she said wryly. "Got some nice shots of you." She waved a miniature camera in the air and pulled the rags from her head. Her bangs of red hair fell across her face.

"You look pretty good for a bag lady."

"You're not so bad yourself—for a barefoot expatriate with a funny name."

Fish started to laugh. "I'm not flying for another hour or so. Cup of coffee at Armstrong's?"

"I always wanted to meet a man named Weevil. What did you decide to name that bar of yours, anyway?"

"Cantina del Cielo."

"Why am I not surprised?"

"You should see it sometime. Panoramic view of the bay. Fifteen minutes from the best snook fishing in Baja."

Fish held out a hand. Toozie took it and threaded her fingers into his, the smile spreading across her face like the flight of a white-winged bird.

THE END

EPILOGUE

SEVEN MILES OFF CATALINA ISLAND, CALIFORNIA

Ten minutes after being freed by Weevil and sprinting into the darkness outside Avalon, Octavia snuck back to the waterfront near Armstrong's Restaurant. She had seen the beached dinghy while lying on the sand, her head bleeding, her hands and feet trussed by Rent's shoelaces. She was unaware that the dinghy was owned by the expatriated American who'd arrived earlier with her half-million-dollar ransom.

She slid the dinghy into the water and paddled out past the crowd of buoyed yachts. Then she started the outboard and aimed for the lights of Long Beach Harbor, where her Mercedes was parked. She planned to cross the border before daybreak and drive to Ensenada, where she could renegotiate with the rich American while safely blackmailing Rent with the sex tape until he released her cousin Camacho.

The cool wind felt pleasant against her skin as the dinghy planed across the flat Pacific. She held out her hand and used spray from the wake to wash her head wound and clean the blood from her face. It was near midnight, and the sea was empty of boat traffic. A rare swath of stars shone overhead.

Enlivened by her escape from Rent, Octavia was feeling upbeat about her prospects when halfway across the channel the outboard sputtered and died. Despite her harried efforts to pull-start the engine, lack of fuel destined her to bobbing in the dark. She rummaged for an oar and began to paddle.

Two hours later and just four miles out from the Long Beach ferry terminal, Octavia stopped to rest. She laid her head across the gunwale and was dozing when a supersonic roar rocketed her awake. She bolted upright and squinted through the darkness. A pair of red and green running lights bore down on her.

Octavia jumped to her feet and waved her arms wildly. The lights remained on course. It took only seconds for the shadow of the cigarette boat to form in the darkness and only seconds more for the speeding boat to reach the dinghy. In her haste to jump overboard, Octavia tripped on an oar and toppled to the floorboards. The last thing she saw was a bright yellow hull carving through the dinghy like a welding torch.

The forty-six-foot Rough Rider with twin Cobra 1200 horsepower 700-cubic-inch engines was driven by Stone Henderson, a seventeen-year-old dropout from Manhattan Beach. His parents owned the largest yacht brokerage in the South Bay. Henderson worked part-time and made two hundred thousand a year in commissions without ever leaving the showroom floor. Mostly, though, he liked to pop Adderalls and take his cigarette boat on midnight joyrides.

"Did you feel something, baby?" asked Henderson's girlfriend, twenty-one-year-old Playboy playmate of the year, Aqua Marine. She stood at the helm topless, her fake breasts angling upward with the wind, a nearly empty bottle of five-hundred-dollar Krug champagne in her outstretched hand.

Stone Henderson chugged the champagne. He reached out and tweaked one of her nearly vertical nipples.

"I do now," he said and flung the empty bottle overboard.

ᕯ ᕯ ᕯ

San Diego, California

After three days in jail, Rent Barnhouse was freed on a million-dollar bond. He reluctantly agreed to plead no contest to impersonating a known drug dealer. He hired Tucson's top criminal defense attorney, Curly Cockburn, but Toozie's photographs of the wig-wearing prosecutor and Fish's concurrent wiretapped recording were too much to overcome. Cockburn recommended a plea bargain. Rent reluctantly agreed. He admitted to setting up Ernesto Camacho as a ruse to gain favor with the citizens of Arizona and become the next governor. The district attorney's office accepted the plea, sentenced Rent to six months probation, and fined him ten thousand dollars.

The media coverage was atmospheric. The next day Rent was disbarred. Then came news of a rabid mountain lion roaming a midtown shopping center, and Rent Barnhouse became old news. He also moved out of state.

Three months after his disbarment, Rent sat in an office atop downtown San Diego's most opulent high-rise. He'd passed an online paralegal class and found a job assisting Derek Moneymaker, one of the country's most successful tort attorneys. Rent seemed especially proficient at writing fraudulent complaints in meaningless legalese. The former federal prosecutor quickly rose through the assistant ranks and was soon senior paralegal.

As he stared across the Coronado Bridge, Rent dictated a laundry list of bogus claims against a bubble bath manufacturer, making sure to mention "bad faith" at least three times a page. Then he snatched a bottle of blue pills from his desk drawer and skipped into the foyer, pausing at his secretary's desk. Joy Finglass wore a sheer blouse and was snapping a piece of chewing gum in her open mouth.

Rent peered down her blouse. "Can you blow bubbles?"

Joy puckered her mouth and produced a tangerine-colored bubble the size of a crabapple.

"Not bad." He tossed the miniature cassette into her lap. "This doozie should be good for at least a million in settlement."

"Mr. Moneymaker will be thrilled."

"He'll be even more thrilled if you joined me for an early happy hour."

"Really?"

"Cross my heart and hope to die."

"Are you sure we never met?" Joy asked for the second time since he'd hired her that morning.

"I'd remember."

"You look familiar. Maybe at a rodeo or something?"

"You like rodeos?"

"And circuses."

"Circuses?" Rent croaked. He was beginning to blush.

Joy twirled the gum around her finger. "I've got a thing for clowns."

Magdalena Bay, Baja California, Mexico

Sunlight brought Edwin from his slumber. He was naked, lying in a strange bed, and, for the first time in his life, happy. He glanced around, expecting to see Peggy standing over him with a morning smile and maybe a Bloody Mary. Instead, he saw a well-muscled man with a crimped goatee and a scaly fisherman's cap.

"Peggy tells me you're a tuna man," Fish said, tying back the curtains on the open window.

"Um…"

"Yellowfin and albacore, right? But then you mix in a few skipjack, of course. Maybe a mackerel or two. Who will know? Those cans can hide the darndest things, don't you think?"

"Well—"

"I used to be a regular on those long-range fishing trips. Aboard the *Wahoo Rhapsody*. Caught boatloads of big tuna. Used to trade them at the dock for pre-canned stuff. Local company named Topwater Tuna. Ever heard of it?"

Edwin fidgeted.

Fish tilted back the brim of his cap, and Edwin saw the pattern of scales glimmer in the morning light. "Peggy's quite a gal. I understand you two just met."

"Yesterday."

"Strange place for a first date."

"Huh?"

"Magdalena Bay. It's not much of a tourist destination."

Edwin shrugged uncomfortably.

"Isabela says you were asking about the *Wahoo Rhapsody*?"

"We…" Edwin's voice trailed off.

Fish waited.

"I guess I'm just not cut out to be a drug dealer. Because of Peggy my plans have changed. I don't care what La Cucaracha says. He can keep his drugs and his money."

"*Her* drugs and money."

"Huh?"

"La Cucaracha is a woman."

"But Memo—"

"Is dead."

Edwin's eyes widened. "Dead?"

"Along with Socorro."

"But the boat—"

"Is no longer involved in smuggling operations."

"What about La Cucaracha?"

"Disappeared."

The door swung open, and Peggy entered with a tray of cut mangoes and papayas. She spritzed the fruit with half a lime. "Anyone hungry?"

"Peggy, we're free!" Edwin said, leaping from the bed. He raced into her arms, knocking the tray to the floor.

Peggy gave a crooked smile. "Free from what?"

"La Cucaracha."

"The cockroach?"

"It's a—"

"I'm looking for a cannery man," Fish interrupted. "To produce fish oil for boats."

"The cannery burned down," Edwin said dejectedly.

"I was thinking Juneau. Alaskan salmon is the most sustainable fishery in the world. Peggy's already agreed to represent me in the purchase of an old warehouse on the wharf. Power of attorney's been signed, and the money should be chugging into San Diego any minute. All you need to do is stop by the dock and pick it up on your way to Alaska. Captain Winston's removed it from the hull and boxed it up for me. Big Joe's even agreed to donate his old woody for the drive north. This time of year should be a beautiful drive."

Edwin's mouth fell open. "You'd trust us to take your money and a truck all the way to Alaska?"

"Something tells me I'd be foolish not to."

"Then it's a deal," Peggy squealed. "Now get dressed, Edwin. You've got to see the man's beach. He owns this whole island. Oh, and his workshop is incredible. Wait 'til you see what he's doing with shrimp skin."

"Boots?" Edwin said eagerly.

"Oh, you're a Parrothead too!" Peggy trilled. She wrapped her arms around his neck and kissed him.

"I'll be in touch," Fish said with a wink. "Right now I've got a mule to feed and a bar to open."

⌙ ⌙ ⌙

Sunrise, Pacific Ocean, Mexico

Four hundred miles off of Cabo San Lucas, the sea was slick as polished turquoise marred only by the wake of the sixty-eight-foot sloop *Hodad's Revenge* on its way to Hawaii. Vanda Duncan was at the helm while her husband Drake reached over the stern rail and sunk a gaff into a large bale covered in black plastic and barnacles. It was attached to red fishing floats, and jutting from the top was a small black antenna.

"What is it?" Vanda asked.

"Dunno, but it's heavy."

He hauled it to the dive step and slit the plastic covering with a knife. The ocean breeze filled with a familiar pungency.

"Hot damn!" Vanda exclaimed, wiggling her nose. "Is that what I think it is?"

Drake didn't answer. He held up a small black box with an antennae poking out like a fuse. "I think this thing's got a tracking device."

"You mean that little box covered in barnacles?"

Drake yanked it free. "Yep. But the little red light isn't blinking. I think the batteries are dead."

"Our medical marijuana's almost out."

"And Hawaii's still a week away."

"It'd be a shame to see it go to waste."

"Indeed it would," Drake said, rearing back his arm and heaving the tracking device into the sea.

AFTERWORD

While this is a work of fiction, much of the mayhem takes place in locations familiar to Baja California travelers. The bars in Cabo San Lucas are depicted as I remember them, though my time there was hardly sober. The parrot most certainly exists at the Giggling Marlin. His name is not Pez Gallo. For years the dead tree at Squid Roe held a Jet Ski. It may or may not have been driven off by a drunken gringo.

The island owned by Atticus Fish is one of the most beautiful places I've ever visited. May it never be sullied by developers' greed. And yes, black snook lurk in the Magdalena mangroves. No offense to Randy Wayne White who valiantly tried to catch one. I know the secrets, and I'm not telling.

Cows grow horns as big as bulls. Big sharp ones. I learned this on a bad stretch of Baja back road. Thankfully, she didn't gore anyone in the car. An Appaloosa can also refer to a breed of mule.

To the best of my knowledge no one has yet attempted to smuggle drugs inside the bellies of dead yellowfin tunas. My sincerest apologies to the San Diego fishing fleet if law enforcement finds the idea credible. Then again, a drug enforcement agent would need to read this book, and having been stopped by my share of this particular breed of government official while crossing the border from Mexico, I feel confident our little secret will remain safe.

The aquarium bar at the Fish Market does not exist. The Fish Market does. If you crave shellfish and are ever in San Diego, stop by and order a Ducket's Bucket. But be mindful of the after meal toothpick.

Topwater Tuna does not exist, but the setting for it does. It's the two-story building on the east side of the 5 Freeway just north of SeaWorld Drive. The one with towering game fish painted on the wall. And speaking of game fish, the use of vodka sprayed over the gill plates is an old Hawaiian trick I picked up years ago. It works better and more humanely than any fish bat on the planet.

Lastly, I know a lawyer who sued God and won. He is not a billionaire, and he did not flee to Baja California. At least not yet.

ACKNOWLEDGMENTS

I am forever indebted to the kindness of Baja's outback residents. They live a difficult life and yet always welcome me with wide smiles and open hearts. On more than one occasion, *pangeros* at a remote fish camp freed my vehicle from axle-deep sand and expected nothing in return. Fresh oysters, fossilized clamshell, and ancient shark's teeth have been delivered to my campsite just for conversation. If bad roads make good people, the inhabitants of Baja are some of the best.

To the trailblazing *norteamericano* of yore like Erle Stanley Gardner and Fred Hoctor, I thank you. The former for his books about Baja treasure that fired my imagination, and the latter for his hospitality and for pointing me to some of the more spectacular sights in Baja California.

To my father, who first took me to Mexico as a kid and introduced me to a life of adventure. And to my mother, who taught me the love of fishing at the age of two. I hope the marlin are running thick up there, Mom. Rest in peace.

A shout-out to the real Captain Winston, whose love of all things Baja rivals my own. A better traveling buddy there is not.

And to Doug McFetters, who's been here since the beginning. Your advice will always be a welcomed sea breeze.

A boatload of gratitude goes to Tyler Dilts, author of *A King of Infinite Space* and English professor extraordinaire. Your deft critique of manuscripts is surpassed only by your passion to help writers succeed. Thanks for getting me here.

To Bela Mogyorody, owner of Viento y Agua coffee shop in Long Beach, California. Much of this book was written at that little table in the back. Thanks for keeping the creative pistons firing with hugs and yerba matés. Thank you Randy Denis for your artistic brilliance and those whimsical Atticus maps that introduce us to Baja California. And *muchísimas gracias* to Claudia Solórzano for fixing my characters' Spanish. My daughter Maggie is lucky to have a teacher as skilled as you.

To my extraordinary editor Alex Carr and the entire team at AmazonEncore including Sarah Tomashek, Jacque Ben-Zekry, Sarah Gelman, and Nikki Sprinkle. To Jessica Smith who fixed my mistakes with frigate bird eyes, and to Sarah Burningham for casting her publicist net far and wide. I am forever indebted to you all.

And lastly to my wife, Amanda. Your wit and humor shine through these pages. I'd spend every moment of my life turning our adventures into stories. May this be but the first.

ABOUT THE AUTHOR

Photograph by Renee Warr, 2008

The author with dinner caught from a surfboard at Scorpion Bay fifty miles north of Isla Santo Domingo.

Shaun Morey is the author of the bestselling *Incredible Fishing Stories* series and a contributor to magazines and newspapers worldwide. He won the inaugural Abbey-Hill short-story contest and is a three-time winner of the *Los Angeles Times* novel-writing contest. Over the years, he has worked as a fishmonger, a tennis instructor, a bartender, an associate literary agent, and an attorney—who could never quite figure out how to sue God and win—until he wrote *Wahoo Rhapsody*. Please visit www.shaunmorey.com for more information.